# Love and the Game 2

# Love and the Game 2

*Johnni Sherri*

www.urbanbooks.net

Urban Books, LLC
300 Farmingdale Road, NY-Route 109
Farmingdale, NY 11735

Love and the Game 2

ISBN 13: 978-1-64556-031-9
ISBN 10: 1-64556-031-7

First Trade Paperback Printing May 2020
Printed in the United States of America

10 9 8 7 6 5 4 3 2 1

Distributed by Kensington Publishing Corp.
Submit Orders to:
Customer Service
400 Hahn Road
Westminster, MD 21157-4627
Phone: 1-800-733-3000
Fax: 1-800-659-2436

# Love and the Game 2

by

*Johnni Sherri*

# Chapter 1

## *Perri*

"Y'all, I have loved this woman from the very first moment I laid eyes on her. Tell 'em, Ma," Derrick said as he stood in front of all my family. Staring down at me with intensity in his eyes, he licked his lips and clasped his hands. "What I tell you that night?" he asked, then waited for me to recall. "If it was the last thing on this earth I did, I was gon' make you my lady," he said.

Derrick paused and gave a hesitant smile before dropping down on one knee. Gasping from shock, I covered my mouth with my hands and gazed into his dark brown eyes. My heart started going crazy, thumping loudly inside my chest, as I tried not to be too presumptuous. Without uttering a word, I narrowed my eyes to question him. When I saw his eyes immediately soften in response, this told me what I already knew.

He pulled my hands from my face and kissed the back of one before licking his lips once more. "Will you do me the honor, Ms. Perri Daniels, of being my wife?" With his other hand, he reached into his pocket and pulled out the most beautiful pear-shaped diamond ring I had ever seen. It was so big and sparkly, something I didn't think he could possibly afford.

After releasing the breath I had been holding, I immediately looked over at my brother, Tez, whose eyes darted toward the back of the room. When I turned around and allowed my gaze to follow his, I was met with the sight of Plus, who was shaking his head.

"Don't do this, Perri," he mouthed. The wrinkles that were etched into his forehead revealed the stress he was under. And after his latest confession, when he told me he loved me, was actually *in love with me*, I knew exactly why he had just mouthed these words.

"Ma," Derrick called again, regaining my attention. "You know I love you, right?" he asked in his deep voice. As he softly stroked my cheek with his hand, I nodded in response. "A nigga's about to go to the NBA, and I need you, Ma. I need my wife by my side."

Behind me, I heard Plus shout, "Perri!" and I swallowed hard. When I briefly closed my eyes to take it all in, I could still taste the sweetness of his tongue in my mouth from earlier.

My heart picked up speed as I turned back and looked at Plus once again. His deep brown eyes held a sadness that I had never seen before, and just like that, I felt torn. Torn between the man I was currently in love with and the boy I had loved my entire life. Throughout the whole graduation ceremony earlier that day, I'd let Plus's words replay in my mind. *I love you, and I'm in love with you.* Why, after all this time, had he revealed that he was in love me? Did he really want to be with me, or was he just saying that because Derrick and I had grown so close? My mind was spinning in that moment.

"Ma, look at me," Derrick said, snapping me out of my thoughts. I turned around to face him and saw nothing but sincerity in his eyes. "I love you," he whispered, but not to the point of begging.

I was tired of stringing Derrick along. So, even though I was choked up and downright confused by it all, I finally decided to tell him the truth. Gently, I caressed the sides of his face and felt the hairs of his low beard prickle the tips of my fingers. Swallowing the dry lump that had formed in my throat, I looked right into his eyes. "I love you too," I assured him.

And I did love Derrick. He had been nothing but good to me time and time again. Although we weren't as familiar with one another as Plus and I were, we had slowly become good friends. Derrick cared for me like no other man had done before, and whenever he looked at me, I swore I felt like the most beautiful woman in the world. Everything I had prayed for in a relationship with a man, I could honestly say I had found with him. There was no longer a need to make him wonder if I finally felt the same way he did, because I did. I truly loved him.

"Will you do me the honor?" he asked again, this time with a bit more conviction and strength behind his voice.

I looked over at my father, because I still didn't know what to say to that question. Of course, he was no help. He shrugged his shoulders slightly and held both of his hands up, as if to say that he was out of it. I then cut my eyes over to Ms. Tonya, who looked as if she was holding her breath, waiting on me to respond, just like everyone else. When I locked eyes with Derrick again and saw that he was still patiently waiting for an answer, I said the only thing I could.

"Yes, Derrick, I will marry you."

A series of loud gasps filled the room—Plus's was the loudest—so I knew I had to elaborate.

"I will marry you . . . *when* the time is right." I closed my eyes and slowly shook my head, thinking of how exactly to explain it to him. "Right now, I think we're both too young, and we've been dating for only a year. Let's not rush it, okay? I promise . . . you have my heart." I placed my hand over his chest.

Derrick's expression was filled with such sadness and defeat, and this, of course, hurt me. He was such a tall, strong man, so to know that I had made him weak with my words just did something to me. I immediately leaned down to kiss his lips, in hopes of repairing some of the damage I might have done to his ego. He kissed me back tentatively, then lifted both of my hands and kissed the backs of them.

"So then we will marry? When the time is right?" he asked, looking for clarification, as he studied my face.

When I nodded my head in agreement, his lips curved up into the slightest smile, exposing his deep dimples. His freckled face and eyes lit up with hope as he slid the diamond ring onto my finger before lifting me up from where I sat in front of him. He wrapped his strong arms tightly around me, and I found myself on the tips of my toes, holding on to him.

"I love you, Ma," he whispered in my ear, sending a cascade of chills down my entire spine.

"I love you too," I whispered back.

And just like that Derrick and I were officially engaged.

Later that night, when everyone had gone their separate ways, I found myself back at home, sitting at the kitchen table with my daddy and sharing a pitcher of homemade sweet tea. He and I both sat in silence for a while. Today had been one of the biggest milestones in my life to date, next to graduating from high school and giving birth to Camille. For the first time, I could actually say that I was a college graduate, as I had finished a two-year program at a community college. The quietness in the house enabled both of us to reflect upon this moment.

"So what are you going to do now?" my father asked, interrupting my thoughts.

Chewing on the corner of my lip, I hesitated. "I applied to Georgetown University."

He sighed. "Georgetown, huh?" he said, rubbing his chin.

Just from the way the words rolled off his tongue, I knew he was against it. If Camille and I left, my father would be all alone in this house, and for some reason, that made me feel guilty. Although my father was a strong man, he was sensitive when it came to his family. The death of my mother had crushed all of us, but him more than anyone. And while I didn't want to be the cause of any more pain for my father, I knew that it was time for me to grow up and leave home.

"Tez wants me and Camille to come live with him so that I have a shorter commute to school. He's gonna pay for tuition and even buy me a car," I explained.

"Hmm," was all he said. "And what about Camille?"

"Day care during the week and back here with you and Ms. Tonya on the weekends, I guess."

"Hmm. I see."

We sat there for a few more moments, sharing nothing but an awkward silence between us. I just looked down nervously and played with my nails, wondering if my father would end up protesting my decision. Wondering if the decision I had made was the right one, after all.

He finally cut through the silence and asked, "Is this about being closer to Derrick?"

"No," I answered honestly.

"Plus?"

"Yes, somewhat. I mean, I do want Plus to have more access to Camille. She needs to be around her father, and I really could use his help," I explained.

When Plus and I had lost our virginity to one another that night after prom, neither of us had known I'd end up pregnant. With a newborn to care for, I had ended up settling for community college, while he got to live out his dreams by playing basketball for Georgetown. Now, finally, it was my turn to attend a four-year university. There was no way I could pass up the opportunity. And despite our differences over the years, Plus had proven to be a damn good father to Camille. Us being in the same city, raising her together, would only be an added bonus.

"Well, you're twenty years old now, Perri, old enough to make your own decisions, and I have to respect that," he said before taking a swig of his sweet tea.

"But you don't approve?" I just had to know.

He shook his head. "It's not about me approving or disapproving. It's just about me accepting the fact that you're a woman. And accepting that I won't see you and Camille on a daily basis . . . All of that's gonna be hard for me." After sitting up straighter in his chair, he turned toward me, a serious expression on his face. "You also know what your brother has going on, and I don't want you and Camille to get hurt behind any of his foolishness. You understand me?"

"Yes, sir." I nodded.

"I keep telling Tez that his lifestyle is gonna catch up to him one day, but he's his own man, and I have to accept that too," he said somberly.

Suddenly, the room grew quiet again. Both of us were overwhelmed by the realization that Tez and I were finally grown up. My mother hadn't been around to witness it, but my father had actually done a good job over the years. Sure, Tez hadn't turned out like my father had hoped, but he was doing well for himself. He was no longer a corner boy hustling in the streets. He was now a boss and was trying to go legit. And I was pursuing my second degree and had matured into a responsible young mother. Daddy's job with us was done, and soon he'd have an empty nest.

"Daddy?"

"Huh?" he said, cutting his eyes over at me.

"How did you know Mama was the one?"

He leaned back in his chair and let out a soft, light-hearted laugh. Then he cast his eyes to the ceiling, as though he had to think hard to recall. "Actually, I didn't at first."

My eyes widened a little in surprise before my eyebrows dipped in confusion. "You didn't?"

"No, your mama wasn't exactly my type back then. She was a good girl, ya know. Wore long dresses and even wore glasses on her face." He shook his head at the memory. "Your mama went to church faithfully . . . every Wednesday night and every Sunday." The corners of his lips gradually curled up into this sneaky little smile. "She just wasn't fast enough for me."

"Daddy!" I gasped.

He laughed some more, holding his belly this time. "What? She wasn't," he said with a shrug. "Shoot, back then, I liked girls with grown-woman figures . . . and the ones who wanted to do more than just talk."

"Dang. You just like the rest of 'em, Pops." I shook my head.

"Yes, a man will be a man, Perri, and don't you ever forget that. We're all just stupid when it comes to women anyway. But at the end of the day, there are still some good ones of us left out there."

I sat up and tilted forward into the table a bit. "So when did you realize that she was the one?"

He threw his eyes up toward the ceiling once again before casually scratching the side of his nose. "I remember when a couple of knuckleheaded boys in our old neighborhood were picking on your aunt Yvette this one time. She was only, like, seven years old, I think, and the boys were both around twelve or thirteen. They had pushed her off her bike and were teasing her. Just being boys, I guess . . ."

"Bullies," I said, clarifying the matter. I remembered exactly what it felt like to be teased for simply dressing like a boy.

"Yes, bullies," he said, nodding his head. "But, anyway, when your mama was walking home from Bible study that Wednesday evening and saw what those boys were do-ing, she went and slapped them both across their faces. Threatened to tell both of their mamas if they didn't stay away from her, and by the end of it, she ended up bringing Yvette home in the pouring rain. By the time they made it to the house that night and I opened the front door, Yvette was crying hysterically and had scrapes and bruises all over her knees and elbows from where she'd fallen. Her clothes were disheveled, and her hair was sticking up all over her head. And even though she was finally home, for some reason, she just wouldn't let go of your mother. She had her arms locked tightly around her waist and . . ." He let his voice trail off.

"And what?" I asked eagerly, inching up a little bit in my seat. Elbows propped up on the table, my chin resting in the palms of my hands, I anxiously waited for him to tell the rest of the story.

"Just wouldn't let go. Like she had known your mother her entire life, or like Camille was some sort of superhero or something." He jerked his neck back at the notion. "When I was finally able to pry little Yvette away and get her into the house with our mama, I went back to the door and thanked Camille properly," he said softly. The look in his eyes gave me the impression he had fallen into a daze.

He went on. "I mean, I had seen her before . . . around the neighborhood and in school over the years. We were both about eighteen at the time. But that night . . . that night was like seeing her for the very first time. Her hair wasn't all pinned up, like it usually was, and she didn't have those thick, ugly glasses sitting on her nose. Instead, her long brown hair was wet and curly and stuck to the sides of her pretty face, and I remember her skin and clothes being damp from the rain." He smiled, still staring off into space. "And when I looked into those big, pretty, bright eyes of hers . . ." He paused, briefly closing his eyes and shaking his head, as if the memory alone was almost too painful to bear.

After swallowing hard, he continued in the softest voice I had ever heard coming from a man. "When I looked into those eyes, which looked identical to yours, I swear, I saw right into her heart and soul that night. I was in the presence of an angel."

"So what did you do?" I asked, not able to take much more suspense.

"I played it cool for a while after that, but then another guy, named Carl, from the block started sniffing behind her." He let out a light snort of laughter at the thought. "Man, I shut that shit down quick!"

"Daddy!" I squealed, because it was rare to hear my father cuss.

"What? I did," he said, and we both laughed. "I laid my cards all out on the table for her and told her exactly how I felt. Told her that she was the most beautiful creature I had ever laid my eyes on and that there wasn't a doubt in my mind that God had created her just for me." He then leaned over, and with a sly grin on his face, he whispered, "Ya know, playing into her devotion to the Lord."

"And just like that?" I asked, smiling. I was enjoying every minute I was hearing about my mother and seeing the love in my father's eyes as he spoke.

"Just like that, baby!"

"And what did she say?"

"She said that she had been waiting on me all along. Said she had had a crush on me for quite some time, but I had been too busy chasing behind fast-tail Tina, coochie-giving Carla, and some of the other girls from the neighborhood," he said with a light chuckle that suddenly trailed off into silence.

I looked over at my father and saw tears starting to form in his eyes, and I knew almost instantly that he was missing my mother some kind of bad. I got up from my seat and went over to him and leaned down. First, I wrapped my arms securely around his neck, and then I gave him the tightest squeeze. "Thank you, Daddy."

He pulled back and asked, "For what?" as he quickly thumbed away a tear before it had a chance to fall.

"For telling me that story. For being such a good father to us all these years." I shrugged.

"I don't know . . . for everything."

He gently grabbed the sides of my face and kissed my forehead, which instantly reminded me of Plus.

"Always follow your heart, Perri. No matter what," he said. "Always."

# Chapter 2

## *Nika*

For the past two weeks, Jorell had been back home in Alabama, where he would spend the summer. It was weird, because I had talked to him only twice since the day he left. Whenever I would call him, he'd send me straight to voice mail. That was bothering me, because for over the past six months Jorell and I had talked on a daily basis either by phone or in person. Now that he was gone, his behavior had changed drastically, leaving my mind and even my heart in an unfamiliar state of confusion. Although I had played hard to get at times and had acted like I wasn't all about Jorell, I was. I was truly head over heels in love with that country-ass nigga.

As I sat on the edge of my bed, I grabbed my cell phone and dialed his number for the fifth time that day. His phone rang only once before he sent me to voice mail, just as I had expected. By this time I had already left two voice-mail messages for the day, so I knew leaving a third wasn't going to do me any good. I tossed my phone on the bed. Suddenly, I started to think that perhaps something bad had happened to him, and this threw me into a panic. I picked up my phone again and hurriedly dialed a number. This time I called Plus, Jorell's teammate and also my friend Perri's baby's daddy.

"Yo," he answered on the second ring.

"Plus, hey. It's me, Nika," I said.

"Oh. Whaddup?"

"Have you heard from Jorell since he went back home?" I asked.

"Yeah, I just talked to that nigga earlier today. Why?"

My eyebrows rose from my confusion, while my heart dropped down into the pit of my stomach. "He didn't change his number, did he?" I asked in a low voice, feeling almost ashamed.

"Nah," he said. Then he paused for a moment, realizing, it seemed to me, that he might be giving away too much information. "But wait—"

I hung up on him, and I immediately felt the urge to cry, but my pride just wouldn't let me. After knowing Jorell for well over a year, I had yet to meet his family. So even if I wanted to call his mother, I couldn't. I lay back on my bed, took the pillow, and smothered my face. "Ahh!" I yelled into it, feeling my frustration seep out.

I hated that Jorell had this effect on me. No matter how many times I told myself, *Fuck that nigga*, and promised myself that I wasn't going to call him, I would dial his number anyway. It was sad to say that sometimes it was just to listen to the sound of his voice during his message. I had it bad. I didn't mind admitting that over the years, I had had my fair share of boyfriends, but none of them, not one of them, had ever had this type of hold on me.

All of a sudden, I heard my bedroom door swing open. I removed the pillow from my face and saw Perri and Camille standing there.

"You a'ight?" Perri asked.

"Yeah, I'm fine," I lied, sitting up in my bed to look them over. Immediately, I noticed that both Perri and Camille were dressed in black Nike basketball shorts and white tees. On their feet were black-and-white Jays with low black ankle socks. I shook my head.

"What?" Perri asked.

"Plus gon' kick your ass for dressing her like a little boy," I told her, still shaking my head.

"She's not dressed like a boy. She's dressed comfortably. And besides, she got her earrings in her ears."

I laughed at her rationale. Looking down at baby Camille, who was now sixteen months old, I smiled. A soft halo of curly black hair framed her light brown face, while her golden eyes sparkled back at me. Perri, who had ahold of Camille's chubby little hand, wore her long brown hair straightened, with a part down the middle. It was summertime, which of course meant the basketball shorts were out and in full effect. But I was at least proud of the fact that Perri kept up with her hair, which I had done for her just two days prior.

Just as I was about to get up from the bed, my cell phone started to vibrate next to me. Both my and Perri's eyes darted toward the screen at the same time. Plus's name and face popped up before I swiped my finger across the screen to ignore his call.

"What's Plus calling you for?" Perri asked as Camille squirmed out of her hold.

"I called him to see if he had talked to Jorell."

"He's still not answering for you?"

I shook my head no in response and lowered my eyes.

"So what Plus say? Has he heard from that nigga?" she asked.

"Yeah . . . earlier today," I sighed.

She sucked her teeth. "Stop thinking about that nigga, 'cause he obviously ain't worried about you."

"Gee, thanks," I muttered, rolling my eyes. "I know you gotta fiancé and all now, but that doesn't mean you weren't in my shoes with Plus just a few months back," I added.

She and I glared hard at each other for a minute. The only sound in the room was Camille's babbling. Then, at the very same time, we both fell out laughing. She and I had never had a real argument, and we weren't about to start now.

"Yo, you stupid. I wasn't never calling Plus back-to-back like that. 'Cause that nigga knows better than not to answer for me," she said, sitting down on the edge of my bed.

"That's 'cause y'all got a baby together—"

"Even if we didn't," she said, cutting me off with her words as well as her hand, which she had raised in the air. After lying back on the bed and resting her weight on her elbows, she then proceeded to say, "Nah, but me and Plus's relationship is different. He's my best friend above anything."

"Yeah," I said, understanding what she was trying to say.

"Now, that doesn't mean that nigga's never broken my heart, 'cause you already know."

"But he's trying to make amends," I said, picking Camille up and sitting her in my lap.

"Niggas always try to make amends when it's too late," she muttered.

"Ain't that the truth. So then, are you and Derrick getting married or what?"

Flipping back her long hair like a *girly* girl, she pursed her lips to the side, then gave a faint smile. "I don't know."

"Whatchu mean, you don't know?"

Looking up at the ceiling, she tried to conceal the blush on her cheeks and her smile, which was now fully formed.

"I mean, I love him, but . . ."

"But you still love Plus," I said, finishing her thought.

"I didn't say that." She tried downplaying what we both knew to be true. "I just got a lot on my plate right now. I mean, I'm starting Georgetown in the fall, and I've decided to try out for their basketball team in another few weeks—"

Hearing that she wanted to play basketball again made me so excited. "Oh my God! Perri, you are?" I squealed.

"Yeah." She smiled. "I'ma see if I still got it." She shrugged coolly, like it was no big deal.

"Oh, girl, please. You still got it, and you know it. But, anyway, what does all that have to do with Derrick?"

"Look, that nigga is about to be drafted into the NBA. He'll be halfway across the country somewhere, with half-naked girls being thrown in his face on a daily basis. I don't want to compete with that."

"So what will happen if Plus gets drafted?"

"*When* Plus gets drafted," she said, correcting me, "I guess we'll just have to find a way to co-parent."

"I'm still rooting for y'all. Don't get me wrong. I like Derrick and all, but the way Plus looked at you that night your brother got shot . . ." I paused and shook my head as I reimagined the love I had seen in his eyes. "He loves you, Perri."

"So he says. Everything's just . . . a lot right now. I'm tired of even thinking about it." She looked over at Camille, who was reaching out for her from my arms, then took her from me. "Ain't that right, Mommy's sweet girl?"

"Mama weet wirl," Camille said, trying to repeat what Perri had said. We both laughed, and Camille mimicked that too, exposing the tiny Chiclet teeth in her mouth as she giggled.

Feeling hot from the extra bodies and the laughter that filled my room, I got up to cut on the ceiling fan. Meanwhile, Perri sat up and cut *Doc McStuffins* on the TV for Camille. Just as I was making my way back over to the bed, I had a thought.

"Hey, what are you doing for the Fourth of July?"

"Um, I don't know. Derrick will be in New York, and I'm definitely not going with him, I know that. Why?"

I didn't respond to her question; instead, I grabbed my phone off my bed and dialed Plus's number.

"Yo," he said.

"Hey, my bad for hanging up on you. That was by accident," I lied. I knew he wouldn't buy it, but I had to say something so I wouldn't come off as rude.

"Yeah, a'ight," he said.

I glanced at Perri, who was facing the television, fully engaged in *Doc McStuffins* right alongside Camille. "So I was wondering, What are you doing for the Fourth of July?" I asked.

"I 'on't know. Shit, prolly. Why?"

"You down for a road trip?"

"A road trip?" he repeated.

"Yeah, a road trip. To Alabama."

"Oh shit," he muttered, already knowing what I was up to. "I'll go only if Perri goes," he said, trying to be slick, but little did he know, I was even slicker.

"Perri will go, but only if you promise to keep your mouth shut." Perri peeked at me over her shoulder after hearing her name. I winked at her. "Don't tell Jorell we're coming, 'cause I'm popping up on that nigga."

"Oh shit," Perri muttered, shaking her head.

# Chapter 3

## *Myesha*

For the past three days, I had busied myself around the house, cooking and cleaning, and had ordered clothes and meaningless items off the Internet. I had grown both tired of being Tez's housewife, minus the ring and commitment, and I was bored. Not to mention, I was two months pregnant with his first child and too scared to tell him. Actually, the word *scared* was putting it mildly. *Terrified* was more like it. He had made it clear from the beginning of our relationship that he never wanted any children. *Like ever.* And after three measly days of missing the pill and having to wait until the following month to start a new pack, I had ended up breaking our agreement.

Since the day I'd found out I was pregnant, several fearful thoughts had scurried frantically through my mind. One was that he would break things off with me, and I was absolutely head over heels in love with that nigga. Two, he would ask me if it was his. I prayed that he wouldn't, not because I had ever cheated on him, but because when Tez got angry, he could be cruel with his words, and that question alone would break me. And three, the most frightening thought of them all, he would ask me to get an abortion. I knew right off the bat that I wouldn't. That third thought was the one I constantly buried in the back of my mind, because imagining that scenario itself made it hard for me to even breathe.

If things didn't work out with Tez, I didn't have any family that I could go running to. He was my family. The only sisters I had were Perri and Aria, and the only mother figure I had was Ms. Tonya. Just the idea of being all alone in this world again was insufferable. Honestly, that was why I secretly hoped one day he'd change his mind about having kids. I had grown up in the system, as a ward of the state, and my dreams as a young girl had always been filled with having a big family.

"Bae-bae!" I could hear Tez holler as he came through the front door.

I got up from where I sat on the couch and placed my laptop down on the coffee table. Before we had even moved in together, Tez had made it very clear that he liked to be formally greeted by his woman as soon as he came through the door. No matter the time of day or night, I fulfilled that requirement happily. Tez carried himself with so much power and authority that for me, it was actually a turn-on to submit to his requests. Some of them at least. I wasn't with him for his notoriety in the streets or even for his money; in fact, it was just the opposite. Despite him being this tough guy with a rough, formidable presence, he was kind and down to earth and easy to talk to at home. And he actually liked to cuddle in bed.

As I approached the foyer, I saw him bending down to remove the white sneakers from his feet. This was something he did every time he walked through the front door, and he expected all our guests to do so as well. When he stood up straight, I inspected his tall frame from head to toe.

Slim light blue jeans sagged slightly around his trim waist, while a white V-neck tee clung to his immense chest and arm muscles. Some of the violent graffiti tattooed on his skin extended down his bulky arms and went up his thick, sculpted neck. His light brown locks were pulled back into a single braid, and when he finally looked up at me, I caught a glimpse of those light amber–colored eyes. Something else that drove me completely insane.

"You gon' stare at a nigga all day, or you gon' come give me a kiss?" he said. His bright eyes looked me over lustfully as he licked his lips, exposing the gold tray on the bottom row of his teeth.

I walked over and wrapped my arms around his neck, swaddling it. I immediately inhaled the smell of his new Prada cologne as I pressed my breasts against him. His strong hands slid down the small of my back all the way to my ass, which he gave a tight squeeze. A low groan escaped from his throat as he pressed himself against me. When our lips met, he sucked on my bottom lip before slipping his tongue in my mouth.

"Mmm," he growled, grinding his hardness against me.

The usual throbbing I felt between my thighs when he was this close took over, and my pulse quickened beneath my skin. Tez and I had been together for almost two years, but every time we touched like this, my body reacted as if it was our very first encounter. The way he made my body feel was something I didn't think I could ever get used to. Needless to say, our lovemaking sessions were everything but normal.

After pinching the cotton fabric of the pink maxi dress I wore, he gathered it up around my hips. The aggressive fingers of his left hand slipped down between my legs and started to play against my naked skin. "Damn. You ready for a nigga, huh?" he whispered into the crook of my neck.

Unsure if he was referring to the fact that I wasn't wearing any panties or to the fact that I was dripping wet, I threw my head back and relished the feeling of his lips on my neck. His tongue snaked around my flesh, causing an involuntary purr to come from my throat.

Then, all of a sudden, I felt both of his hands on the tops of my shoulders. A firm, dominant grip became a forceful push to the floor. "Handle your business, My," he said sternly, calling me by the nickname he had given me.

I felt the cold marble of the foyer tile beneath my knees as I kneeled down in front of him and hurriedly unbuckled his pants. I slid them halfway down before slipping my fingers inside the elastic band of his briefs. Before I could even lower them all the way, his long, meaty dick flew out, begging for my attention. Tez was a beautiful man from head to toe. The bulging veins of his shaft were perfectly placed, the skin was all the same shade of delectable caramel, and his mushroom head was big yet well proportioned.

I took ahold of his muscular thighs, then popped his throbbing member into my mouth with no hands, which was how he preferred.

"Gahdamn, My," he moaned. He sank his fingers deep into my scalp and got a firm grip on my curly hair. I slithered my wet tongue all around him before slowly guiding him to the back of my throat. Then I began my suction, applying just enough pressure to make him go wild.

"Suck that shit, bae," he hissed beneath his breath. Thrusting his hips into my face, he grasped the crown of my head with one hand. I looked up just in time to see his eyes roll to the back of his head and his jaw clench with determination.

I continued that motion, that sloppy suction, for quite a while, humming to myself when I felt the tingle of my own sex. My body suddenly ran hot and my legs trembled from an impending explosion. It was crazy that I didn't even need to have him inside me. His sexy grunts and growls alone were enough to send me over the edge.

"Fuck, shorty," he groaned, sounding almost as if he was surprised by my work. When I looked up again and we locked eyes, I felt his body tense. His jaw slowly dropped, then just hung there. As he swelled and pulsed in my mouth, I knew exactly what was coming next, and I silently shuddered from my own orgasmic pleasure.

"Every. Last. Drop," he muttered slowly, his eyes still on me.

And when he closed his eyes, bit down on his bottom lip, and jerked within my hold, I swear I almost died. I always swallowed everything he gave, which was another one of his requirements. In the past I'd always been happy to oblige, not just because I loved him, but also because he tasted so sweet. But now that I was pregnant with his child, it just didn't feel right doing that.

"Aargh!" he yelled.

I pulled back and removed my hands from his thighs just in time to allow his release to pour onto them.

"Fuck! Gahdamn, bae," he gasped, completely out of breath.

I stood up and quickly spun around to go wash my hands in the bathroom. As I was in there washing them and rinsing out my mouth, I looked up and saw that he was behind me. There was an angry, confused scowl on his face as he glared at me in the mirror.

"The fuck was that, Myesha?"

"What, babe?" I asked innocently, knowing full well what he was referring to.

"Since when don't you swallow?"

"Oh, that," I said, widening my eyes and spinning around on my toes to face him.

"Yeah, *that*," he said mockingly, with his eyebrows pinched.

"My stomach has been a little upset lately, and I didn't want to make it worse." That wasn't a complete lie.

"Prolly would have made that shit feel better. You know, something to coat your stomach." He smirked.

I hit him playfully in the chest and sucked my teeth. "I swear, you so damn nasty, Montez."

"Yeah, a'ight." He shook his head. "Now go on and take some Pepto-Bismol or something, 'cause you got some redeeming to do later on tonight."

*Fuck.*

He gave me a frisky smack on my behind as I passed by him to exit the bathroom. Tez was a sex-crazed maniac, and I was more than happy to be his little freak, so I knew I couldn't avoid telling him much longer.

We both headed to the kitchen, and Tez pulled the oven door open. The robust smell of baked lemon-pepper chicken and garlic potatoes filled the room.

"What else we having?" he asked.

"I was thinking asparagus and maybe some dinner rolls." I looked over at him and waited for his approval.

He gave a slight head nod before coming up behind me. He ran his hands across my swollen breasts before he gave a little squeeze to my nipples.

"Ow, Tez! Shit!" I fussed, because they were so sore. "Why am I always cooking anyway? You and I are the only ones here!"

"The fuck?" he muttered, cocking his head to the side. He was confused, and I couldn't blame him, because my emotions were all over the place. "I thought you liked cooking for me?" he asked, almost sounding hurt.

"I do, but it would be nice having a family to cook for," I said softly, hoping that maybe he'd had a change of heart over the years. I mean, we hadn't talked about having kids since we'd first met.

"Oh, we gon' have family here. Perri and Camille moving in at the end of the summer."

My mouth instantly dropped. This was the first time he had mentioned that. Before I could regain my composure, Tez tapped my chin twice with an upward motion.

"Close ya mouth, sweetheart. Wouldn't want you to catch a fly in that muhfucka and end up upsetting yo' fucking stomach," he said with a sarcastic snort before coolly walking out of the kitchen.

I rolled my eyes and sighed before finishing up our meal. I knew I needed to tell Tez about my pregnancy sooner rather than later, but I just didn't know how. Not knowing if our relationship could survive something like this was stressing me out awfully bad. So for now, for tonight at least, it would just remain a secret between me and the man upstairs.

# Chapter 4

## *Plus*

Early Friday morning I was cruising along I-85 beneath a pitch-black sky. The clock on the dash read 3:56 a.m. and ironically, the only sounds that could be heard were the barely audible lyrics of Donell Jones's "All Her Love," which was playing on the radio. Well, that and Perri's faint snores coming from the passenger seat. I glanced in the rearview mirror to look in the back and saw Nika all curled up, sleeping in the fetal position. It was the day before the Fourth of July, and we were making a so-called "pop-up visit" to Jorell's place all the way down in Prichard, Alabama.

Although I didn't want to do my man dirty like that, I couldn't give up an opportunity to be in Perri's presence without that nigga Derrick breathing down her neck. Every time I thought about her actually being engaged to that nigga, I had to fight off this crazy rage that flamed up inside me. Being this close to her now, I couldn't help but steal glimpses of her while she slept. Her long brown hair, smooth caramel skin, and pouty pink lips, which hung slightly open when she dozed, were merely a few of the beautiful things I'd taken for granted over the years.

After driving several hours more, I heard Perri start to stir in her sleep. Stretching her arms out wide, she let out a soft yawn that was a little louder than the music I was playing. She blinked rapidly, allowing the morning's sun to reflect off her brightly colored eyes, as she attempted to wipe the crust out of the corners.

"Yo, where we at?" she asked after another little yawn.

"We going through Atlanta now," I replied, looking through the window to see green highway signs pass us by at a high rate of speed.

She swiveled around and glanced in the backseat. "Damn. We left you up all by yourself?"

I let out a little snort and shrugged my shoulders. "It's all good. Doesn't bother me none," I said.

We rode for a while, just listening to the Biggie Smalls CD I decided to pop in. Both of us quietly rapped the lyrics, trying our best to not disturb Nika, who was still sleeping in the back. Perri and I had never talked about her impending marriage or the passionate kiss we shared right before her graduation, but that didn't stop us from having moments like this, moments when she and I just vibed like in the old days. When the beat in the song finally dropped, I looked over at Perri and saw the sleek little grin on her face, an expression that mirrored mine.

"What's beef? Beef is when you need 2 gats to go to sleep. Beef is when your moms ain't safe up in the streets," we rapped in unison just above a whisper. Our index fingers were pointing and hammering to the beat of each of Biggie's words. And our heads bobbed rhythmically as we cruised along.

"One more time," I sang out loud, causing her to laugh.

"Yo, I swear you always thought you could rap," she said, shaking her head.

"Thought? No, I always *knew* I could spit. Just so happens that I can ball even better," I told her with a wink.

She sucked her teeth. "Man, you so cocky, Plus. You think you're the best at every damn thing."

"Well, not the best at everything . . . apparently," I said, then instantly regretted the saltiness in my tone.

Perri's eyebrows gathered together. "And what exactly is that supposed to mean?"

I shook my head and kept my eyes on the road, in hopes that she would just drop it. But, of course, that didn't happen.

"No, tell me," she said, not letting up.

Biting back my anger and distasteful words, I swallowed hard and cleared my throat. "I guess I wasn't the best one for you," I said, still keeping my eyes on the road.

"Plus . . . ," she sighed, and from my peripheral vision, I could see her gripping her forehead with her hand. She had been avoiding me, or rather this conversation, for the past few weeks, and I guessed now she was just frustrated.

"Did you fuck him?" I whispered, surprising myself by asking a question I really didn't want to know the answer to.

She let out a deep, shaky breath but didn't speak, which was all the confirmation I needed. Perri and Derrick were too affectionate with one another not to be fucking, so I could have kicked my own ass in that moment for asking such a dumb-ass question. My chest literally burned and ached at the thought of the two of them being physical together.

With my eyes still on the road, I thought about what my next move might be. Tossing around the idea in my head of asking her what I really wanted to know, I gripped the steering wheel a little tighter. Trying to deepen my shallow breaths, I glanced over at the passenger seat and licked my lips in an attempt to find the right words.

"Do you still love me?" I finally asked her.

She turned her head and peered at me, then widened those golden eyes just before opening up her mouth to speak.

"Where we at?" Nika asked groggily, interrupting my moment with Perri.

I silently clenched my jaw out of frustration. Concentrating on the black tar road ahead, I tried to get my emotions back in check.

Perri turned around in her seat and tilted her head to the side. "'Bout time yo' ass woke up," she said.

"My bad, y'all. I'm tired as hell for some reason. We almost there?" Nika said.

Frustrated, I sighed before clearing my throat. "We got about forty more minutes until we get there."

"And you didn't tell him that we were coming, right?" Nika asked, leaning forward in her seat.

Looking at her in the rearview mirror, I shook my head. "Nah. I did my mans dirty for you."

"No, you didn't, Plus. We're just surprising him, is all." Nika gave a wink and a cunning little smile, revealing that she was absolutely up to no good. She ran her hand over the wild cinnamon-colored curls on top of her head before falling back against the seat.

"Yeah, a'ight. Let's just hope that he's the one surprised and not us," I muttered.

"And what's that supposed to mean? Do you know something that Nika should know?" Perri asked, cutting those eyes over at me for the first time in minutes.

I shook my head in response. In all honesty, I didn't know anything specific that Nika should know when it came to Jorell. But I did know niggas. If he hadn't reached out to her after all these weeks, it had to be for a reason. Jorell was one of the biggest hoes on campus, and him being a basketball star only added fuel to his fire. After getting with Nika, he had slowed down a lot, which told me he really cared about her, but I knew that fire was still in him. There wasn't a party we attended where he didn't flirt or exchange numbers with the opposite sex. I just hoped we weren't driving all the way down there to get Nika's feelings hurt.

We pulled up on John Helm Street at exactly 2:09 p.m. and turned past an old faded white sign that read HOPE IV FAMILY. Small one-story redbrick homes line the narrow street, and right away, I could see it was a typical hood, much like the Millwood Projects. Dusty children were out playing hard in the streets, looking as if they hadn't even washed their faces that morning. Some were on bikes and others on Big Wheels as they ripped up and down the broken sidewalk. As we drove along, we noticed that different cliques had gathered on various porches, and these people also looked like they'd just rolled right up out of bed.

"There that country-ass nigga go right there," Nika said, pointing out the window.

As I pulled up, I could see Jorell sitting alone on his front stoop. A few broken white plastic lawn chairs sat on the porch behind him. His shoulder-length dreads with the honey-blond tips hung freely around his face as he sat slumped over on the top step. From what I could make out from the paper bag in his hand, he was drinking a forty-ounce bottle of beer. A white tank top, red basketball shorts, and long tube socks covered his tall, lanky frame. On his sheltered feet were these tattered black house slippers that had a small hole in one of the toes. I let out a snort of laughter at the sight.

When I pulled into the driveway, he stood up, squinting and shielded his eyes from the sun. He must have made out my car, because his gold teeth began to shine through the space between his lips when he smiled. I put the car in park, and as soon as we all climbed out, I immediately felt the scorching Alabama heat. I stretched my limbs before looking over at Jorell, whose eyes moved to the back door. His smile dropped slightly at the sight of Nika, but then he quickly got his face together.

"Dere go my li'l baby," he said, with a chuck of his chin.

"Don't 'little baby' me, nigga. I haven't heard from yo' ass in weeks," she fussed, rolling her eyes.

After making my way over to the porch, I dapped him up before bringing him in for a brotherly hug. Meanwhile, the girls gathered a few things from the car.

"So it's like that, playboy? Y'all just popping up on niggas now?" he muttered low enough for only me to hear.

With my palms out, I shrugged my shoulders. "Hey, I thought you'd be happy to see a nigga."

Perri then walked up behind me with her arms open, ready to hug Jorell.

"Oh! Now I see what it is." He looked over at me and smirked before hugging Perri.

Nika was last to approach Jorell, and judging by her body language, which was filled with attitude, and by the frown that was etched on her face, I knew her greeting wasn't going to be a pleasant one.

Jorell must have noticed it too, because he let out a light little laugh as she trudged her way over. "Come 'ere, my li'l baby," he said with his arms out wide, ready to embrace her.

She held her hand up and shook her head. "No, not this time. I'm not falling for it." I watched as she placed her hand on her hip and shifted her weight to one side of her stance. "Now, why haven't you called me? Why you keep sending me to voice mail, Jorell?" she asked.

Jorell played it cool, running his hand down his face before licking his lips. He had another arrogant grin on his face when he reached out to touch her arm. "I been dealing wit' family shit, shawty."

Nika jerked her arm away from his hand and shook her head. "Nah, uh . . . don't touch me. You can answer the phone for Plus, but you can't call me!" She folded her arms across her chest.

I didn't even have to look at Jorell to know that he was looking at me. I could feel the burning glare from his eyes. "Snitching-ass nigga," he muttered under his breath.

"Yeah, whatever, nigga," I said, waving him off. Perri and I walked up on the porch and sat down on the plastic chairs, while Jorell stepped out farther to meet Nika where she stood.

Gripping the sides of both her arms, he pulled her in close and attempted to kiss her. Instantly, he was shot down: she yanked her head back and turned her face away.

"Don't be like that, li'l baby," I could hear him murmur. "A nigga had family shit going on, shawty."

She looked up into his eyes, and I could tell just by the way her shoulders dropped that the nigga was finally starting to break her down. "Family issues? Like what, Jorell?" she asked softly, combing back her curls with her hand.

"I was gon' tell you, if you would just stop being so damn stubborn, Nika. Shit," he fussed, calling her by her first name, which was very rare.

"Uh-huh . . . It had better have been life or death too. I'm not for all the games, Jorell," she scolded.

He pulled her into him again and loosely draped his arms around her neck. Pressing his forehead against hers, he silently asked for forgiveness. He kissed her brow and then followed that with a long sensual kiss on her lips. Nika had been playing so tough over the past few days, including the entire time she was awake during the car ride. But now that she was here, in front of him, it seemed as if she was surrendering to his touch.

They tongue wrestled in front of us for a while, making it completely awkward for both Perri and me. Finally, Nika looked down, pretending to flick something from her nails, while I just casually looked up and down the

block. Jorell buried his face in the crook of Nika's neck
before they finally broke apart.

"Now come on in here and meet my mama," I heard
him mumble. Excited, Nika smiled and clasped her
hands together. She bounced on the tips of her toes
before letting out a childlike squeal. Jorell then turned
back toward the porch to face us. "Mane, y'all come on in
the house. I wanna introduce y'all to my mama," he said.

We all followed behind him and entered the small
house, which felt only a few degrees cooler than outside.
In the first room an old wooden ceiling fan whirled about,
carrying the scent of what I presumed to be that morning's bacon and eggs. Old brown shag carpeting covered
the sloping floor beneath my feet and stretched across
a room that could not have been more than twelve feet
wide. It housed two faux suede sofas, both pea green. The
tops of them were a slightly darker shade, indicating that
they had become worn and stained over the years. A large
entertainment center stood against one of the four plain
white walls and held a large old-fashioned television in
the center. Then there was the collection of DVDs, family
portraits, and knickknacks all around the room.

As we followed Jorell farther into the house, I began to
hear the soft sounds of gospel music. When I entered the
kitchen behind Jorell, my eyes fell upon a dark-skinned
woman with long dreads and glasses on her face. She was
sitting at the table, and her eyes were glued to the book
lying in front of her. She glanced up, then did a double
take, having noticed the three of us standing behind
Jorell.

"Mama, my peoples here from school," Jorell said.

"Oh," she said with a polite smile.

Pushing the glasses up farther on her face, she leaned
over the table to cut off the little radio, the source of the
gospel music. When she stood up, I noticed right away

that she was a petite woman and actually looked too young to be Jorell's mother. Her skin was smooth and tight, and her body looked youthful in the long floral maxi dress she wore.

She immediately went over to Nika, I guessed because she was trailing close behind Jorell. "And you are?"

"I'm Nika Turner . . . Jorell's girlfriend," she said, hesitantly introducing herself, as she extended her hand.

Jorell's mother stretched her eyes wide before looking up at her son. "Well, I see," she said, a hint of laughter in her voice. Jorell shrugged his shoulders and conveyed a pleading message with his eyes to his mother. She turned back to Nika and looked down at her hand, which was still out in front of her. Softly, she pushed it down, and she shook her head. "No, we do hugs in this house. I'm Ms. Annette, baby," she said, pulling Nika in for an embrace.

As she hugged Jorell's mother, Nika was all smiles. Jorell, on the other hand, looked a tad reluctant. His shoulders were hiked up a bit more than usual, and he gripped the back of his neck.

After releasing Nika, Jorell's mother looked at me. "And who are you?" she asked.

"I'm Ahmad, but everybody calls me Plus," I said, leaning forward for a hug.

"Oh yes! Plus," she said, hugging me tight. Then she released me and looked behind me at Perri. "And I guess this is your girlfriend?"

"Nah, that's his baby mama," Jorell announced.

Perri cut her amber-colored eyes at him and cocked her head to the side. "I done told you about that baby mama shi . . . *stuff* once before, Jorell." She rolled her eyes. "But nah, Plus is my best friend, and yes, we have a daughter together."

"Oh, wow! That's beautiful. How old is she?" Ms. Annette said.

While I responded, "A year and a half," Perri said, "Fifteen months."

"I told you that after she turns a year old, you can stop counting in months, P," I said.

"I know, but that's how I still keep up."

"I did the same thing when Jorell was a baby," Ms. Annette said. She then looked over her shoulder at the stove. "I know y'all drove a long way to get here. Are y'all hungry?"

"Oh no. We're fine—" Nika started to say, but I spoke over her.

"Yes, ma'am, I can eat," I said. I was starving like Marvin, and I wasn't going to stand there pretending like I wasn't.

"Is spaghetti all right?" she asked.

Perri spoke up before I could. "Yes, ma'am."

"Y'all are just so respectful," Ms. Annette said before turning around to busy herself at the stove.

"Well, some of us are," Jorell said, looking at Perri.

Perri pursed her lips to the side and gave him her middle finger behind his mother's back.

"Yo, leave my baby muva alone," I teased, using that same colloquialism I knew she hated.

Perri smirked and gave me the finger too.

Later on that evening, after eating and catching up with Jorell, Perri, Nika, and I got up from our seats in the living room and started for the front door, in hopes of finding a hotel for the night.

Just before we headed out, Ms. Annette came into the living room. "Y'all aren't leaving, are you?" she asked.

I turned back and saw that she was standing there in a long black nightgown and that her hair was tied up in a colorful scarf. "Yes, ma'am, but we'll be back in the morning. Jorell said his cousin was having a cookout tomorrow for the Fourth, so we gonna roll with him to that," I said.

"Nonsense. We have enough room for you all here," she insisted.

"It's up to y'all, breh. Y'all are welcome to stay if you want to. You and Perri can take the little room, and Nika can sleep with me," Jorell said. Wetting his bottom lip with the tip of his tongue, he tossed a suggestive wink in Nika's direction.

"Jorell!" Nika gasped from embarrassment, her eyes large.

Ms. Annette frowned at his comment and shook her head before giving Jorell a scolding glare. "Uh-uh, Jorell! Won't be none of that in my house. You already know." She then nodded her head toward me. "Plus can stay in your room, in that other twin bed, and the girls can take the little room. I've already changed the sheets in there and placed some clean towels on the bed."

"Thanks for your hospitality, Ms. Annette," I said.

"Y'all are more than welcome. Please make yourselves right at home." With that, Ms. Annette headed back down the narrow hall, calling it a night.

# Chapter 5

## *Perri*

It was a little after one in the morning when Plus and I lay back in the full-size bed and stared up toward the ceiling. We looked like twins in our matching white undershirts and navy blue shorts. As we lay there, we listened to the soft taps on the wall we shared with the bedroom next door as Jorell and Nika got it in. It had been well over an hour since Jorell kicked Plus out of his room and asked Nika to join him. She had been hesitant at first, trying to be respectful of his mother's home, but eventually she had given in to his request.

"What's 2200 times 765?" I quizzed.

"Uh, 1,683,000."

"What's 927 times 59?"

Plus let out a deep breath and swiped his hand down his face. "Yo, how much longer they gon' be at it?" he asked. "They in there fucking like rabbits, yo."

"I know, right? I don't know how much longer I can take listening to that damn headboard knocking or Nika's dramatic-ass moaning."

"I mean, I know he's trying to beat that thang up right, but shit. I ain't trying to hear all that. Especially since I ain't getting none."

As soon as he said that, a tightness developed in my chest and I grew uneasy. Whether Plus knew it or not, he'd instantly created an awkward moment for us with just that one little statement. Plus and I hadn't had sex in well over a year, let alone talked about the passionate kiss we'd shared right before my graduation. Too many emotions had been wrapped up in that kiss, making me not even want to address it. Since that day, I had tried my best to act normal around him. I'd encouraged the tight-knit friendship we had always shared and the co-parent-ing we did for Camille. But this, being this close to him and hearing the erotic sounds of lovemaking next door, felt tense.

Just when I felt I couldn't get any more nervous around this man, who I'd known practically my entire life, Plus turned his body toward me and propped his head up with his hand. I glanced over at him and saw his dark brown eyes scanning my face with hesitation, like he wanted to tell me something but didn't know the right words. His soft curly black hair had grown rather long over the past few months, which only added to his handsomeness. In the semidarkness I couldn't help but admire his milk chocolate skin, full brown lips, and dark slanted eyes, which always somehow managed to see through me.

"So you never answered my question," he said quietly. My eyes followed his inviting mouth as he licked his lower lip.

I swallowed hard, trying to calm myself in this intimate moment fostered by us being this close. "What question?" I whispered.

He leaned over and softly grazed my cheek with his lips. Pulled away a few strands of my hair that threatened to enter my mouth as he studied my eyes. "Do you still love me?" His voice was so low. His eyes never left mine as he hovered over me, patiently waiting. I swear, I could feel the beat of his heart, as I was that close to him. The warmth of his fresh breath swept across my face. When I tried to turn my head and look away, he gently pinched my chin between his fingers and forced our eyes to meet. "Do you?"

Releasing the breath held hostage in my lungs, I closed my eyes. "Yes."

"Yes what?" he asked, forcing me to divulge my feelings.

"I love you." As soon as the words crept out of me, I could feel Plus's weight gently bear down on me a little bit more.

When he kissed my forehead, I unconsciously closed my eyes. Things between us were feeling all too familiar in the moment, and I suddenly felt confused. When Plus's soft lips migrated from my forehead to the tip of my nose and he followed that with a wet kiss on my chin, a tremor traveled down my spine. I could feel my body instantly melt into the mattress beneath me as a rhythmic tempo started to stir between my thighs.

"So you still gon' marry that nigga?" he asked in between the soft sucks he gave my chin.

With just that one mention of Derrick, my body froze in place, as I realized what was happening between us. It was like being awakened from a wonderful dream. All my muscles locked up at once. Softly, I shook my head and placed my hand on Plus's muscular chest.

"I . . . I can't," I stammered in a whisper. "I'm with Derrick now, and I . . . I don't want to . . ." I paused, choking on my guilt. "I don't want to hurt him."

Plus collapsed a little bit more on top of me, breaking my hold on his chest. He was now suspended directly over me, and less than an inch of space separated our lips. The warm air from his nostrils and the crisp smell of peppermint lingered just above my face. Both of our hearts were racing, trying to catch up with the other, as we stared intensely into each other's eyes.

"And what did I tell you about that nigga?" he asked, licking his lips. "I. Don't. Give. A. Fuck. About that nigga." Plus had never sounded more dominant and more certain than he did when he said those words. The throbbing between my legs suddenly intensified, and my body warmed all over. When he positioned himself between my thighs, I could feel the pressure of his hard dick against me.

"But—"

Before I could even utter my next string of guilt-ridden words, Plus covered my mouth with his. He sucked on my bottom lip before slipping his tongue inside. With one hand gently gripping the back of my head and the other hand at my waist, he pressed our bodies together. With our lips still locked in what felt like the most powerful kiss ever, he ground on top of me and let out a soft groan.

"I need you so bad right now, P," he said after ending the kiss. The bass in his voice was so low and sensual that I barely even heard him. His words sent chills down my body, and in no time my legs succumbed, wrapping themselves around his waist.

I gripped the bottom of his shirt, pulled it up, aggressively, and raised it over his head. The beautiful brown muscles of his arms and chest were flexed and completely exposed. In contrast to Derrick, Plus had not one tattoo inked on his flawless skin. While both of their athletic bodies were strong and sexy in their own right, in that moment I appreciated the smooth, perfect torso in front of me. I leaned up and allowed my mouth to connect with Plus's chest and greedily sucked on his flesh. My hands slid down his back as he worked his hips against me, grinding with our clothes still on. I ran my tongue from his chest all the way up to the center of his neck and sucked a bit more, enjoying the taste of his skin.

Leaning down, he gently grabbed the sides of my face before gazing directly into my eyes. "I love you, P. I always have, and I always will," he said in a low voice.

I nodded my head, knowing firsthand the sentiment behind his words. His mouth then overpowered mine, seizing the breath from my lungs.

His fingers lightly skimmed the waistband of my shorts before I felt him trying his best to tug them down. As wrong as I knew it was for me to be cheating on Derrick, my body wanted this. I craved this connection with Plus like never before, and the moisture building between my thighs was proof of that. I lifted my hips, and he proceeded to slide the shorts down from my waist, then carelessly toss them to the floor.

"Fuck, P," he gasped, staring at my sex, which was totally exposed.

He lowered himself and placed gentle kisses on my thighs. I was panting like a bitch in heat, but when I felt his slick tongue slither between my folds, I lost all control.

"Aahhh," I wailed. Back arching up off the mattress, I gripped the sides of his head firmly and felt his soft curls slide through my fingers as I pulled my bottom lip between my teeth.

As he buried his face deeper between my legs, I could feel his strong hands cupping my ass. The rapid flicks of his tongue danced all around my bud as I tried my best to hold on for dear life. Teasing waves of an impending orgasm had me right on the edge, until I could no longer take it, and a soft cry came from the back of my throat. Legs trembling and my center throbbing from the overwhelming pleasure, I tried to get my breathing and whimpering under control.

He sat up on his knees in front of me and slid down his basketball shorts, freeing his long erection. We looked each other over lustfully as my chest heaved up and down.

Seeing the slippery head of his beautiful throbbing dick had me curious. My mouth watered at the mere sight. I leaned up from the bed and placed my hands on the sides of his muscular thighs, fully ready and willing to taste him. Just as I opened my mouth up wide and stretched out my anxious tongue, the bedroom door flew open.

"Ahhh!" Nika screamed, then immediately slammed the door shut.

Being caught in such a compromising position brought me back to reality quickly. I flopped back on the bed and covered my face with my hands.

"Shit," I heard Plus mutter.

The next thing I felt was his weight dipping in the mattress beside me.

"You okay?" he asked, pulling up his pants.

With my hands still covering my face, I shook my head. I couldn't even look at him. I was too embarrassed, too engulfed in guilt.

"Talk to me," he pleaded.

After a few seconds of me not responding, he began peeling back my fingers from my face. I timidly looked over at him and saw that his eyebrows were raised with concern. Closing my eyes, I sighed, as I knew I had to address what we had just done and what we were getting ready to do.

"I'm sorry," I confessed, just above a whisper.

"For what?"

"For leading you on. For giving you mixed signals . . . ," I sighed and gave a little shrug. "I don't know."

"Look, everything that happened between us, I wanted to happen. Okay?" When I didn't respond, he delicately pulled at my chin, forcing me to look at him. "Okay?"

Although I nodded, pangs of shame for cheating on Derrick were still very present.

Plus then leaned over and gently kissed my forehead before getting up from the bed. He headed to the door, and just before he reached it, he looked over his shoulder. "Good night, P."

"Night, Plus."

*Fuck.*

# Chapter 6

## *Jorell*

"Mane, y'all ready?" I hollered behind me, holding open the ripped screen door.

Plus was the first one to appear behind me, wearing a black tank top that hid his thin gold chain, army fatigue cargo shorts, and black Jays on his feet. The black Yankees cap he wore on his head was pulled down low, almost hiding his eyes. But even with that, I could still see the mass of overgrown curls around his ears and beneath the back of the cap.

I, on the other hand, had on the latest black Gucci tee, which had red and green stripes across the chest. With my black Gucci shorts, the black Jays on my feet, and a modest Jesus piece that swung from my neck, you couldn't tell me shit. Locks were pulled back into a simple ponytail, and I had small diamond studs in my ears. True, I was a Bama nigga who grew up right in the Hope IV Projects of Prichard. Typical "Ain't shit nigga" who didn't even know who my daddy was. My mama, like most single mothers in our hood, had been on the system for most of my life, and over the years we had struggled like hell to get by. But the one thing I could do better than any nigga in the Hope IV was ball. Because of that, I had a promising future and an image to uphold. Everyone around the way knew that I was most likely going to the NBA, and as a result, I always got girls. A nigga always

had friends, and I was always able to cop shit for the
"low-low." Hence the Gucci fit I had on today.

"Damn, nigga. I thought you said we was just going to a
cookout," Plus said.

"Yeah, breh. My cousin Nard having a little set at the
crib and shit. But you know," I said, smiling, my gold
fronts visible, and popping my collar for effect.

He let out a light snort and shook his head. "Where the
girls at?" he asked.

"I don't know, mane. Still getting ready, I guess. Probably
gossiping and shit about how you and Perri got caught
fucking last night." I said and chuckled.

"Nah, ain't shit happen."

He was lying his ass off, because after Nika had caught
them in the act, she'd run back in my room and told me
what she saw. Even if she hadn't told me, the slick little
grin on his face as he scratched above his ear was a dead
giveaway.

"Oh, a'ight," I said, not wanting to get into his business.
I left all that messy gossiping shit to the girls.

Just as I was about to holler again for Nika and Perri to
hurry up, Nika appeared, with Perri trailing behind her.

"Dere go my li'l baby," I said.

My eyes slowly roamed over Nika's petite, curvy frame,
and not that I didn't like what I saw, but I just didn't
approve. She had on this thin white tank top that stopped
just above her belly button. I knew for certain that she
wasn't wearing a bra, because her stoned nipples were
peeking through the lightweight material. To make mat-
ters worse, she had on these tiny jean shorts that barely
hit the tops of her thighs. As I let my eyes travel down her
beautiful oiled legs, I saw that she even had on the white
cork-wedge sandals I had bought her for her birthday last
month. I shook my head.

"What?" she asked, noticing the disapproving look on
my face.

I pointed toward the back of the house. "Go take that shit off, Nik. It's gon' be too many niggas where we going at."

Her glossy lips pushed out into a cute little pout as she innocently fluttered her eyes. I halfway rolled my eyes at that shit, hating that every time she made that face, a nigga instantly felt soft. Looking her over one more time, taking in just how pretty she actually was, I sighed. Those wild cinnamon-colored curls were pushed back into a semi-Mohawk, highlighting her mocha-colored face and the simple gold hoops in her ears. Her fly definitely matched mine, that was for damn sure.

"A'ight, fuck it. Let's go!" I said. With just one look she had worn me down, something that was all too familiar.

I looked back and saw Perri following behind Nika. Her long silky brown hair cascaded well past her shoulders, and she wore an all-white Yankees baseball cap. Her fitted long jean shorts reached just above the knees, and while she, too, wore a white tank top, it was clear that she had on a bra. Her feet were in a clean pair of white Converse, and in her ears were gold hoops similar to the ones Nika wore, just smaller. She had kept it cute and casual, which I liked, as opposed to her normal *nigga* attire.

"You all right?" Plus asked her in a low tone of voice.

"Gravy, nigga," she muttered before pushing her way past me and going out the door.

After loading up in my Chevy Impala, we headed over to Heritage Estates, where Nard lived with my aunt Kathy. The houses over there were much bigger and nicer than those in the Hope IV, but it was still hood as fuck. Just so happened that Aunt Kathy was out of town for the holiday, so Nard had the crib all to himself. I knew Nard and the people we both hung with, so I was already prepared for a wild night.

It was a few minutes past five when we pulled up to the two-story home. The sun was still shining bright, and the temperature was still high. After getting out of the car, I slid my Gucci shades on my face and smoothed out the wrinkles in my clothes. As we all walked up to the door, I could hear music thumping loudly and I could smell the scent of barbecue drifting in the air. I rubbed my hands together, because I was ready to grub. As soon as Deja opened the door and gave me a hug, I could see her glaring at the girls, who were behind me. Her eyes scanned Nika and Perri as her nose flared a little in disgust. Deja was one of Nard's baby mamas, and like me, she stayed in the Hope IV, right around the corner from me.

"Who you bringing over here?" she asked, not letting us through the door.

"Dis here is my li'l baby Nika from back at school. My teammate Plus and his baby mama—" The daggers shooting from Perri's eyes stopped me cold. "I mean, his daughter's mother, Perri."

Deja scoffed and pursed her lips to the side. "You're li'l baby, huh? And where Meechie at?" She was now rolling her eyes, with one her hand on her hip. The other hand casually patted the gold finger waves on top of her head while she waited for a response.

"I 'on' know. Now, you gon' let a nigga in, or I gotta call Nard out here?"

Deja sucked her teeth and moved out the way, and this way because, I knew, she didn't want to deal with Nard. Nard handled all his women the same way, which was a little rough. And not that I agreed with what he did, but I just didn't want to put up with Deja's ghetto ass.

When we walked in, I immediately inhaled the fresh smell of Kush that lingered in the front room. "Yo, who gon' hook a nigga up with some dro?" I hollered, making my presence known.

The front room was packed full of folks from around the way. Half-naked girls and the niggas I had grown up with were all smoking, drinking, and dancing to Lil Jon's "Snap Yo Fingers." After dapping up some of my people, I walked to the back of the house, where the kitchen was. There were even more people packed in there, either drinking from the red cups in their hands or eating plates full of grilled food. Some sat at the table, playing cards and talking shit. I opened up the fridge and grabbed me and Plus a beer before making my way outside to the back deck.

"Whaddup, playboy?" I said, dapping up my cousin Nard, who was handling the grill. Nigga always reminded me of the rapper Juvenile. His complexion was the color of peanut butter, while his big lips were dark from smoking weed. He, too, had gold grills in his mouth, and he wore thin gold-framed glasses on his face. His hair was cut in a low fade that had a deep curve sliced at the top, and just like me, he was a Bama nigga through and through.

"What's up, li'l nigga? I see you shining," he replied. He used the white hand towel that was draped around his neck to wipe the beads of sweat from his forehead before cutting his eyes over at the girls, who had followed me outside. He licked his lips. "What's up, li'l mamas?" he asked, flashing the gold in his mouth. Given the fact that Nard was only twenty-three years old but had four babies and three baby mamas, you could say that he was a bit of a ladies' man.

"Oh, these my peoples from back at school. My li'l baby Nika right here." I pulled Nika in close to me and grabbed her around her waist.

Nard smiled and gave a nod of approval. "A'ight, I see you, li'l cuz."

"And dis here is my homeboy Plus and my homegirl Perri."

"Perri, huh?" Nard repeated, rubbing his hands together. Lust took ahold of his eyes as they traveled every inch of her body, like she was his prey.

Perri paid him no mind and continued to stare out into the backyard, which was filled with more people having a good time.

Plus, on the other hand, stepped up and offered Nard his hand. He dapped him up, then said possessively, "Yeah, and this is my baby's muva." That sure got Perri's attention, because she whipped her head around to look at Plus.

"Oh, he can call you baby mama, but I can't," I joked before taking a swig of beer.

She rolled her eyes but then let out a little laugh.

"Well, no disrespect, but your girl is beautiful, mane." Nard was laying it on pretty thick. He and I were cut from the same cloth, so I peeped his game right off the bat.

"Yeah, she is beautiful," Plus said in a low voice, looking over at Perri.

I could see Perri swallow and tense up under Plus's covetous gaze. "I-I'm not his girl," she said reluctantly.

Nard smirked, then pulled his fist to his mouth and gave a light chuckle. "Oh shit!" he said, looking at Plus for a reaction.

"No, you're not. Not yet anyway," Plus said with confidence.

Perri let out a small snort of laughter and shook her head before stepping down into the yard with Nika.

While all of us watched the girls walk through the yard, Nard leaned over to Plus and said, "You got a tough one on ya hands, mane."

"Yeah, tell me about it. Shorty paying me back big-time for picking Tasha's trifling ass over her."

"Breh, Perri been over that shit with Tasha's dumb ass. I really think she just in love with that nigga Derrick now," I said.

That must have struck a nerve, because Plus's jaw clenched tight and a vein bulged in his brow. "Fuck that nigga! She wasn't thinking about his ass last night," he muttered.

"I knew you hit! Lying ass," I said.

He shook his head. "Nah, I ain't hit, but like I said, she damn sure wasn't thinking about no fucking Derrick last night, when we were together."

Just then Deja came out on the back deck and asked Nard if he wanted a beer. When he told her yes, I asked if she could bring me another one too.

"Nigga, you better ask your li'l baby out there," she responded and pointed at the yard, in the direction of Nika. She and Perri were sitting by themselves beneath a pop-up tent, hiding from the blazing sun. "I should call Meechie up here right now on your ass," Deja threatened.

Instantly agitated, I ran my hand down my face. "Breh, call Meechie. I don't give a fuck. Me and her not together no mo'."

"Mm-hmm. Whatever, nigga. I know y'all still fucking around, because she told me. And what about Jornelle?"

I almost lost my cool when she said my daughter's name. "What *about* Jornelle? My daughter is taken care of, and she ain't got shit to do with what's going on between me and her mama!"

Nard must've heard enough, because he looked back at Deja with a scowl on his face. "Deja, take your ass on in the muthafuckin' house and bring me my gahdamn beer. Always trying to start some shit."

Deja rolled her eyes and huffed yet still found herself stomping inside the house.

Plus cut his eyes over at me, his eyebrows pinched in confusion. "You still ain't told Nika about your daughter?"

"Nah. I just wasn't expecting shit to get so serious between us the way it did. Damn sure wasn't expecting no pop-up visit." I intentionally delivered a hard glare in Plus's direction so that he'd know that was a dig at him.

He held his hands up in surrender. "Yo, my bad. I just wanted some time alone with Perri. It's like I only see her now if it's concerning Camille or on some family get-together type shit. I'm ready for us to move forward and be a real family . . . before I get drafted, ya feel me?"

"Yeah, I feel you. I mean, at least you know what you want. This shit with Nika . . ." I shook my head, letting my voice trail off. "She got my nose wide open, breh, and I ain't ready for all that shit."

With his back toward us as he faced the grill, Nard let out a light chuckle, which confirmed that he had been listening to our conversation. Then Deja waltzed out with three beers in her hands. She handed one to me, then one to Plus, before going over to Nard and giving him his. Nard slapped her hard on the ass and told her to stay in the house unless he called for her. Surprisingly, she nodded her head submissively before going back inside.

"Damn, nigga. You got your woman like *that*?" Plus asked jokingly.

"You mean *women*," I said, correcting Plus.

Nard let out a light snort of laughter, because he knew I was right, but he didn't address the topic. "Deja know not to play wit' me," was all he said while he continued to cook on the grill.

"So back to you and Nika . . . I think you should just tell her," Plus said. "She's cool people. She wouldn't judge you or no shit like that."

"Mane, it's not about me being ashamed of my daughter, 'cause I could never be that. It's just that when I went up to Georgetown, it was specifically to play ball, get my degree, and then get into the NBA. That's it!" I sliced my hand through the air for dramatic effect. "Everything else was just supposed to be for fun. Hell, me and Meechie were still together when I left home for school." I swiped my hand down my jaw, thinking of how everything had played out.

"Breh, listen, if you bringing shawty"—Nard pointed out toward the yard with the metal spatula in his hand—"over here in front of all your peoples, knowing these all Meechie's peoples too . . ." He let out a breath, clearly amused, before shaking his head. "Breh, then she must mean something to you. It's obvious. Tell her about Jornelle now, before she finds out later on from someone other than you. Then just let that shit play out how it's gon' play out. Ya feel me?"

"Yeah, I feel you. I'ma just tell her tonight, or maybe tomorrow, before y'all leave." I shrugged, then looked over at Plus.

As the night went on, we all were having a good time. Nard could really throw down on the grill, so I had chicken, ribs, and steak, in addition to some of the sides Deja had cooked. I even shared a blunt with Nika, Plus, and Perri, along with a few rounds of Hennessy. It was a little past eleven when Plus and I sat at the kitchen table, across from Nard and Big Tee, playing a game of spades. Nika sat behind me, rubbing my back every so often, while Perri sat behind Plus.

"Don't even think about throwing that bullshit out there," I threatened Nard. He threw the little-ass Joker on the table anyway. "Breh, you killing me. I tried to warn you, big dog." I came right behind him and slammed the big Joker down on the table. Shaking my head, I let my gold grills shine through the gap between my upturned lips as Plus collected the book. "I tried to warn his ass, didn't I, big mane?" I gloated, looking at Big Tee. We all laughed and talked more shit, which was something I absolutely loved to do.

Just as the next hand was being dealt, Meechie walked into the kitchen with Jornelle on her hip. As soon as she and I locked eyes, a scowl became etched across my face. I instantly turned toward Deja, who was standing next to the stove, pretending like she was putting the food away.

"So this what we doing now, Jorell?" Meechie asked, pointing at Nika.

"Fuck is you talking 'bout, Meechie?" I waved her off and looked back down at the cards in my hand.

"Yeah, I heard you been around here all day, flaunting your li'l girlfriend. Is that why you didn't want me to come over here?"

Nika leaned forward. "What is she talking about, Jorell?" she asked, panic evident in her tone of voice.

I knew I needed to explain, but I couldn't address Nika in that moment. Instead, I closed my eyes and gritted my teeth to keep from getting too upset, but it was already too late for that. "Bitch, don't you see what time it is? How the fuck you gon' have my daughter out here this time of night? Niggas smoking and drinking and shit, and then you got the nerve to come at me with some bullshit while she sitting there in your arms!"

"Daughter?" Nika mumbled.

Meechie's eyes doubled in size when she heard that. Then she stepped up closer to the table. She stared at Nika. "Oh! You didn't know? Yes, this nigga got a whole two-year-old daughter by me, boo-boo. We been together since high school and fucked just as recent as last week." Meechie looked over at me and sucked her teeth. "And now that the nigga 'bout to get drafted, he wanna act funny. Trying to leave me and Jornelle behind. I see how it is, nigga. Bringing this little college girl all the way down here to tell me what? What, nigga?" She clapped her hands together, jerking my daughter around in the process.

Just seeing my daughter like that and hearing Meechie talk shit got me pissed beyond the point of control. I stood up from my seat so fast that the chair flew back with force and my tapered locks flung around in my face. Before I knew it, my hand was wrapped around Meechie's throat and I was backing her out of the kitchen. The only thing that spared her little ass was the sweet and innocent sound of my daughter's voice as she called, "Daddy."

I removed the grip I had around Meechie's neck and took Jornelle from her arms. "Come 'ere, Daddy's baby," I said, kissing my daughter on the cheek and rubbing her back. Glaring at Meechie, I pointed toward the front door. "Let's go," I said through gritted teeth.

She looked over at Nika and rolled her eyes before making her exit out of the kitchen. After stepping out into the humid night, we walked over to her car. I strapped Jornelle securely in her car seat and shut the back door. Meechie was standing there with her head cocked to the side and her arms folded across her chest. An irritated frown had taken over her pretty pink lips, and her eyes were dancing all around in an attempt to avoid me.

"So when were you going to tell me you got a new girlfriend?"

"Do it matter? You and me not together no mo', Meechie, so what difference do it make?"

She sucked her teeth. "You better not have her around my daughter either, nigga."

I let out a sarcastic laugh, which apparently didn't sit well with her, because she rolled her eyes and her nostrils flared.

"I'm not kidding, nigga. I'm serious," she said.

"Look, I'll bring my daughter around whoever the fuck I want to. Just stop with the childish shit already, Meechie. Damn!"

Her head suddenly dropped in a defeated manner. "So then, that's it? That's it for you and me? What about last week?" Her voice had softened and was almost like a child's. She glanced back up at me, waiting for a response.

Feeling guilty, I rubbed the back of my neck before lowering my voice and saying, "Last week I fucked up. And, shawty, I'm sorry if you thought that it was more than what it was. But check it. I'm with Nika now."

"That's real fucked up, Jorell. Real fucked up." Those were her last words before she got in the car and started the engine.

Just as she drove off into the night, I could see colorful fireworks scattered across the pitch-black sky. I also heard sporadic gunshots in the distance. When I made my way back inside the house, Nika, Perri and Plus were all standing in the living room, not far from the front door.

"Yo, Nika's ready to go, man," Plus said, his chin raised, hands tucked in the pockets of his shorts. He gave a shrug.

Nika wouldn't even look at me as she hugged herself for comfort. I knew I had fucked up with her big-time, and seeing the hurt look on her face only made me want to hurry up and fix this shit between us. Nodding my head, I removed the car keys from my pocket and went right back out the front door. Nika, Plus, and Perri followed me.

"Holla at me, playboy!" I could hear Nard hollering behind me. I threw my hand in the air to acknowledge him before going down the steps and heading for the car.

The entire ride back to the Hope IV was quiet and awkward as hell. As soon as we entered my house, Nika stormed back into the bedroom that she and Perri were sharing and shut the door. I knew I needed to talk to her before they left in the morning, but I didn't know how, especially when she wouldn't even look at me.

That night I didn't get a wink of sleep, thinking of all the ways I needed to get my life in order. Nika had come in like a thief in the fucking night and had stolen my heart. That was some shit I had never experienced before, and I wasn't prepared for it. But now here I was, thinking of how I could change all my doggish ways just to do right by her. Whatever the plan was, I knew I needed to move fast, or else Nika's pretty ass was going to slip away.

# Chapter 7

## *Perri*

With just three more days to go before the kickoff to my first semester at Georgetown, move-in day at Tez's mini-mansion in Bowie had finally arrived. Derrick had offered to help me out, but since Plus had offered first and was going to be hanging out with the family anyway, I had told Derrick I had it all under control. The two really didn't care for one another these days, and I just didn't want any trouble in Tez's home. Ever since that night with Plus and me in Alabama, things between us had felt a bit tense. I felt this awkwardness about the situation, and I knew that it was because I was confused. Well, beyond confused. If I had to be honest, I thought I was actually in love with two niggas at the same damn time.

Hoping to get some clarity on the situation, I'd distanced myself from Derrick over the past few weeks. We had met up only one time since the Fourth of July, and I always made sure to cut our phone conversations short. And while I really couldn't avoid Plus the same way, due to us having Camille, I found other ways for us not to be alone together. Being alone with him only complicated things. Just the mere sight of him would spark the attraction and chemistry we shared. No matter how many years went by, that same quivering and pulsating between my thighs would still occur. The same clammy hands and the moisture in the seat of my panties. The way my body reacted, you would think we didn't even know each other or, better yet, have a child together. At times I wondered if Plus would always have this hold over me.

"Where do I put this?" Plus peeked his head in my bedroom. He was carrying a box of Camille's belongings.

I looked up from where I sat on the unmade bed and pointed in the direction of the bedroom next door. "Put it in there please." Plus's soft curly black hair was pushed back in a white cut-off sleeve, and because it was hot outside, he didn't have on a shirt. Beads of sweat had gathered around his collarbone and had slid in between his muscular pecs. I subtly rolled my eyes. He got on my damn nerves, with his fine ass.

Even after Plus walked away, my stare lingered where he had stood by the door. It was as if my brain was involuntarily engraving the image of his heavenly body in my mind as some sort of keepsake.

"So Camille's gonna have her own room?" Myesha asked, taking me out of my trance. She was sitting on the floor Indian-style, folding up a few of my things. Her curly black hair was pulled up into a neat little bun that sat right on the top of her head, showcasing all the delicate brown features of her face. Her Asian-like eyes blinked back at me as she arched her neck up for a response.

"Yeah, Tez said that Camille needed her own room. Why? Should I use another room for her instead?"

Myesha hesitated at first, then shook her head. Things about her had been off as of late. We usually talked several times throughout the week, but lately, she'd been distant. She and I had actually grown pretty close over the past couple of years, and now that I considered her to be family, I knew I needed to ask her what was up.

"So what's been going on with you?" I asked, changing the topic of the conversation.

"Girl, nothing." She paused, lifting her shoulders dismissively. "Just the normal stuff, I guess."

"How've you and my brother been?" I asked, prying a bit deeper. I didn't do a whole lot of snooping into other people's business, but I wanted her to open up to me. Part of that was because I felt like she was holding back, while the other part was because now that we were gonna be living together, I wanted someone other than Nika to confide in.

A light breath left her lungs as she casually scratched at her temple. "We straight, I guess. I mean, I'm here all day. Doing nothing actually, and Tez . . ." Her voice dropped off before she pursed her lips to the side. It looked as if she was going through a mental Rolodex of sorts as she carefully chose her words. "Well, Tez is Tez."

"What? He fucking wit' you? You want me to talk to him?" I was trying to understand her evasive answers.

She shook her head and waved her hand at me. "No, your brother's good to me. Treats me like a queen. I just . . . I just don't think we want the same things future-wise."

The corners of my lips curled up into a sheepish smile. "You wanna get married, huh?"

"Yeah—"

Just then Tez walked into the bedroom and unintentionally cut her off. "My, come order us some food before Pops and them get here."

As she got up from the floor, she gave me a closed-lip smile, then attempted to slip past Tez and exit the room. But before she reached the door, he slapped her on the behind. He then grabbed a handful of her ass through the purple cheerleader shorts she wore, then leaned back and gave her a wet, playful kiss.

"Ew!" I complained as I observed their display of affection. Myesha laughed and walked out the door.

Tez's eyes narrowed in my direction. "And don't be in here filling my girl's head up with no dumb shit either, yo."

Gasping, I facetiously threw my hands up on my chest. "Dumb shit? Who me?" I batted my eyes dramatically.

"Yeah, you." He pointed his finger at me. "I know how y'all women do. Always creating problems when there ain't any."

I knew Myesha would kill me for asking him this, but I wanted to know where my brother's head was at. "You ever think you might want to get married one day?"

Tez's neck jerked back, and his eyes opened wide. Covertly, he looked over his shoulder into the hallway, then returned his gaze to me. He licked his lips. "Yo, that's what the fuck y'all was in here talking 'bout?"

Trying to stifle a hearty laugh, I let out a light chuckle. "No, dummy. I just wanted to know where your head was at."

Running his hand down his jaw, he let out a sigh that I could somehow tell was an expression of both relief and annoyance. "Perri, I'm telling you now, don't come up in here and start no bullshit between me and Myesha." His voice was stern but low, like he was trying to whisper. "Our li'l thing we got going on is one hunnid. I don't want her getting no ideas in her head, fucking up what we got going on."

"It was just a question, Tez. Damn."

I watched as a serious expression slid over Tez's face as he shook his head. "You already know how I feel about marriage and kids. I'm out here in these streets every fucking night. Praying that my ass make it home safe and that I don't get caught. Fuck I need a commitment like that for? I 'on't need no extra weight on my shoulders right now, ya feel me? I mean, I couldn't do what I do knowing I had a family at home that I could possibly leave behind."

I rolled my eyes at his brainless rationale. It didn't matter that Myesha wasn't his wife or that they didn't have kids, because if anything were to happen to him, she would be just as devastated. And that whole spiel about not wanting to leave his family behind was just gibberish too. If Tez were to leave this earth or be put behind bars, he would be leaving my father, Ms. Tonya, Plus, Aria and, more importantly, *me* behind to pick up the broken pieces. We were his family, and we would all be lost without him.

"Tez, a wife and kids don't constitute a family. What about me?" I pointed to my chest. "I'm your family. I don't know what I would do if something were ever to happen to you." Hearing my own voice crack helped me to fight back the tears that were threatening to fall from my eyes.

Right away I could tell he sensed my vulnerability, because his eyes softened a bit. "Ain't shit gon' happen to me, P. Stop talking reckless," he said.

Plus's hands, which were clad in fingerless leather gloves, gripped each side of the door frame before he abruptly leaned into the room. "Aye, you gon' come help with the rest of these boxes downstairs, or you gon' sit here and look pretty all day?" he asked, looking at me.

"Nigga, stop flexing and put your shirt on, yo. It ain't that gahdamn hot outside," Tez joked, lifting the mood in the room. We all fell out laughing.

"Yeah, a'ight. Whatever, nigga," Plus said.

Tez didn't let up. He continued clowning on Plus. "Nigga, we know you play basketball. Perri ain't trying see all that shit," he teased, then pulled his fist up to his mouth for a laugh.

A childish play fight erupted as Tez and Plus jabbed gently at each other's chest and abs. This was something they had done often with each other over the years. I got up from the bed, hoping to slip past them unnoticed, but before I could leave the room, Plus's strong arm slipped around my waist and pulled me back into his chest. I closed my eyes, and when he leaned his head down and brought his mouth close to my ear, I could smell the faded scent of his Burberry cologne.

"Let me holla at you for a minute," he whispered in my ear, and I savored the warmth of his breath on my skin.

A mischievous grin took over Tez's lips. "Uh-huh," he mumbled. "I see you two need some privacy."

"No! You don't have to leave," I said, panicking, truly not wanting to be left alone with Plus.

"Yeah, man. Give us a minute please," Plus said, over-ruling me.

As soon as Tez had left the room, Plus shut the door and pressed my back up against it. My chest heaved up and down as he held both of my hands above my head. With his damp body, he covered my own and then buried his face in the crook of my neck. While my mind was telling me to push him away, it was like my body had its own agenda. My eyes instantly closed, and my pussy began to ache.

"Why you been avoiding me?" he asked in a whisper.

The muffled sound of his voice and the feel of his lips brushing against my skin created butterflies in the pit of my stomach. Squeezing my eyes tight, I swallowed hard and deceitfully rocked my head from side to side.

"Yes, you have. Stop lying," he whispered.

With his face still nuzzling my neck, he removed his hand from one of my wrists and slowly slid it down my body before removing his leather glove with his teeth. After tossing it to the floor, he swiped my cheek with the back of his hand before slipping it down to my breast. My chest swelled and tightened from his touch, a clear indication of the breath I had been holding. When his hand gradually snaked down between us and skimmed the elastic band of my shorts, a moan escaped my lips, filling me with a sense of shame.

I shook my head harder, silently protesting the feeling of his hands on my body. When his fingers found their way to my wet center and plunged deep into my throbbing core, I knew I had to say something. "Plus," I cried, letting my head fall back and hit the door.

Just as his fingers began traveling in and out of me with ease, the tip of his wet tongue slithered against my neck. Betraying everything I had been fighting against, I suddenly wrapped my arms around his muscular back. My hips willingly danced on his fingers, and my eyes rolled to the back of my head. I soon reached the point of no return. Biting down on my bottom lip, I tried to barricade the sound of another moan, but it was of no use. When Plus's fingers picked up speed, my body first quivered and then contracted, and I experienced a euphoric high.

"Argh!" I wailed. Tears sat at the corners of my eyes as I slowly ground on his fingers.

As I came down from my euphoric high, he lightly pecked away at my face, giving me the sweetest, most delicate kisses imaginable. When he pulled back, it felt as if my feet hit the floor, and I carefully opened up my eyes. A reluctant plea was on the surface of his gaze as he peered at me with those dark brown eyes. Both of us had been rendered speechless in that moment, but somehow our eyes, which remained locked to one another's, found a way to speak. They conveyed the uncertainty of our colorful past yet left the unanswered questions about our future up for debate.

"I'm gon' always love you, shorty," he said, breaking the silence. As he stared up at the ceiling, he swallowed hard, fighting against his next set of words. "No matter what, I'm gon' still love you, a'ight?" He looked at me, to guarantee that I fully understood.

And I did. Slowly, I closed my eyes, then nodded my head. The brimming tears were now falling freely down the curves of my face as I acknowledged the fact that perhaps Plus was finally letting me go. Would he no longer fight for me or interfere in my relationship with Derrick? My heart was torn.

With his hand cupping the back of my head, he pressed his soft lips into my forehead and held them there for what felt like an eternity. Memories of every moment we had ever shared flooded my mind at once. He leaned down and softly kissed me on the lips one last time. I tasted the salt of my tears as he took my breath away. He drew his face back from mine and pecked the tip of my nose before pulling the door open behind me and walking out of the room. With my back against the closed door and my shorts still around my ankles, I slid down to the carpeted floor. Overwhelmed and confused by what it all meant, I sobbed into the palms of my hands.

It took me exactly forty-two minutes to get myself together and leave my room. When I walked downstairs and looked out the windows, I could see that night had already overtaken the sky. Ms. Tonya and Daddy were sitting in the living room, watching TV, while Myesha was in the kitchen. I made my way over and greeted Ms. Tonya and Daddy.

"Hey, y'all. Where's my baby at?" I asked.

"Plus took her in the kitchen with Myesha a few minutes ago, I think," Daddy said, stretching his neck to see.

I walked into the kitchen and saw Myesha. She was leaning against the counter, with both of her arms out straight, supporting her weight. Her head hung down low between her shoulders, and I could hear her releasing short breaths from her lungs.

"What's wrong with you?" I asked.

"Nothing," she mumbled, her head still hanging low.

"Well, where's my baby?"

"Plus took her downstairs . . ." Her words struggled against a gurgling sound in her throat, and so she paused. "You know that's where your brother's at," she added.

I could tell she didn't feel well. "You sure you're all right?"

Myesha nodded her head but didn't speak. She just continued with those short breaths. When I turned around to head out of the kitchen, I heard what sounded like a bucketful of water spilling on the floor. Quickly, I turned back around and saw Myesha standing over a large puddle of orange-colored puke.

"Oh my goodness! Myesha, are you all right?" I exclaimed.

"Yeah, I'll be fine," she said weakly. Swiping her mouth with the back of her hand, she cut her eyes over at me in a way that revealed her little secret.

"Oh shit! Myesha, you're pregnant?" I let out before covering my mouth.

"Pregnant?"

I stiffened at the harsh sound of Tez's voice booming behind me and at the sight of the sheer horror that instantly covered Myesha's face

# Chapter 8

## *Tez*

The look on Myesha's face told me that I had heard right. Battling against the anger I felt surfacing, I let out an irritated snort of laughter. "Fuck, nah," I muttered, shaking my head.

"Baby, let's go upstairs and talk." The panic in Myesha's tone was evident as she tried to take control of the situation. Just hearing her voice caused heat to course through my veins and my breathing to pick up speed. However, I tried my best to remain cool.

"Nah, I ain't going upstairs. Say what the fuck you got to say, Myesha," I said. I kept an even tone as my eyes seared into her.

Perri must have sensed my anger, because she let out a sigh. "Y'all two just need to talk this out. I'm going downstairs with Plus and Camille," she said before brushing past me.

My eyes, however, stayed fixed on Myesha, who was still frozen in place, with vomit on the floor at her feet. "How far along?" I asked.

When she briefly closed her eyes and tucked in her lips, I knew she was far along. Too far along for a fucking abortion.

I snapped. "The fuck, Myesha! I told you from the jump I didn't want no fucking kids!" I shouted, venting the rage I had been trying so hard to suppress .

Covering her mouth with her hands, she shook her head. "I swear, it was an accident, Tez. I'm sorry," she cried.

"Accident?" I yelled, throwing my arms up in disbelief. "How many months?" I asked again, needing to know for sure that she was far along.

She cast her wet slanted eyes down to the floor before she twiddled her fingers in front of her.

"How many fucking months!" I yelled, this time louder, causing her to jump.

"Four," she whispered.

"Four . . . four fucking months," I mumbled in disbelief. Before I knew it, my hand was wrapped around the cold glass of water that sat on the quartz countertop, and I flung it hard across the room. "Fuck!" I snarled. When the glass shattered loudly against the wall, Myesha screamed.

Godma rushed in and stood next to me as my chest heaved up and down. My wild eyes were filled with nothing but pure anger in that moment. Fists clenched and jaw tight, I glared at my girl with resentment for the first time. She wouldn't look at me, though. Just continued to cry into the palms of her hands, so bad that her shoulders shook.

Godma's wide eyes observed Myesha first, then she saw the putrid vomit on the kitchen floor. When her eyes scanned the room and fell on the shattered glass and the water dripping down the white wall, she gasped. "What in the hell is going on in here?" she asked.

Not responding, I turned around and started walking away, but not before punching a hole in the wall. "I told you I didn't want no fucking kids!" I yelled. By then my father, Plus, and Perri were standing in the kitchen, trying to comprehend what was happening.

"What's wrong, son?" my father asked, placing his hand on my shoulder. I glanced over at Plus. He was standing next to Perri, who had Camille in her arms. I jerked away from my father's grasp and walked past him to head out the door.

"Hold up," I could hear Plus yell behind me, but I ignored him.

I jogged down the brick steps to the circular driveway and slid into my brand-new white Audi Q7. I smelled that new car scent and felt the buttery soft leather seats beneath me before cranking up the engine. After hearing a quick knock on the window, I looked over to find Plus trying to open up my passenger door. I quickly hit the LOCK button, and then I peeled off so fast that the rubber from my tires burned, leaving a trail of gray smoke behind me.

Although Plus was like my little brother and I knew he just wanted to be there for me, I needed to take this ride alone. I needed to clear my head and calm the fuck down. With my music turned up all the way, I bobbed my head, trying to relax. Before long I jumped on highway 295 North, toward Baltimore. At this point a fat ass, along with a blunt and a double shot of Hennessy on the rocks, was desperately calling my name.

I hit the Bluetooth and dialed a number I hadn't called in well over a year.

"Hello?"

"I'm coming through. Be there in thirty," I said, then abruptly ended the call.

After a forty-five-minute ride, I cut off my music before turning down Woodbrook Court. It was a nice, well-lit road in Randallstown, with similar-looking houses lining each side of the street. When I pulled up to the two-story gray home with vinyl siding and creeped up the driveway, I noticed that all the lights were off with the exception of the one on the porch. I hit the button to open up the garage door and carefully pulled in with ease. Using my own key, I quietly let myself in through the garage. The house still smelled the same, like cinnamon, and the stove light was on in the kitchen, just like old times.

I trudged through the kitchen and threw my keys on the counter before opening up the fridge. A brand-new bottle of Hennessy was in there, on the top shelf, already chilled. I grabbed a glass from the cabinet above and filled it halfway before eagerly tossing the drink to the back of my throat. Allowing that warm, burning sensation to coat the inside of my chest somehow soothed me. Running my hand down my face, I took another deep breath, filling my lungs, before pouring myself another.

As I climbed up the narrow stairs, with the glass of Hennessy in my hand, the smell of fresh marijuana became more apparent. I reached the top step and began walking down the dark hall. I saw a sliver of light peeking beneath the bedroom door. I took another deep breath, followed by yet another, to calm my nerves. When I walked in the room, everything was exactly how I'd left it, with the exception of her.

"Long time no see, baby," she purred. Her short brown hair and light buttery skin glistened in the candlelight.

Shayla was a chick I had grown up with in the Millwood Projects. She and I had been fucking on and off for years, since the tender age of fourteen. That was up until God spared my life two years ago, after getting shot. After that, I had decided to commit myself fully to Myesha. She had been there by my side when I had needed her the most, and I felt that I could no longer deny my love for her.

Shayla was cool peoples, though, and was as loyal as they came. She had never pushed a relationship on me, not even after I had got her pregnant when she was seventeen and asked her to get an abortion. In fact, she had even done a few illegal transports for me back in the day and had risked her freedom in more ways than one. For those reasons alone, I had bought her a little house out in the county about three years back and made sure to take care of her monthly bills. She didn't complain about not being with me, as long as her financial needs were met. And I knew that whenever I called, if I ever called again, she would be there waiting.

As I meandered over to the bed, with my body slumped, in a dejected state, she sat up on her knees and reached up to hug my neck. I wrapped my free arm around her tiny waist and felt beneath my hand the smoothness of the silk robe she wore. Shayla still smelled the same, like sweet vanilla extract. Her full breasts pressed up against me, causing my dick to swell in my pants.

"Somebody's been missing me," she whispered. Peering up at me with those big doe-like brown eyes, she slid her hands around my shoulders, then firmly down my back. I couldn't deny that I missed her touch.

I smacked her hard on the ass before sitting my glass down on the nightstand. After taking a seat on the edge of the bed, I removed the gold chains from around my neck, then set them aside. As I kicked the Tims off my feet, she shot up from the bed and went into the en suite bathroom. I could hear her starting the shower.

Leaning out the bathroom door, she asked knowingly, "You wanna jump in the shower while I roll?"

I looked her over, taking in her short, sexy little frame, before licking my lips. "Yeah."

She took out a fresh towel for me, along with a new bar of Dove soap, before helping me remove the rest of my clothes.

While showering for almost thirty minutes, my thoughts were filled with nothing but Myesha, and what I considered to be her betrayal. As the hot water cascaded down my body, I thought back to how I had met her and how we had fallen in love. She had come into my life without warning, like a tornado or maybe even a hurricane.

*One rainy morning I stood in the middle of Cedar Hill Cemetery, visiting my mother's grave. It was something I randomly did when I had her heavy on my mind or when I was going through some shit. As I was stooping down to place the pink tulips beside her headstone, I heard the cries of someone behind me. After sliding my umbrella to the side, I looked over my shoulder and saw this pretty brown china doll with wet curly black hair sticking to the sides of her face. No umbrella or raincoat, just her, standing there in the rain. She was looking down at the grave in front of her and getting soaking wet. Even though she was pretty as hell, I wasn't going to push up on her or even talk to her, given where we were. But when I heard her whimpers, which gave the impression that she was suffering terribly, it just did something to me. I swear, that shit was the saddest sound I had ever heard.*

*I walked over to her, held my umbrella above our heads, and cautiously put my arm around her shoulders. She didn't know my ass from a can of paint, but for some reason, she let me comfort her that morning. She just stood there, looking down at the tombstones of a Barry and Monique Hudson, crying to them about how much she missed them and how much she really needed them. For almost an hour, we stood there shivering, until our feet were damn near buried in the mud.*

*Eventually, the roar of thunder escaped the boiling sky above our heads, and cracks of lightning flickered all around us. I knew we had to leave right away. What made things worse was that I had to physically make her leave the cemetery that day, had to usher her toward the street. When I asked where her car was, she told me that she'd walked. And when I asked where home was, so that I could drop her off, she told me that she didn't have a home. Up until she graduated high school a month before, she had been living in a foster home, and she said that the day she crossed the stage was also the same day she ran away. For the past month she had been living in the streets, going from shelter to shelter, with no real food and no family to her name. Hearing her story just did something to me.*

*Sure, a nigga like me was all about my money, and no, I wasn't no Captain Save a Ho, but the sadness behind her beautiful slanted brown eyes just couldn't be ignored. I put her up in a nice hotel that day, made sure she had good food, and even bought her new clothes. I did that shit for two months straight, never telling a soul about her. Just kept her to myself.*

*Over that time, the ironclad walls she had built up slowly came down, and I learned a lot about her. She shared that her parents had been murdered when she was thirteen years old and that she'd fallen victim to the foster-care system. Her description of the rape and abuse she endured during that time was enough to make even the toughest nigga cringe. But beyond her desolation and vulnerability, I could recognize her beauty and her strength. It was something that reminded me of Perri and my mother. Over those months we connected so much that she even had me telling her my business. Which was some shit a nigga like me just didn't do. I told her stories about my mother and how I'd lost her to cancer when I was just nine years old. I told her how I had got tired of going to school with holes in my shoes and eating ramen noodles for dinner every night, which had ultimately led to me being in the streets.*

*As the months went by, she and I became friends, then eventually lovers. I ended up moving Myesha to her own little apartment, and I even got her something to ride in. But I was still fucking around with Shayla during that time too. And it was all good up until two years ago, when a nigga caught three bullets and was in the hospital, fighting for my life. When I came home from the hospital, Myesha took good care of me. My need to have her on a daily basis intensified, matching the need she already had for me. And somewhere, somehow during the course of all that, she told me she loved me. But what surprised me the most was when I had to fight myself not to say those three little words back. Although I never said them, I couldn't deny that the feelings were there, and outside of my family, no one had ever gotten that out of me.*

*Hell, a nigga didn't think I was even capable of feeling the things I felt for her, but I did. That love bullshit happened all at once, hitting a nigga like a ton of bricks. But even though I thought I might possibly love her ass, not once did I waver when it came to not wanting kids. She was the one who convinced me to stop using condoms, saying that it felt better without them and that she was on the pill. I watched her take them faithfully for several months before I gave in and stopped using condoms. And even then I would occasionally ask her, just double checking that she was on the pill.*

She knew how big of a deal that was for me, so I didn't know now how she could have fucked it all up. Just as my mind started to entertain all the reasons why Myesha would purposely try to get pregnant, I felt a cool breeze coming from behind me. I turned around to see Shayla, who was wearing nothing but her birthday suit. Her skin was already glistening from the steam as she gingerly stepped inside the tub. Her skin was smooth and all the same shade of vanilla, with the exception of her hardened nipples. Her short brown hair was brushed back off her face, exposing her big brown eyes and the high set of her cheekbones. When she closed those pink, heart-shaped lips of hers, I immediately envisioned them wrapped around my dick.

"You're taking an awfully long time in here. Thought you might need some help," she said, grabbing the soapy cloth from my hand.

I put my hand up to stop her, because I had already washed. "Nah, shorty, I'm good."

She put the cloth aside and quickly dropped down to her knees in front of me. As her warm mouth took me whole, my head involuntarily fell back, allowing the water to flow down both of us. I could feel my long locks slapping against the top of my ass as she grabbed the sides of my thighs for support. Swallowing my dick up to the back of her throat, she moaned and gagged from my size. Repeatedly, her soft, wet tongue swiped up and down my shaft, and she sucked me deeper, until my toes finally began to curl.

"Shit," I hissed.

I looked down at those big doe eyes, which were fervently trained on me. Water cascaded down her entire face as I slipped in and out of her lips. I thrust my hips forward, grabbed the very top of her head, met her face with several gentle strokes of my own. The sounds of her slurping and moaning caused a tightness to stir in my groin and sent the rest of my body into a seizure-like frenzy. I clenched my teeth to hold back my bitch-like moans, but it was of no use. With a firm grip on her head, I grunted out and finally came.

"Fuck, Shay!"

After we got out of the shower and got in bed, Shayla admitted that she was hoping we could fuck. And not that she wasn't tempting, but I was just too mentally and physically spent to do anything more. With the lights completely off, I closed my eyes but struggled to actually fall asleep. For most of the night, my guilt and anger battled against one another inside my head.

Of course I was angry about being forced into father-hood but, on the other hand, I felt guilty too. Guilty for being here with Shayla, but mostly for not hearing Myesha out. Maybe there was a good reason she had let four months pass by without telling me she was pregnant with my seed. From day one, Myesha had shown me she had a pure heart. She wasn't like these other birds out here, trying to trap a nigga for his money. Shorty truly loved me for me. But even with that said, it didn't change the fact that I didn't want to be a father. At least not now, with the way my life was set up. I wanted to get this bread while I was still young and able, and I wanted to come home at night to my woman and a quiet house.

Before the sun could even come up, I slipped out of bed and put my clothes back on.

"You're leaving?" Shayla asked softly from the bed. Her bare shoulders appeared from the top of the thin white sheet as she rubbed her eyes.

"Yeah. I'ma check you later, a'ight?" I looked down and saw a subtle sadness wash over her face.

"Don't be a stranger for too long this time," she whis-pered.

I leaned down and kissed her forehead as she reached up to gently touch my face. "I won't."

"Promise?"

"I promise, shorty," I said before letting out a light chuckle.

After going downstairs and entering the garage, I got in my ride. As daylight was breaking through the sky, I cruised down the highway, heading back to Bowie. Thoughts of how to make this shit right with Myesha played heavily on my mind. I kept rehearsing over

and over in my head what I wanted to say to her. Kept
thinking of her potential responses and envisioning how
this shit was all going to play out.

When I finally made it home, it was 6:51 a.m. After
entering the quiet house, I disabled the alarm before
heading upstairs to our master suite. I pushed the double
doors open to find our bed empty and neatly made. I
went into the master bathroom, but Myesha wasn't in
there either. My heart was beating so loudly, I could
literally feel it pulsing inside my throat, and all of a
sudden my stomach just didn't feel right. I pulled open
the door to our walk-in closet and instantly noticed the
empty hangers. Every piece of clothing she owned had
been removed. My chest tightened at the sight, and a
nigga felt like he was suffocating.

I rushed out of the room and first flung open the door
to my office, then went down to the guest room. No signs
of Myesha could be found in either room. Panicking, I
knocked hard on Perri's bedroom door. Surprisingly, a
heavy-eyed Plus answer my knock and opened the door. I
peeked in the room and saw that Perri still asleep in the
bed and that on the floor beside it was an all too familiar
pallet, which I assumed was his.

"Where'd Myesha go?" I asked, trying to disguise the
fluster in my voice.

Sighing, Plus ran his hand down the top of his head,
pushing his curls forward. He glanced up in a sympa-
thetic manner before walking over to the bed.

"Aye yo, P! Perri!" he called, shaking Perri's leg.

Perri struggled a bit before she finally woke up and noticed me standing by the door. Her eyes held the same look
of pity and compassion that Plus's did. Without even asking,
I already knew, but I just needed to hear Perri to say it.

I swallowed hard, ignoring the constriction forming
inside my chest. "Where did Myesha go?" I asked, then
licked away the dryness from my lips.

Perri reached for a sealed white envelope on her nightstand before shuffling her way out of bed. "You made her leave, yo," she whispered, placing the envelope in my hand.

I ripped the envelope open in a hurry, and pulled out a simple folded white sheet of paper. I just stared at it, too afraid to read what I knew could be her very last words to me. With shaky hands, I somehow mustered up the courage to unfold the letter. I immediately saw her beautiful handwriting in dark blue ink.

*Dear Montez,*

*After you left last night, I did some serious soul-searching and took the time to really just reflect. I came to the conclusion that I betrayed you in the worst possible way. The only stipulation you ever gave me in this relationship was the one I defied, and for that, I truly apologize.*

*You saved me—no, you loved me—during a time when I didn't think I'd ever receive love again. I was broken down, abused, and all alone when you swooped in and changed all that for me. You revitalized my worth as a human being and, more importantly, as a woman. You don't realize this, but you've now given me something even greater. . . . You've given me a family, something that was taken from me almost eight years ago. This little piece of joy I'm carrying inside me now will always be my family. Someone for me to love and someone who will love me back unconditionally, without stipulations. And for that, I'm forever grateful.*

*Every day I'll cherish the memory of you, of us, through this gift you've given me. But I will no*

*longer be a burden to you or be made to feel that
I've interrupted your so-called lifestyle. Take care
and know that I'll always love you.*
   *Myesha*

A nigga hadn't cried since I was nine years old, but
in that moment it was just impossible to hold back my
emotions. The tears had already begun to blotch the ink
when I reread her letter a second time. Perri wrapped
an arm around my back and cried right alongside me,
leaning her head against my shoulder. Plus, on the other
hand, just stood there looking helpless, rubbing his hand
down his jaw, unsure of exactly what else to say.

"I gotta go get my family back, yo," I said with a sniff. "I
gotta go get my family."

# Chapter 9

## *Perri*

As I sat down on the bleachers to ensure that my sneakers were tied tight, I looked clear across McDonough Arena. Girls who resembled me were either passing the ball or standing in line to attempt a layup shot. It was finally the day of the women's basketball tryouts at Georgetown, and for some reason, I was nervous as hell. Given the rapid beating of my heart and all the sweat on my hands, I didn't know how I was going to perform.

"Perri Daniels?"

Hearing my name, I lifted my head up to see a tall white lady with icy blue eyes and short chestnut-brown hair looking my way. Coach Cindy Barrett was the head coach for the women's basketball team at Georgetown. She had the reputation of being a bulldog, vicious and strong willed. And judging by the stern glare and the frown she was giving me, that description seemed pretty accurate.

"You Daniels?" she asked again, pointing at me.

I nodded my head, stood up nervously from the bench, and walked out onto the court.

After lifting the whistle up to her lips, she blew it loudly, getting everyone's attention. "All right, ladies. Listen up! We've got twenty-four of you trying out this year, but we're taking only three. I'm gonna start by counting you all off into six groups of four. Line up!"

After we had lined up on the court, she counted us off and told us that we were going to play a few games of four on four. I sat back down on the bench with some of the other girls and watched the first game play out. There were several girls playing that were actually pretty good, but one in particular really stood out. She was a tall dark-skinned girl with a scar across her cheek. She had big pouty lips and a wide nose that was pierced with a tiny diamond. On top of her head was a bush ball that bounced as she ran up and down the court with her long colt-like legs. The girls who sat beside me cheered every time she made a shot, affectionately referring to her as KiKi. She was clearly my competition.

At the end of a six-minute game, KiKi and her crew were the winners, and they headed over to the bleachers for some water and much-needed rest.

"Good game," I said to Kiki, giving her a high five.

"Thanks," she said before squeezing the bottle to squirt water in her mouth.

It was now my turn to get out there and show what I had. After swinging my arms around my chest to stretch, I walked out on the floor with the other girls who were scheduled to play in the next game. I closed my eyes and said a silent prayer in hopes of performing my best.

When the whistle blew, it felt like a switch turned on inside me. I opened my eyes and effortlessly rushed down the court. All my nerves had suddenly subsided, and although I could still feel my heart galloping inside my chest, it was game time. As soon as the ball was passed to me, I pulled up on the three-point line and took a shot. The swishing sound of the ball going through the net caused a temporary smile to grace my face, but I kept my focus and ran back down the court to get in position. I was defending this short, pretty little white girl who, I had to admit, had some sick ball-handling skills. However, her skills just weren't as good as mine. As soon as she went up for a three-point jumper of her own, I smacked the ball in midair and took it down to the other end of the court. I passed it to a teammate, who did a chest pass right back to me, and I went in for an easy two-point layup. When I felt that rush of excitement coursing through my veins, I knew I was on one.

As the game continued, I made several rebounds and three more successful shots, scoring eleven out of the total seventeen points my team racked up. When the game was over and we had won our six-minute set, all the girls were patting me on my back, cheering, and giving me high fives. I felt so alive, it was as if I was made whole again. That piece of me that had been missing for the past few years seemed to have finally been restored.

After all three games were played, Coach Barrett told us to go shower in the locker room. She said that by the time we were done, she would have the names of the girls who had made the first round of cuts up on the board. I was nervous as hell. When I later came out of the locker room, I saw Derrick standing against the wall of the gym, with his hands tucked in his pockets. His dark eyes lit up when he saw me, and the dimples in his cheeks deepened as he smiled.

I walked over to him and gave him a tight hug around his neck, smelled his signature cologne. "What are you doing here?"

"I came to see if my fiancée made the team," he said, using that word *fiancée* again.

I let out a nervous little giggle. "Well, I guess we'll see."

He sucked his teeth and waved me off, as though I was talking nonsense. "I just know you made it, Ma. My girl got skills."

His eyes went to my lips before his tongue slowly licked his own. After stepping forward, he pinched my chin between his fingers and leaned in for a kiss. My eyes couldn't help but close, but before his lips could merge with mine, we heard, "Ahem."

My eyes flew open, and I saw Plus standing off to the side of us with a dozen red roses in his hand and Camille down by his side.

"Mommy," she said, pulling away from Plus's hand to run toward me.

I picked her up and kissed her chubby cheek before returning my gaze to Plus. Standing there, with navy blue basketball shorts on and a gray Nike T-shirt, he smirked at the two of us. Soft, overgrown curls were pulled back underneath his fitted cap, and his small diamond studs sparkled in his ears. I bit down on my bottom lip, hating the fact that I was *still* so attracted to him.

"Uh, what are you guys doing here?" I asked.

Plus came in closer, passed me the flowers, and congratulated me before stepping slightly in front of Derrick and kissing me on the lips. There wasn't any tongue involved, nor did he let the moment linger, but when he pulled back and I got a glimpse of the expression on Derrick's face, I knew he felt disrespected. His eyebrows were knotted together, and his jaw was tight.

"My man, the fuck is you doing, son?" Derrick all but growled, gaining Plus's full attention.

A cocky little grin was etched across Plus's face, and he coolly licked his lips and ran his hand down his jaw.

Mortified, I pressed my hand against my forehead and closed my eyes. Why did Plus have to kiss me in front of Derrick?

"Oh, my bad. How's it going, D?" Plus asked almost facetiously.

The scowl on Derrick's face couldn't be missed when he stepped up, squaring his big muscular shoulders. A sarcastic snort of laughter escaped his lips before he thumbed one side of his nose. "Not too well, duke, considering you kissing my fiancée all on the mouth. Fuck was that?"

Holding his chin in his hand, Plus allowed his eyes to roam up to the ceiling before he twisted his lips to the side. I had known Plus long enough to ascertain that he was carefully selecting his next set of words. He let out a light snort and shook his head before aiming his finger at Derrick as if it were a gun. "Look, I'm gon' keep it all the way one hunnid wit' you," he said, stretching his thumb back toward me and Camille. "This here is my muhfucking family. You can call her your fiancée all you want, but it doesn't change the fact that her heart belongs to me."

"Ahmad!" I gasped, hoping that he would stop.

Derrick cocked his head to the side, ready to speak up, as well, but Plus kept on, holding his hand up in the air. "Nah, lemme finish! She ain't been wearing yo' fucking ring, and she damn sure ain't been running around here calling you her fiancé."

Derrick's eyes shot to me, and I felt so ashamed when I looked down at my bare hand, with Camille squirming unceasingly in my arms.

Plus went on. "Now I'm just gon' say this, and then I'll leave it at that. I'm in love with Perri, and the only reason she's even with you is that I"—he pointed to his chest—"fucked shit up. I was out there searching for some shit I already had right in front of my fucking face. And I swear, yo . . . I swear to God, if I gots to spend e'ry day trying to prove to her that, with all my faults, I'm still the better man, then that's what I'm gon' do."

Derrick's shoulders dropped, and although more words were ready to skate off his tongue, he didn't respond. With a smug grin on his face, he simply nodded his head. The gesture wasn't a sign of defeat but an indication that Plus had perhaps won this round.

Plus turned back toward me and kissed me on my cheek before taking Camille out of my arms. "Again, shorty, congrats on making the first round of cuts. I'll see you back at the house, a'ight?"

Up until that point, I had totally forgotten that I was supposed to check the board. I glanced over to the right side of the gym and saw all the other girls gathered around. Without so much as a good-bye, I ran full speed ahead in their direction with the bouquet of roses in my hand. I literally had to fight my way through the crowd to get up front, but as soon as I got there, I skimmed through the names on the page attached to the board, my finger moving nervously down the list. Some of the names were highlighted, while others were crossed out. The very last highlighted name, at the bottom of the page, was Perri Daniels.

*Yes!* Silently, I did a fist pump before turning back to cut through the crowd of girls. As I started skipping away, I heard my name being called.

"Aye, yo, Daniels!"

I turned around to see KiKi, the tall dark-skinned girl with the bush ball on the top of her head. I lifted my chin to acknowledge her.

"I'll see you tomorrow," she said.

Nodding my head, I smiled, then rushed back toward Derrick and Plus. Only it appeared that Plus and Camille had already left. I should have felt relieved that I was no longer going to be caught in between Plus and Derrick, but I didn't. Instead, I felt sad that Plus wasn't there to share my moment. Then I realized that he had congratulated me already, and I wondered how he had known then that I had made the team. Then I figured he, being so clever, must have checked the board the moment the names were posted.

"So I'm guessing that cheesy-ass smile on your face means you made it, huh?" Derrick joked.

"Yes," I said, cheesing more.

He gave me a tight hug, then picked me up before spinning me around. "Congrats, Ma. You deserve it," he whispered in my ear. As confused as I was when it came to him and Plus, I had to admit that it felt good being in his arms. When he put me back down, he asked me if he could take me to dinner. Knowing that I hadn't been out with Derrick in well over a month and that I had constantly been blowing him off, I agreed.

When we got out to his car, he went to open up the door for me but suddenly stopped. Narrowing his eyes, he tucked in his lips.

"You gon' open up my door?" I asked.

"Yeah, I'm gon' open up your door, Ma." With a serious expression on his face, he let out a snort before licking his lips. A split second later, he glared at me and said, "But let me just say this right quick before we go. Unless you are telling me that you don't want to be with me like that, please put that ring back on yo' finger, and don't take that shit off, a'ight? That's disrespectful as fuck, Ma."

My mouth dropped a bit, as I had been rendered speechless. Nonetheless, I nodded my head, because he was right. I was playing a dangerous game with all our emotions. Finally, he opened the car door for me, and I slid in the seat, feeling a tad awkward. Once Derrick got inside and cranked up the engine, he reached over to hold my hand, instantly putting me at ease.

Over the course of dinner at Hwy 55, Derrick and I fell back into our normal vibe, laughing and talking just as we had before summer break. It was nice being around him again, and while I was inarguably still in love with Plus, I couldn't deny that my feelings for Derrick were still very much present.

When Derrick walked me up to my door that evening, he closed the space between us before leaning down to kiss my lips. At first he gave me a soft peck, but it gradually transitioned into a slip of his tongue. The undeniable chemistry we shared was evident, as my knees buckled beneath me. Just as he pulled back and I was able to catch my breath, the door opened behind me. Plus was standing there, holding Camille in his arms.

*Ugh!*

Derrick's nose flared slightly as he backed up a bit more. "Yo, you staying here now?" he asked, tucking his hands in his pockets.

"Why you worrying about it?" Plus said, glaring at Derrick.

Patting Derrick softly on the chest, I told him that I would call him later. After watching him jog down the stairs to his car and pull off, I stormed past Plus, who was still standing in the doorway. The startling sound of the door slamming shut behind me caused me to turn around.

"What is your problem, Ahmad?" I fussed.

"You." He pointed at me. "You're my fucking problem."

"Well, then, you know how to fix it. Just leave already."

"Is that what you want? You want me to leave?" he asked in a low voice, walking into my personal space.

Even with Camille in his arms, my breath contracted, and I had to turn my head and look away. My chest was heaving and a pout had formed on my lips when he peered down at me. He gripped one side of my waist firmly and pulled me in close as he waited for eye contact. I always felt like this with him. Whenever the two of us got close, a warmth would spread throughout my entire body, I would blush like a schoolgirl, and moisture would collect between my thighs. It never failed.

"You want me to leave?" he whispered again, pressing his body even closer to mine.

"Daddy no weave, Mommy," Camille said.

I looked up and saw her brandy-colored eyes sparkling back at me, along with the ridiculous smirk on Plus's face. I rolled my eyes before he and I both fell out laughing. Camille giggled, too, like she knew what we were laughing about. I had to admit that it was the cutest thing: those two joining forces against me.

When the humor settled, Plus licked his lips and tightened his hold on my waist. "I guess it's settled, then," he said evenly, gazing down into my eyes. "Camille has spoken, and Daddy ain't going nowhere."

# Chapter 10

## *Nika*

With only ten minutes to spare until my next class, I rushed out of the science building. There, leaning back against the brick building that was Chesapeake Hall, stood Jorell, with some tall light-skinned girl by his side. While she stood there laughing and smiling in his face, he appeared to be soaking it right on up. He was flashing those gold front teeth of his flirtatiously and moistening his lips every so often with the tip of his wet tongue. His long locks lay underneath a backward baseball cap, and his eyes were curiously low as he propped one foot up on the wall.

Rolling my eyes, I walked past him and kept going until I heard him call my name.

"Nika! Hold up, shawty!" he shouted.

I turned around to see him jogging toward me, holding up the crotch of his sagging pants as the gold chains around his neck swung back and forth.

"What do you want, Jorell?" I asked, glancing down at the watch on my wrist.

"Damn, shawty. It's like that? A nigga drove all the way up here to see you, and you ain't even got five minutes to holla at me?"

Here it was, ten days into the month of September, and I hadn't even seen or spoken to Jorell since the Fourth of July. I had been so hurt—no, *distraught*—to learn that

Jorell had been keeping his daughter a secret from me. After I'd left Alabama the very next day, I'd cut Jorell off completely, blocking all his calls, texts, and emails. I had been avoiding contact with him at all costs, even by distancing myself a bit from Perri and Plus. It was the only way I knew to protect myself from him. And now here he was, at my school, standing in front of me and acting as though I was the one who had done him wrong.

"Look, I didn't ask you to come all the way up here, Jorell. I have eight minutes to get to my next class, so if you need to tell me something, I suggest you get it off your chest now!" I spat, snaking my neck.

"Damn, li'l baby. I miss all that feistiness," he said playfully. His gold teeth shined through the crack of his lips as he gave a cocky little grin.

Beyond fed up with his slick talking and arrogant ways, I rolled my eyes before turning to walk away, but before I could take another step, he grabbed my arm and pulled me back.

"Hold up, shawty. My bad," he said. His dark brown eyes narrowed as a pinched, more serious expression took over his face. His grasp on my arm loosened, and then his hand slid gently all the way down to join mine. "I been trying to call you, but you blocked a nigga," he said in a low voice.

I removed my hand from his and held it up near his face. "Jorell, let's just be real. You kept your daughter a secret from me for almost *two years*," I shouted angrily, holding up two fingers. "Then I had to hear about it not from you, but from your daughter's mother." I sucked in a breath before my index finger shot in the air. "Who, by the way, you were cheating on me with." I was so furious as I recounted all those events in my mind that my hands were actually shaking. "So now you drove all the way up here to say what? What could there possibly be left to say, Jorell?"

Frustrated, Jorell ran his hand down his face before letting out a deep sigh. "I fucked up, Nik. I don't know what else to say." He shook his head.

"Humph," I scoffed, folding my arms over my chest.

His pleading eyes softened a bit more as he stepped in close. "I miss you like crazy, shawty." There was a hint of desperation in his voice, which was low enough for only me to hear.

I pointed back to where the tall light-skinned girl was standing behind us, probably still waiting on Jorell. "Yeah, I can really tell how much you miss me," I said sarcastically.

He cursed beneath his breath after looking over his shoulder. Seeing the girl just waving her hand about, he clenched his jaw. "Mane, I don't know that girl."

"But you want to get to know her, right?" Leaning in for an answer, I raised my left eyebrow.

Sucking his teeth, he shook his head. I knew Jorell was lying, so I trekked over to the girl myself.

"Excuse me," I said, causing the girl's eyes to grow wide. "Was my boyfriend over here, trying to talk to you?" My voice was calm as I pointed my thumb back at Jorell.

Her eyes shot over to him before stuttered words began to fall from her lips. "Um, I . . . I . . . uh . . ."

I peeked back around to see Jorell shaking his head from side to side in an exaggerated manner, obviously trying to tell the girl to say no.

I spun around really fast on the balls of my feet and jumped right in Jorell's face. "Exactly. Now keep your lying, cheating ho ass the fuck away from me, Jorell!"

I left him standing there as I stormed off, heading to my next class. The sound of him calling out my name from behind me eventually grew weak as I placed more distance between us. When I finally reached my classroom door, I hesitated before going in. I had to wipe the moisture from my face and suck in a deep breath to collect myself before stepping inside the classroom.

That evening, long after class was over, I entered the house, feeling both physically and emotionally drained. Grandma Pearl's old gray eyes met mine as she sat on the sofa, knitting something in a pale shade of blue. Her heart-shaped face, which had seemed to age rather slowly over the years, was framed by a halo of curly white hair.

"You want something to eat?" was the first thing she asked. After adjusting the glasses on her face, she cast her eyes back down on her working needles. There was no "Hello" or "How was your day?" "Can I feed you?" was what she asked. That had always been her way of greeting me, and I didn't mind.

"No, ma'am. I'm not hungry. Just going upstairs," I said, raking my fingers through my untamed curls.

As I hurriedly crossed the living room, she spoke again. "So how are things going with that nice boy you brought over here?"

*Really!* Jorell had met my grandmother only three times in the past two years, and the last time he had visited our house was before the summer even began. It was now September. If I didn't know any better, I'd swear she had some sort of grandmother's intuition. Rolling my eyes, I stopped in my tracks and released a small breath of annoyance. "Fine, I guess, Grandma. I don't talk to him anymore."

For the second time since I'd walked through the door, she glanced up at me over her glasses. "Really?" she asked, her voice rising an octave, as though she was surprised.

"Yes, ma'am. I found out that he has a daughter and . . ." I swallowed, hesitating, because the next part really hurt. "He's still involved with her mother, I guess."

"Wow. I see," she said, glancing back down to work the yarn with her needles again. "Well, look, Ms. Bernadine at church has been trying to set you up with her grandson Clarence for the longest—"

*Clarence.* I shook my head to cut her off, because even his name sounded lame. "That's all right, Grandma. I really don't do blind dates."

"Just come to church with me this Sunday. No date or nothing. Just . . . to say hi," she proposed.

Rolling my eyes, I let out another quiet puff of air, trying to remain respectful. "All right. Fine," I said, reluctantly agreeing, because I knew just how persistent she could be.

A victorious smile formed on her mouth as she slowly nodded her head. "Oh, and I made us some turkey wings. Go wash up, so you can eat."

Although it hadn't been but five minutes since I last told her I wasn't hungry, I knew she wasn't going for that. With heavy feet, I climbed the stairs to do just as she had instructed.

Sunday morning had arrived and, just like I had agreed, I was heading into the church with Grandma. I hadn't been to church in a good while, so a lot people were acting shocked to see me. They stopped me on my way to our seats and asked how I'd been or what I'd been up to. After getting through it all with a counterfeit smile and whatever faux politeness I could muster at 8:30 in the morning, I made it to the very first pew just a minute after Grandma. Yes, that's right, front and center. As the mother of the church for the past fifteen years, Grandma wouldn't have it any other way.

As we stood by our seats, I gave a sigh of relief, as I'd noticed that Ms. Bernadine, a prim and proper lady, was sitting alone two seats down from Grandma's. She was fair skinned, and she had large dangly black moles all over her face and neck. Beneath her money-green church hat was a short-cut wig that sat just a tad bit crooked on her head. A few strands of pearls were gathered around her neck, and they complimented her green two-piece ensemble and her flat green Mootsies Tootsies shoes. My eyes traveled slowly down her swollen elephant legs, which she had managed somehow to cross at the ankles.

"So, Ms. Nika, I see you found your way to service this morning," she said.

My eyebrows rose as I forced another tight-lipped smile. "Yes, ma'am."

Just as Grandma and I were about to take our seats, a young man walked past us.

"Oh, here's Clarence now," Grandma said, giving me an obvious wink. Sheer embarrassment consumed my entire being as I looked over at this short, chubby fellow, whose broad smile exposed the gap between his teeth. Pulling his too-small pants up over his protruding belly, he studied me through the thick lens of the glasses on his face. Then he stepped closer to me and extended his hand.

"Clarence," was all he said. I could feel my nostrils flare as I looked down at his dry ashy fingers.

Only a few awkward seconds had passed before Grandma lightly smacked me on my back. My mouth dropped a little as I tripped forward into his personal space. Eyes fluttering, I swallowed, having realized just how rude I was being. He just gave another toothy grin, showcasing that same gap of his, with his hand still extended. Wanting to come off as not being the least bit interested, I shook his hand firmly, as though we were conducting business.

"Nika. It's nice to meet you, Clarence," I said with an even voice before coercing my face to wear another phony smile.

When he turned my hand over and kissed the back of it, I gasped. Immediately, I cringed from the rough feel of his cracked lips against my skin. I pulled my hand back and rubbed where he had just kissed, subconsciously trying to clean my hand or soothe the skin, I guessed.

Ms. Bernadine just smiled as she patted the seat next to her for Clarence to sit. I tried sitting on the other side of Grandma, but she wasn't having it. She simply shook her head before silently telling me with those commanding eyes of hers to sit next to Clarence.

After the three of us took our seats, the overwhelming scent of Clarence's Brut cologne caused an itching in my throat. We were sitting so close to each other that the sides of our arms and legs were touching, and I was desperate for some wiggle room. When the choir came out and began to sing, Clarence sang right along with them. He clapped his fat little stubby hands and stomped his loafer-covered feet to the rhythm. As he rocked back and forth in the pew, he repeatedly bumped into me.

The service hadn't even started yet, and I was beyond annoyed and ready to go. However, when Pastor Strong came out, looking every bit of a distinguished clergyman in his purple robe, and began to preach, I immediately perked up. I hadn't heard one of his electrifying sermons in over two months, so a rush of excitement washed over me. I sat up attentively in my seat, more than ready to be schooled and *sanctified*.

Pastor Strong first instructed us to turn to Proverbs 31:30. Clarence flipped through the good book and attempted to share with me, but luckily, I had brought my own Bible.

"Charm is deceitful, and beauty is vain, but a woman who fears the Lord is to be praised," Pastor preached.

Why, of all the chapters and verses in the Bible, did Pastor have to read that one? Grandma nudged me a few times and cut her eyes over knowingly to see if I had understood the parallel. And I did, I supposed. Perhaps I was too much into looks—my own, as well as those of the one I chose to date. Pastor's selection also reminded me of Perri and how she had been judged her entire life based on her looks.

Perhaps I had been fooled by Jorell's magnetic charm all this time, and I was steering clear of good old Clarence now because of his less than attractive features. *Hmm, I wonder*, I thought as I looked over at Clarence, who was totally enthralled by Pastor's sermon. I noticed the crust in one corner of his mouth, which hung slightly ajar. And I saw that his eyes were completely occupied behind those bifocal lenses as he listened closely.

The sound of Pastor's voice growing louder and the organ abruptly beginning to play caught my attention. Pastor Strong was now in the thick of his sermon, which was apparent from the usual beads of sweat that had already begun to form on his brow. With one hand raised up high in the air and the other clutching the microphone, he shouted and danced, all the while giving thanks to the Lord. Now, I was used to Pastor, and some churchgoers in the pews, catching the spirit, but I was startled by Clarence.

"Praise Him!" he shouted next to me, with a feminine wave of his hand. Clarence had scooched up to the edge of his seat, like he was starving for Pastor's next words. "Praise Him!" he shouted again, this time much louder and almost like he was singing the words.

My eyes shot over in his direction as soon as he jumped up from his seat. First, he swayed, doing a spiritual two-step to the exact beat of the organ playing in the background. Then his arms went up, and he swung them from side to side in the air. Soon his right foot began tapping to a beat all his own, a faster beat, and when he clapped his hands, it was clear to me that he had caught the full-blown Holy Ghost. The next thing I knew, Clarence was singing and shouting, "Won't He do it! Won't He do it!" repeatedly as he ran laps around the church. Yes, that's right. Entire laps around the inside of the church.

Beyond mortified, I shrank down in my seat, which did nothing to drown out the gasps and the low whispers of the other members of the church. Most likely, everyone assumed that Clarence and I were here together, given our *previous* seating arrangement. Sure, I knew I had to start looking at the nice guys, and no, looks and charm weren't all that mattered, but if the choice was between sweetmeat, chubby choirboy Clarence and being all alone, I'd choose loneliness every day of the week.

After fifteen more minutes of Pastor trying to get through his sermon peacefully, Clarence decided to come back to the front pew and join us. On his white shirt were sweat stains that had formed under his armpits and beneath his breasts. When he plopped back down and squeezed right on in between me and Ms. Bernadine, I swear, I was just about to lose it, but Grandma knowingly patted my arm.

Clarence leaned over and whispered in my ear, "Lord knows the spirit moves in this church when Pastor Strong does preach."

I nodded, an abrasive smile plastered on my face.

When church was finally over, the four of us all walked outside together. "Y'all want to go get something to eat, Pearl? This way the kids can get better acquainted," Ms. Bernadine suggested.

I opened my mouth, totally ready to protest, but Grandma perceptively grabbed me by the shoulder. "Not this time, Bernadine. Sorry. Nika has a lot of studying to do."

Clarence looked highly disappointed as he tucked his hands in the pockets of his high-water pants. "Well, maybe next Sunday, then," he said, rocking back on his heels.

Grandma gave me a sharp look that told me to be nice.

"Yeah, maybe next time," I offered.

On the quiet ride home, I allowed the gospel music that played low on the radio to be the only sound until Grandma finally spoke. "So watcha think about Clarence?" she asked, a hint of humor in her voice.

I scoffed. "Not my type, Grandma," was all I said.

"Humph. Well, he isn't the cheating, baby-making type, that's for sure."

"I suppose not," I mumbled.

Hearing her reference to Jorell made me sad all over again. It was like I hated him and loved him at the same damn time. But I knew no matter how strong my love for him was, I couldn't dismiss the fact that he had lied and cheated on me. In my mind, what he'd done was inexcusable. As much as I knew Pastor, and even more so God, would think otherwise, I didn't know if I could ever forgive him. After thinking about Jorell, going to church, and meeting Clarence that day, I knew exactly where my focus should be: on God, myself, and school. After that, maybe, just maybe, I'd resume the hunt for a good guy who had just a smidge of charm.

# Chapter 11

## *Myesha*

It was late Friday night when I found myself in the living room of my new apartment. I was hanging cheesy ornaments on my sad little Charlie Brown Christmas tree as the baby actively moved inside my belly. At seven months pregnant, I no longer had the energy to do the extreme holiday decorating I used to do.

I was now living in a two-bedroom apartment in Alexandria, Virginia. With the money Tez had piled into my savings account over the past couple of years, I managed to support myself fairly well now. I had bought myself a used Toyota Corolla and had even bought some necessities for the baby to be. My baby boy would be entering this world with a brand-new crib, playpen, and clothes, all courtesy of the local Walmart. I knew it probably wasn't what Tez would have bought if he were an actual willing participant in the parenting of our child. Still, the quality of what I had bought was decent, and I was pleased.

Over the past three months, I had tortured myself repeatedly with the notion of going back to Tez. I had hoped that perhaps he'd had a change of heart after all this time, considering our separation. I had thought that just maybe I had rushed such an important decision and that I had been overly emotional at the time. But on quiet, lonely nights like this one, the realization would suddenly hit. He'd told me numerous times over the course of two years that he *never* wanted to be a father. I felt that I had no choice but to respect that.

My heart had shattered to pieces when Tez walked out that door when he found out I was pregnant, and that night I had cried like a baby. I had prayed during my entire bus ride to a hotel in DC that I was making the best decision for both me and my unborn child. I hadn't experienced that kind of hurt since my parents died, but with each day that passed, I grew stronger and more excited about motherhood.

After walking into my galley kitchen, I pulled open the refrigerator door. I stood there staring, as if food would somehow magically collect on the empty shelves. I didn't know why, but it was something I did habitually when I was hungry. After closing the fridge door, I walked out of the kitchen and threw my coat on. After grabbing my car keys off the end table, I cut off the lamp. Only the single strand of Christmas lights on the tree shined in the apartment when I headed out the front door.

After getting into my car, I drove over to the KFC on Little River Turnpike. The drive-through line was incredibly long, so I decided to go inside, though I knew I would have to brave the cold. It was only thirty degrees that night in Alexandria, and with the lashing winds, I could feel every bit of it as I trekked inside. While standing in line behind some girl with a rather large order, I stared up at the menu, contemplating whether I should get a two-piece and a biscuit or my favorite, the four-piece chicken tenders combo. If Tez were here, he would probably tell me to get the chicken tenders dinner, because I was too greedy for just two pieces of chicken and a biscuit, I thought, rolling my eyes. To be rebellious, I ended up ordering the two-piece chicken combo.

In preparation for the cold winter wind I would encounter on my way back to the car, I zipped up my coat as far as it would go. The promise of heat had me walking so fast, you would've thought I was in some sort of race. But before I could even open up my car door, I felt a forceful hand cover my mouth from behind. I was pulled backward, and I struggled frantically to stay up on my feet. I screamed over and over again, the perpetrator's hand just stifled the sound.

I heard the sound of a van door sliding open behind me before a pillowcase was thrown over my head. Locking every muscle in my trembling body, I prepared to be tossed inside the van, but instead, I was lifted off the ground with care, then placed delicately inside the vehicle. The van started up, and the driver sped off. Terrified, I cried and pleaded for over an hour, asking that my kidnapper let me go. And although my hands and feet were not bound, I was too scared to make a move or even remove the pillowcase. I was petrified that my baby and I would be hurt if I didn't play this out right.

When the vehicle finally came to a stop, I heard a man, who I assumed was also the driver, speak. His voice was somewhat familiar, but I couldn't really make out who he was.

"Boss, I got her outside," he said.

No more than a minute later, I heard the van door slide open. My shivering body stilled and I sat frozen in place. Beneath the pillowcase I closed my eyes and silently prayed to God to protect us in that moment. Each second that passed was like torture, as I did not know what he or *they* would do to me. Violent thoughts infiltrated my mind all at once, causing me to whimper uncontrollably. I was so frightened that I actually peed on myself.

"Myesha," I heard someone say.

Instantly recognizing that assertive voice, I sat up straight and removed the pillowcase from my head. My eyes stretched wide from shock when I saw Tez standing outside the van door. He looked more pissed than I'd ever seen him before. His red-rimmed eyes stared at me as he clenched his angular jaw.

I cocked my head to the side, utterly confused. "Tez?" I could feel my eyebrows pinch together as I spoke.

His eyes slowly traveled from my face all the way down to my swollen belly. As they lingered there, I could have sworn I saw a slight hint of tenderness, something that I had never seen before, but had previously dreamed about. That look, however, was short lived. His soft eyes closed, and a grimace gradually appeared on his face.

"Get the fuck in this house. Now!" he demanded, his bare chest and arms flexing above his gray sweatpants. Before I even had a chance to stand up, he reached inside and pulled me out of the van by my arm. As soon as my feet hit the ground, I grabbed the bottom of my belly for support.

"Fucking stupid as shit, yo," he muttered under his breath as he pushed the back of my head softly to steer me toward the house. I just cried the whole way.

As I climbed the stairs, I could see Perri and Plus waiting at the door. The scene that was unfolding before them had rendered them speechless. Both of them looked scared. When I made it all the way to the door, they moved out of the way to let me in, but before I could even cross the threshold, Tez pushed me in the back of my head again. There was something about him putting his hands on me that time that pissed me off right away. Something inside me snapped, and before I knew it, I had turned around to slap him hard in the face.

"Don't put your goddamn hands on me!" I screamed.

One stiff slap on the face quickly turned into multiple blows to his arms and chest. I was crying so hard that I could no longer see what was in front of me. I could only feel his bare flesh beneath my fists. He gripped the sides of my arms firmly and shook me until my punches gradually ceased.

"Calm the fuck down, Myesha, before you hurt my fucking seed. Take yo' ass on in the house and clean ya pissy ass up so we can talk," he said, finally gaining control of the situation.

"Take me back home!" I protested weakly. Abundant tears ran down my face as I tried to move past him, but he blocked me at every step.

"You *are* home! Now, stop being fucking stupid. Had me out here looking for yo' ass for the past three months! Worried sick that something might have happened to you or my fucking seed!" he spat. His anger-filled eyes narrowed into slits, and he squeezed his fists at his sides.

I was appalled by his choice of words, and my neck involuntarily whipped back. "Your seed!" I exclaimed, squinting my blurry eyes. "Since when, Tez? The last thing you said was that you didn't want to be a father. So I did you a favor and I left. Now you want to kidnap me and—"

Running his hand down his face out of frustration, he let out a deep sigh. "Ain't nobody kidnap your stupid ass. Stop being so fucking dramatic, Myesha," he said, his voice a bit softer now. While he had been so uptight just moments before, now he started to relax, indicating that he no longer wanted to argue. "Just go get cleaned up so we can talk this shit out, a'ight?"

I sniffed back the last of my tears and turned to walk farther into the house. Perri, who was still waiting with Plus by her side, instantly pulled me in for a tight hug before rubbing her hand across my belly.

"It's gonna be all right. Let's go get you cleaned up," she said, looping her arm through mine and leading the way.

After going upstairs and entering the master bedroom, I noticed right away that nothing had changed. The same vanilla suede curtains hung from the windows, and the matching comforter was still spread across the king-size bed. And still standing in a back corner of the dresser top was my favorite Vera Wang limited edition perfume, which I'd mistakenly left behind. Even *Sons of Anarchy*, which was one of Tez's favorite shows, was playing on the flat-screen TV that hung on the wall. Absolutely nothing had changed.

I went into the master bathroom and quickly undressed before jumping into the shower. For about twenty minutes I stood there under the hot water, just thinking about what it all meant to be back in Tez's home. *Does he really want this baby? Will he resent me in the long run? Can we eventually be the family I so desperately need us to be?*

After another ten minutes or so, I finished up and cut off the water. When I stepped out and dried off, I realized that I didn't have anything to put on. I opened the bathroom door and went back inside the bedroom to find Tez sitting on the edge of the bed, with his head hung low between his shoulders. His long locks draped his face, which rested against his praying hands. While he sat there, deep in thought, I took in the muscle definition of his forearms, which were laced with lively veins and covered in violent ink.

When I took another step farther into the room, he lifted his head. He locked his amber-colored eyes on me as I just stood there, voiceless, wearing nothing but a white towel. I could see the trouble lines in his forehead slowly fade away as he sat up straight. Hearing the heavy breath he exhaled before he slowly licked his lips made me feel uneasy.

Finally, he moved his head, summoning me. "Getcha ass over here." Although his voice was low, his tone was every bit as commanding as it usually was.

Despite the fact that my emotions were still in a stormy place, I walked over submissively. Less than a foot away from where he sat, I stopped directly in front of him. Feeling more or less like an apprehensive child about to get scolded, I attempted to avoid his intimidating glare. When the awkward silence between us became unbearable, I decided to look down at him. Tez parted his lips, as though he was about to speak, but then he hesitated. Grabbing his jaw, he narrowed his eyes in thought, likely to better articulate his next thought.

"Myesha, where the fuck you been all this time?"

# Chapter 12

## *Tez*

Hearing the shower run, I sat there on the edge of the bed, feeling anxiety of a foreign nature. While I was growing up, when things were hard for us financially, I would worry about how Pops would pay the light bill or if we would even have enough to eat until his next paycheck. Then later, as a teen, I would stress about niggas running up on me or trying to rob me while I was dealing small shit on the block. Before Myesha ran off a few months ago, my worries mostly concerned how to expand and move up to the next level in the game. I was one of the major distributors in the DMV, but at twenty-four years old, I wanted more. More access, more money and, most of all, more power.

However, when Myesha left that night, my worries had somehow seemed to become magnified tenfold. Night and day for the past three months I had agonized over Myesha's safety, as well as the baby's. I had sat and wondered for hours on end what kind of father I could possibly be, given my line of work. Then, as more days rolled by, I had questioned whether Myesha would even come back to me and if I'd ever get the opportunity to be a father at all.

I was so deep in my thoughts that I didn't even hear the shower cut off. The subtle sound of the floor creaking caused me to glance up. Myesha stood there apprehen-

sively, wearing nothing but a white towel and a prominent belly. Her curly black hair was wet and slicked back,
as though it had just been freshly washed. I could see her
bare brown shoulders glistening from the drops of water
left on her skin. She was so fucking beautiful.

With her dark Asian-like eyes, she gave me a tentative
gaze. I responded by subtly motioning her over by raising
my chin. "Getcha ass over here," I said in a low voice.
While I was still angry at her for leaving, I was more
relieved to see her in the flesh than anything.

When she wobbled over to where I sat on the bed, I
thought of the delicate manner in which I needed to
approach her. I didn't want her to snap on me, like she'd
just done downstairs, nor did I want her to run away
again. I simply wanted to get answers and for us to figure
out how to move forward from all the bullshit.

"Myesha, where the fuck you been all this time?"

She pulled her bottom lip between her teeth before
taking a deep swallow. "I-I've been living in Virginia,"
she said shakily.

"Virginia! The fuck!" I could feel my nostrils flare
slightly. "So you was gone just take my child—"

"Your son," she said, cutting off my words.

Stunned, my airway constricted all at once. Stretching
my eyes, I looked at her to be sure I'd heard her correctly.
"A son?" I muttered in disbelief.

"Yes, Tez. Your son," she said softly.

Myesha never looked more beautiful than she did in
that moment, saying those words. I parted the towel
where she had it folded across her breasts, partially
exposing her. Then I slid my hands gently across her
hardened belly as I took in the sight of the dark vertical
line down its center. I leaned up and placed one gentle
kiss after another on her belly until I heard soft moans
seep from her lips. I slowly peeled the towel from around

her body and carelessly tossed it to the floor. At seven months pregnant, Myesha was breathtaking. Her round breasts were fuller, and her soft skin glowed and felt much like silk.

"I've missed you so fucking much, My," I whispered between my kisses.

After delicately positioning her hands on each side of my face, she lifted my head and peered down into my eyes. Her eyes were earnestly in search of something, and without speaking any words, I did my best to reassure her. I stood up and cupped the back of her head. Then I crashed my lips against hers for the first time in months before gliding my tongue into her mouth. I kissed her more passionately, I believed, than I'd ever kissed any girl or woman in my entire lifetime. My hands roamed her body without reserve, exploring every new curve she had developed. The clean smell of her appealed to my senses, and before I knew it, my tongue was trailing down the crook of her neck.

"I missed you too, Tez," she moaned.

My throbbing dick hurt at the sound of her calling my name. As my tongue traveled farther south, I took one of her full breasts into my mouth. Sucked on its hardened nipple as her chest heaved up and down. With her ass in the palms of my hands, I gently squeezed as I steadily glided her breast in and out of my mouth. As her sensual moans grew louder, my dick began to jump in my pants, dying to be freed. My ability to fight off the urge to have her was now beyond gone. Removing one hand from her ass, I softly strummed the front of her clit. Her breathing suddenly intensified, and without warning, I slipped two fingers inside her.

"Baby," she whimpered, holding on to my shoulders for balance, as I plunged in and out of her with ease.

"Fuck, My." She was just too fucking wet, and I knew then that I had to taste her.

As I laid her back on the bed, her dark, slanted eyes filled with pure lust. I took a brief moment to look her over again, reacquainting myself with all her sexy features. From her full, pouty lips to her smooth brown skin, which had remained flawless throughout her pregnancy. I kneeled down beneath her and threw her thighs over my shoulders before tenderly kissing her most sensitive place.

"Ooh, Tez," she moaned, shuddering underneath me. Hearing that bit of encouragement was all I needed to pick up my pace. I flicked my tongue fast against her until she gave a pleasurable cry. "Tez. Baby, wait," she breathed, gripping my locks.

The more she called my name, the more excited I became. I slowly tended to every nook, cranny, and fold of her body as she gyrated her hips against me. And just as I felt her muscles begin to tense up, I stiffened my tongue and drilled fervently inside her.

"Ahhh, Tez," she cried out in release. She gripped my locks tightly as she faced her first orgasm of the night.

After placing kisses on her inner thigh, I slid my pants down and stroked my long, throbbing erection. I hovered over her and slid in with care.

"Gahdamn, My. I've missed this pussy," I hissed, hearing her exhale at the same time.

I didn't realize how much I'd missed her touch until I felt her tight, wet walls clamp down on me. Instinctively, I closed my eyes and bit down on my bottom lip, then released a low grunt. I relished her warmth as I began stroking her insides nice and slow.

"I've missed you so much," she cried softly. Tears spilled from the corners of her tightly sealed eyes as she held on to me.

Her hands clasped the sides of my face as I leaned down to cover her mouth with my own. "Don't ever leave me, My. I swear . . ." My voice trailed off into a low groan that I released inside her mouth. "Don't ever . . ." I stumbled over my words again, feeling my groin tighten. My hips were now working overtime in a slow, steady motion.

"Oh my Gah . . . ," she whimpered out loud. Her body compressed around me and her mouth hung slightly ajar. She was too easy.

"Let that shit go, My. Come for me," I begged, rousing her insides. Just when I saw that she could bear no more, I thrust myself deep inside her.

"Tez!" she cried out, body exploding and tightening beneath me at the same exact time.

Hearing her say my name caused the same sensation to ignite inside me, and before I knew it, I was coming right along with her. "Fuck!" I groaned, releasing inside her.

After we took a shower together, we got back in bed and buried ourselves beneath the thick covers. Our naked bodies were intertwined as I held her tightly from behind. Still in a state of wonderment, I kept kissing her shoulder and smoothing back her damp hair. I was gradually coming to terms with the fact that after all these months, she was actually *here* beside me.

After several moments of silence had passed, I was all but sure she'd fallen asleep, but just when I closed my eyes, I heard her whisper, "Tez?"

"Yeah, baby?" I mumbled.

"I'm so sorry I left you. Had I known you wanted this baby, I swear I never would have left."

I slid my hands down to rub her protruding belly. "Just don't leave again, a'ight? You just gotta be patient with me."

"I know, and I will." She said no more, but the low sound that came from her throat told me there was more she wanted to say.

"What's up, shorty? Talk to me," I said.

She slowly turned over to face me. The light bleeding in through the gaps in the blinds, enabled us to look into each other's eyes. Tenderly, she cupped my chin and traced my lips back and forth with her thumb. "I love you so much, Tez."

I had lost count of the number of times Myesha had told me she loved me over the course of the past two years, but I knew that I had never reciprocated, not even once, and told her that I loved her back. After losing my mother, I had vowed never to love another woman besides Perri. I had decided that there was just too much at stake with that kind of heartbreak and that I absolutely wanted no parts of it.

As I looked deep into Myesha's eyes now, I knew she wanted me to say the words back, but I just couldn't. Not even under these circumstances. I leaned forward and placed a simple kiss on her forehead. "Sleep tight, shorty. Get some rest, a'ight?" was all I could bear to say.

Myesha tentatively kissed my lips, then turned back over to go to sleep. No more than ten minutes later, my cell phone began buzzing on the nightstand next to me. I leaned up and looked at Myesha first. She appeared to be in a deep sleep. Then I rolled over and noticed that the alarm clock read 12:12 a.m. After grabbing my phone, I rubbed my sleepy eyes so that my vision would be clearer. It was a text message from Shayla.

Didn't hear from you today. I was hoping you'd be in my bed tonight.

Running my hand down my face, I let out a quiet sigh of frustration. For the past few months, I had been back dealing with Shayla. I'd been spending a few nights out of the week at her place and fucking pretty regularly. After searching the entire state of Maryland, to no avail, I honestly hadn't known if I'd ever see Myesha again. And while my heart had still been with her, Shayla had been there, available for my every need. Now that I had Myesha back in my life and had a son on the way, this would be my second time leaving Shayla for her. I just hoped Shayla would take the news as well as she had the last time, a couple of years ago, because the last thing I needed was drama when I had just got back my peace.

# Chapter 13

## *Plus*

It was early Christmas morning when I looked up from the floor to see Perri still asleep in her bed. I had continued to spend most nights out of the week over at Tez's house just to be with her and Camille. Although I mostly slept on the floor or on the couch in the basement, I was content. I knew she was trying to remain faithful to that nigga Derrick, and after everything I had put her through over the years, I knew I had no choice but to respect it. Besides, deep down I knew in time I'd have her as my own. Call me soft all you want, but in my mind, we were destined to be together. And the more time we spent together strengthening our friendship and our partnership as parents, the more I was convinced.

Careful not to disturb Perri, I got up and walked out of the room. I went inside Camille's bedroom to see her standing up in her crib, fully awake. Her bright amber-colored eyes lit up at the sight of me, as though she knew it was Christmas Day. "Daddy! Daddy!" she said excitedly, bouncing up and down on the mattress. Frizzy black curls framed her pretty face as she smiled with those white Chiclet teeth of hers.

"Merry Christmas, li'l mama," I said before picking her up and kissing her cheek. After getting her a fresh diaper, I took her into the bathroom to give her a quick washup and to brush my own teeth. We had just finished up and were leaving Camille's bedroom when Perri walked into the hallway.

"Mommy," Camille squealed, running over to her.

With her eyes barely open, Perri appeared to be still half asleep. Her exaggerated yawn as she stretched her limbs and then reached down for Camille made that apparent. After scooping my baby girl up into her arms, she attempted to smooth back her wild hair, which was clumped all over her head.

"Morning, my little troll doll," I teased, sweeping the wooly mass on top of her head back and forth with my hand.

"Yo, shut up," she muttered, playfully smacking me on my bare chest.

When she placed our daughter back down and went into the hall bath, Camille and I made our way downstairs. The smell of pancakes, bacon, and eggs greeted us before we even made it to the kitchen. I quickly assumed Myesha was already up and in the kitchen, making Christmas breakfast. These past few days I had found myself taking full advantage of having her back at the house. Perri's ass couldn't cook for shit, and a nigga was beyond tired of eating carryout. Not only could Myesha throw down in the kitchen, but she also spent lots of time with Camille. These past few nights Perri and I had stayed up playing *Madden NFL* till the wee hours of the morning while Myesha had tended to Camille. That was some shit Perri and I hadn't been able to do since high school.

However, when I walked into the kitchen, I was surprised to see my mother standing in front of the stove and Myesha sitting at the kitchen table, reading a magazine. Myesha had thrown her black curls up in a loose ponytail, and she had reading glasses on her face. Thanks to the open floor plan, I could also see Mr. Phillip, who was Perri's father, and Aria in the living room, sitting on the couch.

"Merry Christmas, family!" I said, grabbing a couple of pieces of bacon off a plate that sat on the counter.

"Nanna! Nanna!" Camille called out, dashing toward my mother's legs.

"Hey, Nanna's sweet girl," my mother cooed, turning around and stepping back. "Ahmad, get my baby away from this hot stove," she fussed.

I picked Camille up, and with her squirming in my arms, I went out into the living-room area, where I could smell the fresh scent of pine. The last-minute Christmas tree Tez had gone out and bought was massive. He had centered it in front of the living-room window, and as I looked at it, I realized it had to be over ten feet tall and five feet wide. Underneath it was an abundance of colorfully wrapped gifts.

Two nights ago Myesha and Perri had decorated the whole tree in silver and gold while Tez and I had just sat back and watched. Hell, up until Myesha had come back, we hadn't thought there was even going to be a Christmas in this house. Perri and I had already made plans to go back home to the Millwood Projects on Christmas Eve. But with Myesha's return, Tez had transformed from the Grinch to motherfucking Santa Claus himself right before our very own eyes.

"Hey, y'all," Aria said with a yawn, acknowledging both me and Camille.

"And Merry Christmas to you too, big head," I teased, prompting her eyes to roll. "Merry Christmas, Mr. Phillip," I said, putting Camille down.

His eyes shifted from the television, which was tuned to ESPN, over to us. "Merry Christmas, Ahmad. And come here, li'l girl," he said, reaching for Camille. She rushed to jump into her grandfather's arms. "Where are my two children?" he asked, shaking his head. "My li'l girl here is ready to see what Santa's brought her."

"Santa ain't buy shit, Pops," I heard Tez mutter from behind me as he entered the room.

"Yo, watch your mouth in front of my shorty, man," I said. Tez was always cussing, and while Perri's mouth had gotten much better since she had Camille, my baby girl was always subjected to it.

Myesha, who was also coming into the living room from the opposite direction, shot him a warning glare. "You can't say stuff like that around kids, Montez."

He sucked his teeth. "Man, whatever," he said nonchalantly, waving her off.

"I'm serious, Tez!" she fussed, holding the bottom of her belly.

"I said a'ight. Fuck else you want me to say?"

Myesha rolled her eyes and attempted to walk back into the kitchen, but before she could leave the room, Tez hurried over to her and wrapped her in his arms. He lifted her chin with his finger. "Gimme a kiss," he ordered.

Hoisting herself on the balls of her feet, she met his lips for a simple kiss. "Can we open up gifts now? I wanna see what you got me," she said, pulling back. She was grinning so wide and clasping her hands together like a kid as she bounced up and down on her toes.

"Should'na got yo' ass shit since you wanna run away from a nigga," he muttered. Although it was intended as a joke, I could tell Tez was still a bit salty from Myesha abandoning him these past few months.

"Shut up, Tez," she said, playfully smacking him on the arm.

"Yo, Perri! Bring ya ass on!" he yelled.

Perri appeared at the top of the stairs, with her pretty face contorted into a scowl. "Stop yelling! And stop cussing in front of my daughter, yo," she told Tez as she made her way down the steps.

"Man, you and Myesha on that same bullsh—"

"Tez!" my mother and Mr. Phillip hollered just in time.

Tez sucked his teeth and waved them both off, but he knew not to finish his sentence. He just had this knowing little smirk on his face, which most likely meant he knew what he was doing in the first place.

When Perri made her way into the living room, I couldn't help but stare at her. Her long hair was wet and curly, as she had just washed it, and her caramel-colored face was completely bare. Just like golden topaz crystals, her bright eyes seemed to sparkle from the morning sun pouring in through the windows. Although she had on gray sweatpants that matched my own and an oversize white T-shirt, she still looked pretty as hell.

*How I could not have appreciated her understated beauty all this time. I'll never understand,* I thought.

"Hey, Daddy." Perri leaned down in front of the couch to hug her father. "You ready, baby?" she asked, reaching her arms out for Camille, who was sitting next to him. Camille just looked at Perri with the cutest expression on her face, like she was totally unmoved. She hadn't even turned two yet, so her concept of Christmas was completely nonexistent.

Once Perri got ahold of her, the three of us sat down on the hardwood floor in front of the tree. We passed Camille her gifts one at a time and let her unwrap them, which seemed to be the most exciting part for her. She got clothes, shoes, books, and even a few toys, most of which Tez had supplied. Me and Perri had limited funds these days, since neither of us had a job, but with the remainder of my refund check, I had managed to buy a few things.

"Here. Open this up." I passed Perri a small box that was horribly wrapped in shiny red paper.

"What this?" she asked, taking the gift from my hand. Before she could get it completely unwrapped, Camille took over and pulled off the rest of the wrapping paper for her. Perri and I just laughed. When the black velvet box was completely exposed, I watched Perri's eyes narrow before they cut over to me.

I knew she was asking what I had got her. "Just go ahead and open it," I said, pressing.

Slowly, she lifted back the top of the box, revealing an eighteen-karat gold necklace that looped through a heart-shaped pendant. The initials P&P were elegantly engraved on the front. Her eyes widened at first, then softened before she glanced over at me. "Wow. This is beautiful, Plus. Thank you," she said in a low voice, pulling the necklace out of the box.

"Open it up," I told her. A puzzled expression was etched across her face, and I realized she didn't understand. "It's a locket," I explained.

As she opened up the locket, I sat up on my knees and hovered over her from behind. Her hand gently covered her mouth when a picture of her, Camille, and me appeared. It had been taken at the state fair this past summer, on one of our happier days spent as a family. When she looked back and peered up at me, she had tears on the rims of her eyes.

"Ahmad," she gasped in a whisper, questioning me with her raised eyebrows.

I didn't know why, but a nigga got choked up from her reaction alone. Swallowing back my emotions, I grabbed the necklace from her hand and secured it around her neck. With tears still clinging to her lower lids, she sat up on her knees to face me. Although I knew we had an audience, it felt like it was only she and I in that moment, gazing into each other's eyes. When she tenderly grabbed me by the sides of my face, I dropped my head a little to hide the sentiment behind my eyes.

"Thank you so much, Plus. I'll wear it always," she whispered, reaching down to clutch the pendant against her chest. Still trying to respect her wishes, I settled for placing a simple kiss on her cheek.

"Ooh, let me see," Aria said, interrupting our moment.

Just as Perri stood up to go show Aria and the rest of the family her new necklace, the doorbell rang. I quickly shot up from the floor to go answer it, then slid across the hardwood in my white socks. Without checking through the peephole, I opened the door to find Derrick standing in front of me. He had a navy blue Yankees cap on his head, he was wearing a navy blue letterman's jacket, and his hands were tucked deep in the pockets of his light blue jeans. When our eyes locked, he removed his hands from his pockets and squared his shoulders, like that shit was supposed to mean something to me. The grimace on his face was no surprise, given the fact it most likely mirrored my own.

"Fuck you want?" I barked, chucking my chin up behind the storm door.

I watched his jaw tighten before he licked his lips. "Is Perri home?" he asked, clasping his hands together in front of him. I could tell it was killing this nigga to be cordial.

Narrowing my eyes, I gave a sheepish grin before opening up the door. He slid past me and entered the house without making eye contact.

"What's up, boo-boo?" he said, looking down at Camille, who had suddenly attached herself to my leg. For sure, the scowl on my face couldn't be missed.

When he reached down to greet her with a high five, she turned her face away like she was trying to hide.

"Oh, I see how it is, boo-boo," he said with a hint of humor in his voice. I pinched the bridge of my nose to calm myself. My tolerance level for this nigga seemed to have diminished little by little since his proposal to Perri last May.

As he walked farther into the house, I picked up Camille, and we trailed close behind him. When he stepped into the living room, I saw that Perri had kneeled down and was pulling more presents out from under the tree. Once her eyes landed on him, they lit up with surprise.

"Derrick! What are you doing here?" she asked, looking confused. "Shouldn't you still be in New York?"

"You already know I wasn't going to miss seeing you on Christmas, Ma," he said, extending his hand to help her up. He then looked over at the rest of the family and nodded his head before taking his hat off. "Merry Christmas, everybody."

While everyone returned the holiday greeting, I caught Tez staring at me from the other side of the room. A dumbass smirk was etched on his face. I was sure he saw the jealousy in my eyes when Perri stood and then reached to hug Derrick around the neck. When she pulled back from his embrace, he slipped his right hand into the pocket of his letterman jacket and pulled out a small rectangular box wrapped in gold paper. I figured it was probably his Christmas present for her, and even though it was childish as fuck, I silently prayed it didn't top mine.

Perri took her time, carefully unwrapping the gift, unlike the one I had given her earlier, the wrapping on which Camille all but destroyed. When the gift was completely exposed, she held it up. "Oh, Dior. Perfume," she said, turning it around so our family could see.

*This freckle-faced nigga*, I thought to myself.

"Yo, Derrick, you see what Plus got her?" Tez's sneaky ass asked, taking a seat on the arm of the chair in which Myesha was now sitting.

# Chapter 14

## *Perri*

With his dimples partially on display, Derrick let out a snort of laughter before looking back over his shoulder at Plus. From the angle at which I stood, I could see Plus shrug his shoulders all cocky like. He had his mouth stretched back, as if to say that his gift to me was no big deal. I, on the other hand, immediately reached up to hold the pendant against my chest. I didn't know why, but guilt had suddenly consumed me.

Derrick turned back. "What he get you?" he asked.

I could feel my eyes widen a bit more and my dry mouth drop, as though I didn't fully comprehend his question. To say that I was uncomfortable in that moment would be an understatement. After a few seconds had passed, Derrick leaned in, like he was waiting for me to get my mind right. I swallowed hard.

Hesitantly, I lifted the pendant up off my chest for him to see. Derrick's nostrils slowly flared with disgust, and his mouth turned down into an ugly frown. I could only imagine what his face would look like if I opened up the locket and allowed him to see the picture of the three of us, *our family*.

Tez must have noticed his reaction, too, because he started doing some overstated bop toward us, pulling up his sagging sweatpants and thumbing the side of his nose real silly like. When he reached us, he placed his hands on each of our shoulders, looked over at Derrick, and cracked a wide smile, exposing the gold grills on his bottom row of his teeth. His light amber–colored eyes were full of pure amusement.

"Nigga, you might as well have come up in this bitch empty handed, son," he said, taking a crack at Derrick's New York accent.

I punched him in the arm. "Shut up, Tez."

"Leave them children alone, Montez," Ms. Tonya said from the couch in an attempt at backing me up.

Tez didn't let up, though; he just started laughing at our expense. "You gon' have to step your game up, homeboy," he said with more laughter.

*Ugh.* I rolled my eyes.

"He can get her necklaces all day, but I'm the one that put that ring on her finger," Derrick said in his defense.

Both Derrick's and my eyes traveled down to my left hand at the same time. If looks could kill, I swear a bitch would have been dead in that moment, as my finger was ring free and completely bare. While Tez let out another chuckle, an angry puff of air escaped from Derrick's nostrils. He closed his eyes and shook his head, as though he was disappointed in me.

"I—I just got out of the shower," I quickly lied, trying to explain.

The truth of the matter was I hadn't worn that ring since the beginning of Christmas break. As soon as Derrick had left for New York, it had felt like a weight of some sort was lifted off me. Whenever Derrick was around, I was constantly having to explain my friendship with Plus to him and the reason why Plus was always around. On the other hand, whenever I was at home, I was constantly having to steer clear of Plus, because it was a serious struggle to be near him every day. Spending time together with Camille like a true family and having Plus sleep in my bedroom almost every night, even if it was just on the floor, complicated things for me.

Deep down I struggled against my desire to have Plus near me. I wanted to be able to kiss his lips, run my fingers through his curly hair, and skate my hands over his smooth chocolaty muscles. But, on the other hand, I was committed to Derrick. A tall, fine specimen of a man. The one who had guarded my heart and made me feel so beautiful whenever I was in his presence.

With his lips tucked in, like he was trying to bite his tongue, Derrick simply nodded his head and patted my hand. "Well, I gotta get outta here and get back on the road," he said.

My eyes lit up. "So soon?" I asked. The hurt look in Derrick's eyes made my stomach contort into knots. "Don't go," I whined.

"Got to," he said.

He glanced over at the rest of the family and said his good-byes before heading for the door. I followed close behind to walk him out, passing Plus and Camille along the way. When we got outside, Derrick didn't even turn around to acknowledge me. He just jogged down the front steps, like he was in some sort of rush, before trekking over to his car.

"Wait!" I yelled, following behind him.

With his car door already open, he looked over at me. I had stopped on the bottom step in front of the house. "What do you want, shorty?"

"Why are you leaving when you just got here? Are you mad?" I asked, even though I knew the answer.

Derrick slammed his car door shut and walked back around the car to face me. "Fuck you mean, Am I mad?" he asked sarcastically, slicing his hand through the air. "Shorty, you ain't wearing the engagement ring I bought you, we ain't fucked in months, and every time I call or swing by, *that nigga*"—he pointed toward the house—"is here! Of course a nigga is pissed!" he barked.

"He's Camille's father. You know this," I said, trying to rationalize with him.

"So because he's Camille's father, you got to wear his name around your neck?" His eyebrows rose.

"He's my best friend, and it's just our initials," I replied, darting my eyes up toward the gray winter sky.

He held both of his hands up in surrender before pushing them toward me, as if he was waving me off or, rather, casting me away. "What-the-fuck-ever, man. When you tired of playing games, just let a nigga know," he said. With that, he walked back and then slid into the driver seat of his car. His engine hadn't even cranked up good before he sped off, leaving a stream of exhaust behind.

I was so furious that I stormed inside the house and let the door slam shut behind me.

Immediately Tez snapped, "Don't be slamming my gahdamn door. Fuck wrong wit' you?"

"Yo, why you always gotta be starting shit? Now he's all mad at me," I said to Tez.

Tez smacked his teeth. "That pussy-ass nigga."

"I'm serious, Tez. He's not fucking with me no more." I heard the emotional crack in my voice, and although I was on the verge of tears, I downright refused to let my whole family see me cry.

"Look, I just told the nigga the truth. If he's trying to win your heart, he better come correct. Not coming all the way down here from New York to drop you off some cheap-ass bottle of perfume."

"It isn't cheap!"

"Yeah, whatever. That shit runs two for twenty at the flea market," Tez said.

I rolled my eyes and folded my arms across my chest.

"That nigga ain't the one for you, no way," he said, crushing me even further.

"That's enough, Tez!" Myesha wobbled over and grabbed his shoulder.

"But I thought you liked Derrick?" I asked, my voice low.

"You putting too much emphasis on the word *like*. That nigga's a'ight," Tez explained.

Not being able to fight back the tears any longer, I ran up to my bedroom, taking two stairs at a time. After shutting the door behind me, I sank down on my bed and pulled the pillow over my head. There, in the darkness, was where I decided to let it all out. My face was covered in tears in a matter of seconds. I was so confused, and all I could hear were Derrick's last words replaying in my mind. It was true that we hadn't had sex in almost three months. Whenever he'd call, Plus would be right there, sitting beside me. Hell, most days Plus and I even carpooled to and from school together. While I was appreciative about having daily help with Camille, this new living arrangement with Plus was making my situation with Derrick all the more difficult.

After an hour or so of sulking all alone in my room, I heard a soft knock on the door. I lifted my head from underneath the pillow to see Plus creeping in.

"Come on, shorty. It's Christmas, and Camille wants to spend time with you," he said.

He was right, so I didn't even put up a fuss. "All right. Give me a minute and I'll come back down," I said.

Once Plus had left, I went into the bathroom to wash my face before making my way downstairs. I found Ms. Tonya, Myesha, and Aria in the kitchen. Everyone else was down in the basement.

"You okay, baby?" Ms. Tonya asked, looking over at me from where she stood in front of the stove. "Want something to eat? You never did eat breakfast."

I shook my head. "I'm all right."

"You wanna talk about it?" Myesha asked, pushing back a loose curl that was dangling in her face. She was sitting across from Aria at the table, looking at baby magazines.

Shaking my head again, I said, "No, I'm good. Really."

"Are you sure? I mean, let's face it. Your heart is torn because you're in love with two men. I've been there before," Ms. Tonya said.

My eyebrows shot up. "Who said I'm in love with two men?"

"Well, Perri, you're right. I don't know if you're in love with Derrick or not, but I know for a fact you're in love with my son." The words left Ms. Tonya's lips with such confidence, she didn't even look at me. She just kept stirring the contents of the pot over on the stove.

I kept quiet, challenging myself neither to confirm nor deny her assumption. Instead I walked across the kitchen and sat down quietly at the table with Myesha and Aria. There was a stack of magazines in the center of the table, so I just grabbed one.

"We're looking for a new crib and stroller for the baby. Tez said that the ones I got weren't worth shit and that he wasn't putting his son in no bullshit like that," Myesha explained, shaking her head.

"I never thought I'd see the day when Tez would actually become a father," I muttered.

"You and me both, girl. But I'm so excited, y'all. I finally get the family I . . ." Myesha's voice trailed off, and she cast her tear-filled eyes back down to the magazine.

I didn't bother pressing the issue, because Tez had already shared her story with me a few months ago. I had learned all about her parents dying and the brutality she had endured while living in the foster-care system. Everything now made sense as to why she'd run away. She didn't want to get an abortion, because she truly wanted a family.

About half an hour later, Ms. Tonya asked me and the other girls to help in the preparation of Christmas dinner, just as we had done for Thanksgiving. I boiled the macaroni and cut up the big block of cheese for the macaroni and cheese. And because I knew Ms. Tonya so well, I figured she would most likely give me full credit for making the entire dish. After a few hours of us slaving away in the kitchen, we all set the big table for Christmas dinner. In addition to my macaroni and cheese, we would be having ham, turkey, stuffing, collard greens, and sweet potato casserole.

Once we were all gathered around the table and Daddy said the prayer, we all dug in and ate like it was our last meal here on earth. As always, Ms. Tonya had outdone herself. Everything had been cooked to perfection. With the big Christmas tree all lit up, a football game on the TV, and the Temptation's holiday CD softly playing in the background, we talked and drank at the table like one big happy family. Everything about that Christmas Day felt flawless, with the exception of my and Derrick's argument that morning. A few hours after Derrick had left, he had sent me a short text message that read **Made it home**. But when I tried to call him back, he sent me straight to voice mail. I really didn't know what to make of our situation or what to do about it, but the thought of losing him permanently scared me for some reason.

Later that night, after Plus had put Camille to bed, he came downstairs to the basement, where Tez and I were. My father and Ms. Tonya had already gone back home, and Myesha had turned in for the night. I was stretched out on the leather couch, while Tez sat in one of his reclining chairs, smoking a blunt.

"Camille's asleep," Plus said.

After lifting my feet, he sat down at that end of the couch. I tried pulling my feet away so that I could make more room for him to sit, but he quickly placed them in his lap. He gripped both of my feet firmly with his hands, then began massaging them through my socks. Enjoying the feeling of his strong hands just kneading away, I closed my eyes. As his warm hands gradually wandered up my bare calves, I could feel the tips of his fingers pressing gently into my skin. Slowly, his fingers worked my muscles over with care, and like always, my body began to double-cross me. Within a matter of seconds, I was throbbing between my thighs and moisture had begun to saturate my panties, which caused me to feel ashamed.

"Aah." The soft moan mistakenly slipped through my lips, causing my eyes to shoot open from embarrassment.

Apparently, Tez didn't hear me, because he was pre-occupied with his cell-phone screen, but judging by the cocky smirk on Plus's face, he did. See, it was when he did stuff like that, that I felt all the more confused. Without a doubt, Plus knew that for me, he was home. Nobody's touch could ever make me feel like his did. We had been in each other's lives for so long that he knew just the simple things to do to get me under his spell.

"Hey, Plus, I—I need to talk to you," I stammered, sitting up straight on the couch. I smoothed back my frizzy hair with the palm of my hand before getting up.

Plus's eyebrows knit in confusion before he licked his lips and chucked up his chin. "A'ight."

He followed me upstairs and into my bedroom, where we both took a seat on the edge of the bed.

"So tell me what's up," he said, cutting to the chase.

I closed my eyes and took in a deep breath, because I knew that what I had to say to Plus would be difficult for both of us. "Um," I said, hesitating, wiping my sweaty palms down the front of my thighs.

"Talk to me, P. What's going on?" He lay back on the bed all casual like, with his elbows supporting his upper body. The muscles of his abdomen contracted beautifully into six mini mounds, and they led all the way down to the trace of hair just above the elastic band of his sweatpants.

*Help me, Father!*

As I continued to look him over lustfully, taking in the sight of his bare chest and arms, I swallowed hard. The thumping between my thighs had magnified tenfold and my pulse had quickened beneath my skin. "I can't do this!" I finally said, a little louder than intended.

With his head cocked to the side and his eyebrows pinched from bewilderment, he asked, "Do what?"

"I need some space, Ahmad! Being around you day and night like this"—I waved my hand up and down his body—"is confusing. It's . . ." Slowly shaking my head, I cupped my hands over my mouth to keep the words in.

"It's what?"

"You being here . . . us being so close is causing problems for Derrick and me."

"I told you, I don't give a—"

"I know you don't care about Derrick, and I'm not asking you to, yo. But I *do*." I pointed to my chest. "I love him, and I don't like hurting him," I finally admitted.

Plus sat up straight and ran his hand down his jaw before narrowing his dark brown eyes. "So you actually love that nigga?"

I swallowed hard and lifted my chin slightly in an attempt to evoke some type of confidence. "Yes, I believe I do," I said.

As he stood up from the bed and towered over me, I could see that his jaw was tightly clenched. He let out a low snort before slowly shaking his head. When he ran his hand over the top of his curls and pushed them forward, his frustration was confirmed. The agonizing look on his face immediately caused pangs in my chest.

"You don't love that nigga, Perri. You're just afraid that I'm gon' hurt you again, and no matter how many times I tell you I won't, you just won't believe me," he said, putting his hands up in surrender. "But check it, I love you enough to let your ass go. If you make shit work out with Derrick, I won't stand in your way. I'll give you your space, a'ight?"

As much as Plus was trying to be the bigger person, the hurt and bitterness laced in his voice couldn't be missed. I didn't know why I gave a shit about his feelings when there were so many times when he hadn't thought about mine, but in that moment I suddenly got teary eyed. I stood up from the bed and wrapped my arms around his neck in a natural attempt to comfort him. But before I knew it, my face was buried in his bare chest, and I was the one sobbing like a baby. As my shoulders shook, he wrapped his arms around my waist and held me close. Just that fast, our roles had reversed. My failed attempt at consoling him had quickly turned into him being there for me. Over the years, I had made a conscious effort to display only a hard shell, to keep an ironclad wall around my heart. Nothing and no one could ever make me this emotional. Except for my best friend, Plus.

After pulling me back from his chest, he lifted my wet face with his hands. As he thumbed away a few of my tears, we stared intently into one another's eyes. And then, without notice, he crashed his lips fervently against mine, stealing my breath away. Our tongues explored each other's mouths for what felt like an eternity before he pulled back a little and held on to just my bottom lip for a split second more, then released me entirely.

"I still love you, Perri. No matter what, a'ight?" he said, repeating those same words he had spoken to me when

I first moved in with Tez. With that, Plus turned and walked out of the bedroom, leaving me all alone with my thoughts.

My head was spinning as my heart thudded in my chest.

"I love you too," I whispered.

# Chapter 15

## *Nika*

I trekked fast through the snow flurries as I made my way toward the front entrance of Mount Airy Mansion with a large gift bag in my hand. It was Camille's second birthday, and apparently, Perri and her family were going all out. From what I understood, this particular banquet hall was one of the most expensive in all of Prince George's County. And judging by the lavish grounds, though they were covered in the whitest of snow, I could see why.

When I walked inside the front lobby, I stomped the snow off my boots and unwrapped the thick purple scarf from around my neck. After removing the matching hat from my head— my grandmother had made it and the scarf—I shook out my curls. As I wandered farther inside the place, I took in the rich craftsmanship on display and the lavish decor. Antique crown molding trimmed the edges of the ceiling, and fancy art and mirrors hung on just about every wall.

Before I could reach the double doors to the room where the main event was taking place, I heard the lyrics of Soulja Boy's "Crank That," and they grew louder with each step I took. When I finally opened one of the doors, I discovered that the room was dim inside. Pink and green strobe lights bounced off the walls, and a full DJ table was set up against the back wall, like in a nightclub. Surrounding an already full dance floor were several tables draped in what appeared to be expensive pink and white linens. This was rather much for a two-year-old's birthday party, in my opinion. However, I knew that if Tez had anything to do with it, he was going to go all out for his niece.

As I stood there at the door, in awe of all the ghetto fabulousness happening in the room, I felt someone bump my shoulder. I turned my head to see big red hair framing a very familiar face. All the way from Prichard, Alabama, was Jorell's baby's mother, Meechie, in the flesh. Rather than say, "Excuse me," she simply rolled her eyes before sashaying across the room. It didn't take a rocket scientist to figure out that she'd run into me on purpose.

*Bitch!*

I stood there for a few more seconds, allowing my eyes to follow her leisurely. Although I didn't want to, I had to admit that Meechie was a beautiful girl. Light skin with a curvy, size ten frame. Her pouty full pink lips and almond-shaped eyes gave her an unwarranted air of innocence. And while I had toned down my sexy style of dress and was wearing simple fitted blue jeans, a teal sweater, and brown snow boots, Meechie wore tight black leggings, a short red silk blouse, and black booties with a sleek five-inch heel.

I knew that she was there only because of Jorell, because Perri wouldn't do me like that. When she finally reached her table, she sat down right next to Jorell, confirming my suspicions. He was holding their daughter in his lap. She must have known I was watching, because it looked almost rehearsed when she leaned over and kissed him smack-dab on the lips. If that wasn't a stiff slap to my withering ego, I didn't know what was. Although I was the one to call it quits with Jorell last year, I had to admit that he looked good sitting over there, like some sort of Nubian king. Even from a distance and in the dim lighting of the room, I could tell his long locks had been freshly twisted. They were neatly pulled back, showcasing the angles of his dark, handsome face.

"Oh, whaddup, Nika?" Plus said, taking me out of my trance.

"Hey, Plus!"

We gave each other a brief hug before he took the gift bag from my hand like a gentleman. "You can sit over here with the rest of us," he said, then guided me over to a seat.

As I walked deeper into the room, I saw that Ms. Tonya, Mr. Phillip, Aria, Tez, and a very pregnant Myesha were all sitting at one of the tables in the front. Perri was out on the dance floor, doing a simple two-step with Camille in her arms. I gave everyone at the table a hug before taking off my coat and sitting down.

"What's been going on, girl? We haven't seen you in a while," Myesha leaned over and said, raising her voice above the music.

"Yeah, I've been busy with school and church. Helping my grandmother out more," I explained.

I sat back and watched as Plus joined Perri and Camille out on the dance floor. The three of them were all smiles as they danced, looking every bit like the Black Family of the Year. I knew Perri had told me that she and Derrick were working things out, but looking at her and Plus together now, with their daughter happily in between them, gave me goose bumps. Even from the outside looking in, you could tell they loved each other.

"Nika, where you been at?" I felt two strong hands press down on my shoulders before I looked back and up and saw Derrick, of course.

"Hey, Derrick." I waved. "I've been around."

He took a seat next to me and watched the crowd on the dance floor like the rest of us. Perri and Plus continued to dance and play with Camille, as if they were in their own little bubble. I would never ask, but I was curious about how Derrick felt watching that scene. Personally, I felt slightly nauseated when I watched Jorell, Meechie, and their daughter sitting all together across the room, and hell, Jorell and I weren't even together. So I could only imagine the amount of grief Derrick's stomach was putting him through.

As I sat there, more people came into the room. Not very many children, mostly adults, and they filled up the empty tables, as well as the dance floor. Myesha told me that Perri and Tez didn't know much of their family, so the majority of people who had shown up were from Plus's side. Even though they weren't Perri's family, I did notice that they all greeted and hugged her like she was one of their own. I guessed that was because Perri and Plus had been friends since before they could probably even speak.

I stood up from the table. "Hey, I'm going over to get me some punch. Does anyone want anything to drink?" I said.

"You can bring me some punch back too, please," Myesha said, while everyone else either shook their head or told me, "No thank you."

As I made my way over to the cake and punch table, I came face-to-face with Jamal and Shivon. "Hey. How you doin'?" a smiling Jamal asked, exposing the gap between his two front teeth.

I hadn't seen either of them since last April, and although Shivon didn't even part her lips to speak, it was still a pleasant surprise to run into her. I was just happy to see that Jamal and Plus were still friends after everything that had gone down with TK and Tasha.

"Hey, Jamal," I said, giving him a friendly hug before waving to Shivon. She just pretended like she didn't see me, but that was cool. I just continued on to the cake and punch table to get myself something to drink.

The elaborate four-tiered layered cake in the center of the table was shaped like a royal castle. Keeping with the color scheme of the decorations in the room, it was elegantly decorated in the soft hues of pink, white, and gold. Cupcakes of the same color surrounded the cake, and the entire table had been sprinkled with glittery confetti. There were even two fountains on each side that had pink punch flowing endlessly from several spouts. They had truly gone all out for baby Camille.

"How it do, la baby?" That all too familiar Alabama accent resonated from behind me. The smell of his Gucci Pour Homme, combined with the scent of the coconut oil he used on his locks, sent an immediate chill down my spine.

After putting on the bravest face I could manifest in that moment, I turned around slowly. Standing before me was the man—or rather boy, I should say—I'd fallen for one random night in a hospital visiting room. His gold grills shined brilliantly through the crack of his cocky smirk, and his long locks were draped effortlessly across his big boxy shoulders. His stance was arrogantly wide and one hand covered his fist as he stared down at me, licking away at his full brown lips.

*Sexy motherfucker.*

"How can I help you?" I asked, swallowing the lump in my throat.

"Oh, you don't know me now?" Jorell looked away, tossing his eyes to the other side of the room, before letting out a small snort of laughter.

"Well, I *thought* I knew you! But seeing as though you had this top secret life . . . no, I guess I don't know you," I replied.

"Mane, there you go," he said, licking his lips again. He stayed quiet for a second, with just those dark eyes honed in on me, adding to my discomfort. He knew it, too, and I was sure it gave him some sort of twisted pleasure to watch me squirm under his lustful gaze.

"You know I still think about you, right?" he finally said before biting down on his bottom lip.

"Yeah, I'm so sure." Dramatically, I motioned with my head in the direction of the table where Meechie and his daughter were still seated. "I can clearly see that," I said.

As if I'd just told some sort of joke, humor filled his eyes and he let out a chuckle. I both hated and missed that sound at the same time. "Shawty, you know I miss yo' feisty ass," he said.

I rolled my eyes and tried to walk around him, but he quickly grabbed me by the waist. Just that minor warmth of his touch sent spurs of electricity throughout my entire body. He leaned down, put his face near mine, and my eyes closed.

"Our story ain't over, li'l baby," he whispered.

Swallowing hard, I peeled his hands from around me. "Yes it is! Now, you need to go back over there with your family!" I pointed.

Again, Jorell leaned down into my personal space, almost destroying the last bit of strength and resistance I had left. My heart thumped so loudly within my chest, I could hear it clear as day between my ears. My chest heaved up and down from my breathing picking up speed. All compliments, or rather side effects, of this Bama nigga named Jorell.

"That's my daughter, but I ain't wit' Meechie no mo'," he explained.

My eyes immediately popped open. "Well, what about the kiss?"

As he recollected, his eyes briefly squinted before widening. One corner of his mouth lifted into that same cocky smirk before his hand went up to hold his jaw. "Shawty, I ain't got no girl no mo', so these lips are up for grabs." He shrugged.

I smacked my teeth. "They were up for grabs even when you did have a girl. Or did you forget?" I snapped, throwing his infidelity back in his face.

He let out another snort and held both of his hands up in surrender. "You got me, shawty. You got me. I fucked up fo' sho', but if I ever get another chance, li'l baby, I swear—"

"Don't make promises we both know you can't keep, Jorell," I said, cutting him off.

Having no more words to exchange, we stared briefly into one another's eyes before I turned back, grabbed my drinks, and walked away. As I sauntered back over to my table, fully aware that I'd have his undivided attention, I caught Meechie glaring at me from afar. His daughter, who I had to admit was quite adorable, sat still in her lap.

"What was Jorell saying to you?" Myesha asked when I got back to the table.

"Trying to run game, girl. What else?" I said, sitting down in my seat.

Shortly after, we sang "Happy Birthday" to Camille, while she, Perri, and Plus all sat in the center of the dance floor. She was so cute in her pink princess dress and gold tiara. Once everyone had eaten cake and she had opened up her presents, people took to the dance floor once again and did the electric slide. *Black folk.* Of course, Meechie was out there doing the most, snaking her hips and shaking her ass with every dip and turn of the song. I knew it was wrong, but I silently hoped she'd get tripped up in those high heels of hers and fall flat on her face.

Perri came over. "Why you not out there dancing?" she asked. She was beaming from so much happiness as she looked down at me with those pretty amber-colored eyes.

My eyes went to Meechie on the dance floor. "Nah, it's too crowded out there for me."

Perri's eyes followed mine. "Oh . . . yeah." She gritted her teeth before twisting her lips to the side. "Her and Jornelle came up a few days ago, and Jorell asked if they could come to the party. Sorry."

"No, it's no biggie," I lied, shrugging my shoulders. "We're not even together anymore."

After another thirty minutes or so, the crowd began to thin and the DJ began packing up his equipment. While I sipped on the last of my punch, I watched Derrick, Plus, and Tez scatter about the room, trying to clean up. My eyes then landed on Perri, who was over talking to Jamal and Shivon. I didn't want to get up from the table, because I knew Jorell and Meechie would be watching me like a hawk, but I also knew I needed to offer my friend some help.

As I hesitantly crossed the dance floor, I kept my eyes trained on my destination, careful not to let my gaze travel over in Jorell's and Meechie's direction. Perri was laughing with Jamal about something as I approached the table, while Shivon appeared to be looking down at her phone.

"Hey, girl, you need some help cleaning up all this mess?" I asked, feeling Jorell's eyes sear into me from a distance.

"Nah, Plus and Tez got it," Perri said.

"And Derrick too, it seems." I smiled as I glanced across the room, in search of the three of them. My eyes locked with Jorell's. He was sneakily gaping at me, with lust in his eyes, as he pulled his bottom lip between his teeth.

*Ugh!*

"Yeah, he's trying. My boo," Perri said, regaining my attention.

My eyebrows rose when I heard that term of endearment leave her mouth. "Look at you, being all . . . mushy," I said.

She laughed, then scrunched up her nose. "Yeah, whateva, yo."

"Still wearing that necklace too, I see."

She clutched the heart-shaped pendant and held it against her chest. "*Please* don't let Derrick hear you say that," she whispered.

"Uh-huh," I said, giving her a knowing look. "Well, I guess if you don't need me, I'm getting ready to head out." I gave her a hug, then turned back to walk across the room.

After gathering up my things from the table and putting my winter gear back on, I gave everyone a hug good-bye.

"Don't stay away too long this time," Ms. Tonya said, rocking back and forth with a sleeping Camille secured in her arms.

"I won't," I told her just before heading out.

I was almost out the door when Jorell and his little family walked up beside me. He looked down at me but didn't say anything, which I assumed was because Meechie was right there. His daughter was also in between us, holding his hand. I gave her a little smile, which she returned, and then I slowed my pace a bit and allowed the three of them to walk a step ahead of me as I watched from behind. Real subtle like, Meechie peeked back over her shoulder at me, then reached down to grab Jorell's other hand.

He snatched his hand away before looking back at me. "Stop wit' the games, shawty. You know we not even like that no mo'," I heard him say.

Not wanting to be in their presence any longer, I rushed past the three of them and through the lobby, then bolted out the front door. The flurries had turned into a steady snowfall, and the ground looked to be covered with at least a half inch of snow. After trekking through the blanket of snow, I immediately got into my car and cranked up the engine. Although I wanted to get out of there fast, I knew I had to warm up my car. Once I had fastened my seat belt and melted back into my seat, my cell phone buzzing beside me caught my attention. I reached over and sighed when I saw that it was a text from none other than Jorell.

My love, our story ain't over.

# Chapter 16

## *Tez*

"Yo, where the fuck she at!" I spat to Levar, who was standing in the waiting room.

"They got her back in observation, duke. She been asking for you," he told me before running his hand down his face.

When he looked at me with his veiny red eyes, I could see the stress and fatigue written all over his face. Having to deal with stupid shit like this at three o'clock in the fucking morning, I could relate. Levar was one of my goons from the Millwood Projects. He was a big dude, standing only an inch taller than me, at six feet four, but weighing close to three hundred pounds. He had skin black as night, a low-cut fade, and a widespread African nose.

"A'ight. Good looking out," I said, dapping him up. "You ain't gotta stay. You can dip."

After getting into it with the nurse behind the desk, I learned that the room number was 317. Anger and annoyance filled my entire body as I stormed through the corridors of UM Prince George's hospital. As I passed by open rooms, I could hear the beeping of several machines and the deathly smell of disinfectant. Ever since my mother had passed, I had hated hospitals, and the fact that I had to be here pissed me off just that much more.

When I entered the room, lit only by a small lamp and the glow from the TV, I immediately saw her lying back in the bed. Her already light skin was even paler, and her short chestnut brown hair was sprawled all over her head. Her eyes were sunken in and her ashen lips were emotionless as she looked at me standing by the door. The sight of the white bandages wrapped tightly around each of her wrists forced an irritated breath from my lungs.

I wiped my hand down my face in an attempt to calm myself. "Shayla," I muttered, shaking my head.

"I-I'm so sorry, Tez," she croaked. Her voice was so weak that I unconsciously cleared my own throat.

"Look, the only reason I'm here is that I care about you. But, shorty, you already know the deal." I kept my voice even so that I would sound stern but not insensitive. After all, she had tried to kill herself over me.

"And I thought I could take it. I swear, I did. I thought I could just let her come and take you away from me all over again, but I just . . ." Her voice trailed off into a gut-wrenching cry.

I could see the veins protruding in her neck as she held her hands up to cover her face, pulling the intravenous tubes in her arms along with her. A nigga almost broke, seeing her like that.

I walked farther into the room until I was directly at her bedside. I placed my hand tenderly over her thigh, which was tucked securely beneath a thick white blanket. "Shayla, you knew what it was from the jump. I never . . . Not once did I ever lead you on."

Her hands fell from her tear-stained face before she peered up at me with that pitiful set of brown eyes. "I love you, though. I've *always* loved you, Tez," she confessed.

Hearing her declare her love for me pulled at my heartstrings, no doubt, but it didn't change the fact that my heart belonged to someone else. Mulling her words over in my head, I swiped my thumb across her wet cheek and inhaled a deep breath out of frustration. "I got mad love for you, shorty. You already know this. But I got a baby on the way, which means I got a real family now. That shit between me and you"—I shook my head—"is dead."

"But she left you, when I was there," she shrieked while stabbing her finger into her chest. "I have always been there!"

Nothing she had said was untrue, which was why I had rushed to the hospital in the first place. Shayla had definitely been loyal over the years, and I couldn't take that away from her even if I'd tried. When she'd called me earlier, talking all crazy, saying how she was going to kill herself, I honestly hadn't believed her. But something in the back of my consciousness had kept recalling the desperation in her voice. The shit had been pulling at me, telling me that shorty wasn't playing at all. That was when I had ended up calling Levar and had had him check in on her since he lived close by.

When he called and said that he'd found her limp body lying in a bathtub of bloody water, I knew then that she had been telling the truth. I just assumed she was like any other crazy bitch, making false threats to get what she wanted. But no, shorty actually tried to take her own life over me, which made me instantly feel like shit. I had been fucking her the entire time Myesha was gone, and as soon as I had got Myesha back, I'd cut Shayla off without sparing her feelings. When I had stopped dealing with her the first time, a few years back, she'd handled it like a G, but this time she was acting different. Somehow, during all that late-night fucking and sucking, she had gotten herself emotionally attached.

"Shorty, where's your family at?"

"I 'on't know . . . They're supposed to be on their way," she whispered, with a sniff.

"I'm stepping out for a minute to make a few calls. Be right back, a'ight?" I gave her a quick kiss on the forehead before walking out of the room.

As I made my way down the long hallway, I noticed that I wasn't getting any service on my phone. I jumped on the elevator and pressed the number one to go to the first floor before letting my head drop back against the metal wall. This shit with Shayla was quickly draining me. I needed to get in touch with her peoples fast, so that they could come and take over, and I could get the fuck on.

After hopping off the elevator, I trudged through the front lobby of the emergency department. The place was packed full of sad, sick-looking motherfuckers who were coughing and wheezing all over the place. Just seconds before the automatic doors slid open, I threw the hood over my head, and then I stepped out into the cold. The pitch-black sky was clear in that hour of darkness, with not a single star in sight. Only the sounds of distant cars and traveling sirens could be heard.

As I stepped over patches of ice and snow on the sidewalk, I look down at my phone. Six text messages and eight missed calls flashed on the front screen. Just as I was about to open up my messages, I heard Shayla's mother call out to me from the parking lot.

"Tez!"

I lifted my head up and saw not only her mother running toward me but also her younger sister Shakia, who was trailing behind.

"What's up, Big Dee Dee? Kia?" I said.

"Oh, my God, Tez! How is my baby? Where is she?" Big Dee Dee asked in a panic.

I had known Big Dee Dee almost my entire life from growing up in the Millwood Projects. She wasn't a fat woman by far, but she was thick and very tall for a female, standing at five feet eleven inches. She had the same light skin tone as Shayla and big doe-like brown eyes. Back when I was just a little nigga selling dope on the corner, Big Dee Dee would allow me to stash product at her house during the day. She would even cook up and bag a little something every now and again, which was actually how me and Shayla had got close.

"She's all right. Upstairs in three-seventeen," I said, giving her a hug.

Just as Big Dee Dee drew back from my embrace, I heard the sound of screeching tires. When I looked out toward the street, I immediately saw that a car had pulled up close to the curb in front of us. It was Plus's Honda Accord.

"The fuck?" I mumbled under my breath.

Plus jumped out from the driver's side in a hurry before jogging around the car. At the same time, I saw Perri was getting out of the front passenger seat.

"Excuse me, Big Dee Dee. I think I see my li'l sister," I said.

As I walked over to the car, Plus was helping Myesha get out from the back. I could see her swollen face and watched her wince in pain as she struggled to get up from the seat. From the quick, short breaths she pushed out of her mouth in intervals, it was obvious that she was in labor. Just as I was approaching the car, Perri ran up to me.

"Tez! You made it," she said.

"Uh-huh, yeah," I stammered, nodding my head.

Myesha's eyes instantly lit up at the sight of me, but I guessed the agony she was in wouldn't allow her to speak. Immediately, I rushed over and helped Plus pull her out of the car. Hearing the panic in her rhythmic breathing, I securely wrapped my arm around her to try to support her weight. As we all began walking inside, Shakia darted out in front of us, her nose flared and eyebrows pinched, giving away the fact that she was about to be on some bullshit.

"Fuck off, Kia!" I spat, walking past her in a hurry.

However, Shakia kept on walking alongside us, matching us stride for stride. "So wait a minute!" Her eyes narrowed into tiny slits. "This the bitch you left my sister for? She's the reason my sister's laid up in the hospital bed!" she snapped. Hearing her call Myesha a bitch caused my blood to boil and my jaw to clench instantly. And although I wanted to slap the fuck out of her, I knew getting my girl inside was more important.

When Myesha's curious eyes peered up at me, I found myself rendered speechless. But before I could even say a word to try to explain, she stopped and hunched down, allowing a low grunt to come from her throat. It seemed as if the pain of her contractions momentarily overshadowed everything else.

"Tez, answer me! You been fucking my sister all this time . . . all these years, and now you getting ready to have a baby with this bitch!" Shakia yelled in my face.

"Go on some-fucking-where, Shakia," I growled, still holding on to Myesha, whose pain was clearly intensifying.

Like me, Perri must have grown tired of hearing Shakia's rants, because she came over and pushed her out of my and Myesha's faces.

"He said, 'Get the fuck back, bitch!'" Perri yelled, shoving Shakia so hard that she fell in a small mound of leftover snow on the ground.

Even though Perri just kept walking along with the rest of us, I knew that wouldn't be the end of it. Shakia was a hood rat through and through and definitely loved to fight. After springing up quickly to her feet, Shakia rushed over and shoved Perri hard in the back, causing her to trip forward a little. My eyes immediately went looking for Big Dee Dee, but she was no longer outside. I figured she'd probably already gone up to see about Shayla.

When Perri turned back around, she stormed past me, and without warning, the two started throwing hands. Poor Plus was doing his best to intervene.

"Plus, get Perri, yo!" I ordered over my shoulder.

Once Myesha and I made it inside the hospital's lobby, the nurses quickly got her in a wheelchair and took her straight up to labor and delivery. Although I hoped Perri and Plus were okay, I knew at that moment my focus needed to be on Myesha and bringing our son into the world. They immediately hooked her up to several monitors and laid her back in a bed to check her cervix. Throughout the whole process, she squeezed my hand so hard, I thought my shit was literally broken.

With apologetic eyes, the nurse removed the bloody gloves from her hands. "She's already eight centimeters," she said. I knew that without saying it, she was telling us that it was too late for an epidural. More than likely, Myesha was so late getting to the hospital because of me.

As I stood at her bedside, Myesha tugged hard on one of my locks and pulled me down close to her face. "I. Can't. Do. This," she whispered through gritted teeth, lips trembling in the process.

I jerked my neck back and could feel my nose simultaneously flare with anger, because my initial reaction was to smack the hell out of her for pulling on my shit like that. But I had to quickly calm myself and remember everything that my girl was going through. "You got this, My. Don't you want to meet our son?" I said in a comforting tone of voice.

Instead of responding to me, she hunched down and grunted again, enduring another hard-hitting contraction. As they started to strike less than a minute apart, each with more force than the last, Myesha's low grunts turned into bellowing cries. Tears were streaming down her cheeks, and beads of sweat had collected at the edge of her brows. If I listened closely, I could even hear the slight chattering of her teeth, and just when I didn't think she could take any more, she let out a piercing scream.

"Argh . . . Fuck!"

Stretching my eyes wide in panic, I yelled at the nurse, "Do something! Shit! Nigga, don't you see she in pain!"

I guessed the nurse had witnessed this display of dramatics several times before, because she gave both of us a blank stare before shaking her head. Moments later she checked Myesha again and told us it was time for her to push. My damn knees almost gave out from underneath of me. For some reason, I was nervous as hell, and Myesha's loud crying and moaning was only making a nigga feel worse.

No more than a minute later, the doctor came in to join us. While he got down at the end of the bed and put on his gloves, the nurse propped Myesha up a bit and picked up one of her legs. She instructed me to hold up the other right before they told her how to push down. With her chin to her chest, Myesha bore down with force and tightly clamped her teeth shut. Trembling, she repeated that motion on and off, every minute or so, wailing and screaming in between.

She endured that same cycle for nearly thirty minutes before my son, Montez, Jr., was finally born. Seeing the doctor hold his tiny body up in the air brought tears to my eyes. Looking back at Myesha, whose exhausted eyes were filled with nothing but love, I realized that the two of them together were everything I had ever needed, but something that I had never known I wanted in this lifetime.

"I'm so proud of you, baby," I whispered before kissing the top of Myesha's head.

She reached up and wiped the lone tear that had *mistakenly* fallen from the corner of my eye. "Aw, baby.

Look at you getting all emotional," she cooed. Her face was misted with sweat as she smiled at me.

After Montez, Jr., was cleaned and weighed, the nurse delicately placed him in Myesha's arms. Both of us gazed down into his sleeping face, taking in all his tiny features. I could already see that he had my nose and my mouth. And although he didn't have a head full of hair like Camille did when she was born, the little he did have was a sandy-brown color, just like mine.

"Damn. Li'l nigga look just like me," I boasted.

Myesha nudged me with her arm. "Don't call him that. And at this point, you can't even tell who he's going to look like."

"Shit! You's a lie! Bet you the li'l nigga got my eyes too," I teased. She nudged me again, and I chuckled. "Come on, li'l man. Open ya eyes up for Daddy." I played with the bottom of his feet, but for whatever reason, he just wouldn't open up his eyes.

Myesha and I were so wrapped up in our son that we didn't even notice the doctor and nurses leave, nor did we hear Perri and Plus creep into the room.

"Hey, y'all," Perri said just before her bright eyes landed on the baby. "Oh, my God," she squealed, making her way over to the bed. She had a small purple bruise on the edge of her jaw, which instantly made me feel bad for getting her wrapped up in my bullshit. However, neither Perri nor Plus mentioned Shakia while they were in the room. And while I knew Myesha would ask me about it eventually, I was just grateful to have this moment of peace with my son.

Plus came over and dapped me up before congratulating both of us.

"Where Pops at? Anybody call him or Godma?" I asked.

"Yeah, they're on their way. Aria's going to stay back with Camille," Plus said.

All of a sudden, the door opened and a wheelchair rolled in, with Shayla sitting right in it. She looked every bit of a psychopath, with the dark rings around her eyes, the wild hair, and the bloodstained bandages around her wrists. She just stared at us with a vacant expression. My chest tightened at the sight of her. *Fuck!* After I left her earlier, I had hoped that they would restrain the bitch or that she would at least stay put in her room now that Big Dee Dee was here. But neither seemed to be the case.

"So this is her, huh?" Shayla asked, her voice trembling and soft, almost like a child's, as she rolled farther into the room.

All eyes in the room immediately went to me, and I swallowed hard. "Shayla, I'll talk to you later. Right now I'm with my family," I said.

"Tez, who is this?" Myesha asked in a low voice.

I shook my head. "Not right now, My. Just worry about my son."

"I'll tell you who I am. I'm the—"

"Yo, do we need to call security on your ass?" Perri snapped. Plus's hands immediately went to her shoulders in an attempt to calm her down. The last thing we needed was Perri fighting again.

Myesha looked over at Perri and put her hand up before cutting her eyes back over to Shayla. "No! I want to know. Who are you, and why are you here?"

Before I could even intervene, Shayla spoke up. "I'm the woman he's been with for the past ten years."

Myesha looked up at me for a response at the same time that my neck jerked back.

"Yo, why the fuck you lying on me, shorty?" I barked.

"So we haven't been fucking since we were kids? You didn't get me pregnant and pay for me to get an abortion seven years ago? You didn't buy me a house and a new car just a few years back . . . both of which I still live in and drive today?" Her left eyebrow rose.

Myesha and Perri both gasped at the same time. A split second later, all sets of eyes in the room were directly on me as they all anxiously awaited an answer. When I looked down at Myesha's dark, slanted eyes, which were begging for a response, *the right response*, I felt an unnatural type of fear. Fear of losing her all over again.

"Tez," she said in a low voice, waiting on some form of a denial to fall from my lips, as she blinked back her tears. But I couldn't. I couldn't deny shit Shayla had just said, because it was all true. And that revelation quickly turned my fear into anger.

"Bitch, you betta get the fuck out of this room before I finish the job you started!" I threatened through gritted teeth.

"Why her over me?" Shayla asked, unbothered by the loudness of my voice.

With adrenaline coursing through my wiry veins, I stormed over and grabbed the handles on the back of her wheelchair. I spun her ass around so fast that she whipped forward in her chair and let out an ear-splitting scream.

"Stop, Tez! Stop!" she shouted, reaching around to claw at one of my hands.

I opened up the door and pushed her ass out of the room, then shoved that chair as hard as I could down the hospital hall. I stood there and watched her fly down the hall.

"Aah!" she shrieked.

Why the bitch didn't use her brakes, I didn't know, but she ended up crashing right into a medical-supply cart.

"Stay the fuck away from me, Shayla! I'm serious as a fucking heart attack, shorty! This ain't what you want," I yelled, threatening her again. My voice boomed down the narrow hall as spit flew from my lips.

A nurse came up to me and asked, "Sir, is everything all right?"

"Yeah. Just keep that psycho bitch away from me and my girl's room. I think she's a psych patient that escaped from y'all's ward."

As the nurse's eyebrows gathered in confusion, I headed back into the room. The first thing I heard was crying. While Plus sat in a rocking chair, holding my son, Perri tried her best to comfort Myesha, who was obviously upset. She was crouched down in the bed, shielding her face with her hands, while Perri rubbed her on the back. I went over and stroked her arm.

"My," I whispered.

She peeled her hand back from her wet face and looked up at me before smacking my hand away. "Don't you fucking touch me! Don't you ever touch me!" she snapped. Both Perri and I backed up a step.

"That shit is in the past. I swear—"

"Get out!" she shouted, cutting me off. "Get the fuck out! Now!"

"The fuck?" I felt my face ball up and my chest rise with vexation when she said that. "Shorty, you got me all the way fucked up if you think I'm gon' leave my son. So you can get that idea up outta ya head!" I spat.

"Why? You didn't even want him, remember!" she threw back in my face.

Shaking my head, I closed my eyes and let out a snort of laughter. That was all I could do in the moment to keep from choking the life out of her. I'd admit that there was a time when I didn't want to be a father, but looking at my son now as he lay there in Plus's arms, there was no way I could deny him.

I briefly pinched the bridge of my nose before I said, "I'm not leaving, Myesha."

"Get out! Leave now, or I'll call security," she warned.

In a state of disbelief, I cocked my head to the side and squinted my eyes. "Are you fucking serious right now?"

"Leave!" she screamed, pointing at the door.

Hearing the sound of my son crying behind me immediately caught my attention. I turned around and looked down at my son, whose bright eyes were now wide open and just as golden as mine.

"You see what you did? Stop being so fucking dramatic all the gahdamn time," I told her.

She grabbed the remote that was attached to her hospital bed and pressed the red button.

"Yes, ma'am?" the nurse chimed through the speaker.

I held my hands up in surrender. "Fuck it! I'll leave. But I'm tellin' you now, I'm coming back to see my son, Myesha. You can't keep him away from me."

She sniffed back a few more tears before she brought the remote up a little closer to her mouth. "I hit the button by accident," she said to the nurse.

I picked my son up out of Plus's arms and kissed the top of his soft little head before looking down into his face. A smile spread across my face as he wrapped his long, tiny fingers around mine and peered at me with those amber-colored eyes.

"Daddy will be back, li'l man. Yo' mama on some bullshit right now," I whispered. "But Daddy will be back. Promise," I added. I cradled him just a few seconds longer before I passed him back to Plus and headed out the door.

# Chapter 17

## *Tez*

It was the first day of spring when I found myself sitting out on the back stoop of Pop's place. For the past two months, I had been staying back in the Millwood Projects, which was some total bullshit. Myesha had kicked my black ass out of my own damn house, and now, at twenty-five years old, I was back to living with my father. It wasn't that I couldn't afford an apartment. I just didn't think she'd be mad for that long. In the past four years, I had bought two homes, with cash, yet here I was, right back where it all started. It was either that or her ass was going to run away again, and I just couldn't allow that, especially now that she had my son.

However, Myesha wasn't a total bitch these days. Almost daily, she would allow me to come by and visit my son. But as soon as she put MJ down for the night, she made sure to send my ass right back on out that door. I was doing everything in my power to win her evil ass over, but she hadn't budged a bit. I had sent dozens of flowers, expensive jewelry, and had even ordered her ass fancy dinners throughout the week, just so she wouldn't have to cook. But even after doing all of that, she acted as if she didn't care.

Hell, a nigga wasn't even getting none anymore, all because she wanted to play games. Sure, I knew Shayla would be more than willing to fuck, but I also knew that even entertaining her crazy ass again was asking for trouble. More than that, I was trying to be a better man these days. Although I wanted to get my dick wet, my desire to be with Myesha overpowered anything else. She was the one for me, and watching her care for my son day in and day out reaffirmed that.

Through the chain-link fence, I looked out into the old neighborhood. It appeared just as sad as the gray April sky that loomed above my head. Trash lined the gutters of the streets, while badass kids played unattended. The same old junkies from back in the day sporadically paced up and down the block, while the young niggas serving covertly prowled familiar corners. Even in broad daylight, the chirps of police cars riding through could be heard mingling with the sounds of the ice-cream truck.

I hated that my father still lived here when I could now afford to have him living better. But since this was the house he had once shared with my mother, he refused to leave. He said every memory of her was embedded in these walls, and even after seventeen years, there were still things in this house that carried her scent. With that being said, I had no choice but to respect his wishes.

I pulled a pre-rolled blunt out of the pocket of my hoodie, and just when I was about to light it up, I heard the back door to the house slam shut behind me.

"Don't be smoking that crap in my house, Montez," my father fussed.

I looked back over my shoulder and saw him pulling up a chair. "Damn, Pops. I'm not even *in* the house. I'm chilling outside," I said.

"If you want to smoke that, then you need to go back to your house."

"Shit, I'm trying to, but Myesha . . . ," I sighed, letting my voice trail off. "She being stubborn as hell."

"Well, she's hurt, but she'll come around."

I placed the unlit blunt back in my pocket and got up from the step to pull up a chair beside him. "How you figure that?" I asked.

"'Cause she loves you, that's how I know," he stated matter-of-factly.

Leaning up to rest my elbows on the tops of my thighs, I glanced over at him and cleared my throat. "You ever go through anything like that with Moms?"

His eyes shot up toward the dismal sky before the edges of his lips turned up into a natural smile. "Once. Before your sister was born."

I waited for him to say more, but he didn't. He just sat there with that silly smirk on his face.

"A'ight, so what happened?" I said, prodding.

"I think you were about two or maybe three years old at the time, and of course, your mother never worked. She stayed home to take care of you, while I went on the job every day. I was working down at the asphalt plant back then, and an old girlfriend of mine, Regina, had just started working there as a secretary. You mother knew of her from back in the day." He shrugged. "And I guess that's why I never mentioned to her that Regina had started working there," he said, shaking his head.

I let out a low snort. "Ma had a fit, didn't she?"

He put his hand up to stop me from rushing the story. "Hold up now. Let me tell the story," he said.

I laughed, because Pops never talked like this. Only when it came to my mother.

"So, Regina and I had started going to lunch a few times a week. Nothing ever happened except maybe some innocent flirting, but still, I was wrong. Well, some of yo' mama's friends from church saw us out one day and ended up telling her."

"Damn. Not the church, Pops," I muttered with a chuckle.

He nodded his head. "Exactly! I came home from work one day, and she had all my shit sitting out there on the front step. All my clothes and shoes packed up in those black plastic trash bags," he said with a laugh. "Tonya let me stay at her place for a few days, until your mama calmed down and let me back in."

"You stayed with Godma?" My eyebrows rose.

He vigorously shook his head back and forth. "No, not like that. I could never mess with Tonya that way. She was like a sister to your mother. Hell, even now I consider Tonya family because of baby Camille. I would never do your mama dirty like that, not even in her death."

I nodded my head, fully understanding what he was trying to say. "You don't ever get lonely, though?" I asked.

"Son, trust me. I received more love from your mother than most men get their entire lifetime. Plus, I have a few friends I can call."

I let out a low snort of laughter. "Playa," I muttered.

He just shrugged, a little grin on his face.

"So when Moms threw you out, what happened to make her calm down and take you back? What did you have to do?"

"The first couple of days out the house, I sent flowers and even wrote her a little poem—"

"A poem!" I shouted, then chuckled. "Moms had yo' ass acting like some soft-ass nigga, huh?" I joked.

He cracked a smile and nodded his head to agree. "But you know what, son? None of that shit worked. The only thing that got us back on track was me giving her time. After she realized that nothing had actually happened between me and Regina, and that I was truly sorry for not being honest with her in the first place, she forgave me."

"Yeah, well, I've given Myesha plenty of time to get over that shit. Hell, two months, to be exact. But she's still not fucking with me." Feeling stressed, I reached in my pocket and pulled out the unlit blunt before placing it in between my lips.

"Go ahead and light it up," my father said, shaking his head.

"'Preciate it, Pops."

As I lit the blunt, he said, "Since you're the one that messed things up, you have to realize that forgiveness is not on your time clock. However long it takes for her to get over what you did is what it's going to be." Holding his hand up, he then said, "And might I remind you that what you did was a hell of a lot worse than just taking someone out to lunch."

After allowing a wisp of smoke to swirl from my lips, I ran my hand down my face and let out a deep breath. "I hear you, Pops. I hear you."

"Also, while I've got you out here, I been meaning to ask you something," he said.

"A'ight."

"Now that you have a family of your own, when are you getting out of the streets?"

I quietly sucked my teeth. "Come on now, Pops. I ain't been in the streets since I was, like, seventeen years old."

"You know what I'm saying, Montez! You may not be out in the streets like that," he said, pointing at the street behind our house, where a few dope boys were standing on the corner. "But you're still out there."

No one in my family knew exactly what I did these days for money. All they knew was that a nigga had his GED and that my former occupation consisted of hugging the block and serving these fiends. Not wanting either to confirm or deny my father's accusations, I chucked my chin up.

He reached over and placed his hand on my shoulder. "Son, all I'm saying is that you can't keep that kind of lifestyle with a family at home," he said.

I nodded my head, because he was right. In fact, my future in the game had been weighing heavily on my mind ever since Myesha first told me she was pregnant. I knew I needed to take another route when it came to making my money, but with no experience in anything else, what could I possibly do?

"You can always come and work with me, doing security," my father said.

I felt my face ball up, because, honestly, I was offended. Even though I had always tried my best to keep a low profile in the streets, as the years had gone by, I'd deservedly earned the reputation of being a boss. And although I would never tell my father, I truly felt like working a minimum-wage security job was beneath me. Now don't get me wrong. I respected what my father did for a living, because it had always provided a roof over our head and our other essential needs. But as a nigga that had over two million dollars sitting in the bank, what the fuck would I look like being a gahdamn *rent-a-cop*?

"Nah, I'm good, Pops," I said, then took a pull on my blunt.

"We've gotten a lot of high-profile cases. A lot of celebrities these past few months. It's not just working at warehouses anymore," he said.

In thought, I felt my left eyebrow lift. *Hmm*, I wondered.

"Anyway," he said, changing the subject, "are you going to Plus's game tonight? Myesha wanted to get out of the house, so Tonya and I are going up to your place to keep the kids."

"Yeah, I'll probably go up there to see him play, if I can get a ticket at the last minute," I said.

Just as I was about to place the blunt back up to my lips, I felt a drop of rain hit my hand. I looked up and suddenly noticed the thick dark clouds rolling in. "Looks like it's about to dump, Pops. Come on. Let's go back inside."

Around eight o'clock that evening, I took my seat in the arena, next to Perri. Myesha's stubborn ass wouldn't even sit next to me, and of course, she looked good as hell. She kept it simple, wearing a navy blue Georgetown Hoyas jersey and some tight-fitting jeans that showed the curves of her plump ass and hips. With an additional fifteen pounds on her since the baby, she was thicker than before. And while she seemed to be self-conscious about it, I actually loved the extra weight.

Myesha's long black curls hung effortlessly underneath the fitted Georgetown cap she wore on her head, and her mocha-colored lips shined, appearing to have been dipped in a clear coat of gloss. From the car ride over to the arena, I could still smell the Chanel perfume she wore. She played too many games, because she knew it was my favorite scent on her.

I leaned over and whispered in Perri's ear, "Tell Myesha I said she looks real good tonight."

Perri faced me with those cognac-colored eyes that mirrored my own before scrunching up her nose.

"Yo, just tell her what I said," I fussed under my breath.

Perri rolled her eyes and huffed before leaning over to Myesha and whispering in her ear.

From my peripheral, I could see Myesha whispering something back to her.

"She said thanks," Perri said, her tone dry, as she kept her eyes fixed on the court.

"That's it?"

Without even looking at me, she nodded her head.

Leaning over, I whispered in Perri's ear again. "A'ight. Well, tell her that I miss her."

Perri cut her eyes at me and jerked her head back. "Nigga, you see her just about every day."

"Just tell her what I said," I snapped.

She sucked her teeth before leaning over and whispering in Myesha's ear again. While I pretended to be focused on the game, I could see Myesha loop her hair behind her ear before responding back.

Perri leaned over to me and said, "Nigga, she said, she know."

I let out a low snort of laughter before running my tongue across my teeth. "Tell her I know she miss this dick," I said.

"Ugh!" Perri groaned, slapping me on the arm. She stood up from her seat and looked down at Myesha. "Look, you need to sit right here, because I'm not gon' be in between y'all niggas all night."

Myesha released a heavy sigh before getting up to switch seats with Perri. Her face contorted from an obvious attitude as she sat down next me.

"So how you been?" I asked.

She adjusted the fitted cap down tighter on her head before looking over at me. "Same as I was yesterday, Tez. I'm fine," she said, sounding annoyed.

"Shorty, you gotta bad attitude, you know that?"

She just rolled her eyes at me before focusing again on the basketball court.

"But I still miss yo' pretty ass." When I said that, I could have sworn I saw the corners of her mouth shoot up into a tiny smile, but that moment quickly faded when she jumped up from her chair and started loudly cheering and shouting Plus's name. From what I could see on the scoreboard, I had just missed one of his many three-point shots.

For the remainder of the game, she pretty much ignored me. She would only talk to Perri and cheer when

Georgetown scored. When the game was finally over, the three of us moved through the thick crowd, making our way back downstairs in the arena. I tried to hold the small of Myesha's back, but she kept walking fast so that I couldn't touch her.

"I think I'm just gonna wait for Derrick and ask him for a ride," Perri said, cutting her eyes over at Myesha for confirmation.

"Fuck you looking at her for?" I asked.

"You cool, girl?" Perri asked, without acknowledging my question.

Myesha cut those dark, slanted eyes of hers over at me before shrugging her shoulders. "I guess."

As Perri headed toward the locker room, Myesha and I walked out to the parking garage. When we got to my car, I stepped in front of her to open up her door.

"You didn't need to open up my door, Tez. It's not like we're on a date," she said before sliding into her seat.

"You still my baby's muva, and a nigga is still a gentleman." I gave her a little wink.

She rolled her eyes at me and pulled the car door shut. After walking around to the driver's side and getting in, I cranked up the engine and pulled off. On the ride home that night, Myesha stared out the window, her arms folded across her chest. I had to play my music loud just so that the car wouldn't be silent. I knew that she was still pissed at me, but after two months of separation, I hoped for at least a little bit of conversation. I mean, shit. We did just have a baby together.

Seeing a collection of red lights in front of me, I slowed down my speed. The traffic on 495 was backed up for at least a couple of miles, which would only prolong the miserable car ride home. With my foot resting on the brakes, I cut the music down and looked over toward Myesha. "So how's my li'l man?" I asked.

Myesha tucked her curly hair behind her ear. "The same as he was yesterday, when you saw him. He's fine,'" she said, still looking out the window.

I let out a heavy breath, because I was getting tired of her funky-ass attitude. After tapping my fingers on the steering wheel for a couple of seconds and calming myself down, I tried again. "You wanna go get something to eat before I take you back? Maybe we can talk."

Slowly, she turned her body toward me and lifted her head, showcasing those dark eyes beneath the brim of her hat. This would be the first time our eyes met that day. And judging by the flare of her nostrils and her full lips, which were twisted to the side, she was still angry at a nigga. "No, I don't want to go out to eat with you. And exactly what is there for us to talk about, Tez?"

Pinching the bridge of my nose, I could feel myself growing pissed. "Why you gotta be so fucking smart, yo? You see a nigga tryin' to talk to you. I been trying to make shit right, but you acting like you don't want me to come home."

"I don't," she muttered under her breath, adjusting her body in the seat.

"What was that?" Even though I had heard her clearly, I wanted her to repeat herself.

"I said, I don't want you to come home, Tez. I'm done."

"You done? Fuck is that supposed to mean?"

"Exactly what I said."

I let out a snort before thumbing one side of my nose. "No, you done when I say you fucking done. You got my son. You living in my fucking house—"

"Take the damn house, Tez. Shit! Just take it! It's just one more thing you can use to try to control me. You're the one that was out there hoeing around while I was pregnant, and now you wanna make me out to be the bad person." Her finger and her head shook at the same time. "I don't think so!"

"Man, fuck outta here with that bullshit, Myesha! Wasn't nobody hoeing around. Had you stayed yo' ass where the fuck you was supposed to, instead of running off like some little-ass brat, then I wouldn't have done shit!" I was so angry and caught up with arguing with Myesha that I hadn't noticed that the traffic in front of me had begun to pull away. The loud sounds of horns honking behind me caught our attention.

"Just shut up and drive, Montez!"

Easing my foot off the brakes, I drove slowly until the next stopping point in the traffic. Not wanting to fight anymore, I released a heavy sigh and ran my hand down the front of my face. "Look, you don't have to go nowhere. The house is yours, a'ight?"

"So, is that what you do? Just go around giving bitches houses?"

My neck snapped back as I cut my eyes toward her. "Is that what you are? One of my bitches?"

"You know what I mean, Tez. I can't believe you bought that crazy-ass bitch a house."

"Man, that was a long-ass time ago—"

"Were you sleeping with her while we were together?" she asked in a low voice, cutting me off.

"No. I told you I ended shit with her when things between us got serious."

"Did you love her?" she asked, but before I could speak, she answered the question for herself. "Well, clearly, you did. You been with the girl since y'all were teenagers, you bought her a whole damn house, for Christ's sake, and she was the first one you ran to when me and you got into an argument."

*The fuck?* "How you gon' ask a nigga a question, then take it upon yo' self to answer that shit? Hell no, I ain't luh that girl. Not once in all the years I dealt with her did I ever tell her that I loved her. Not once."

"Well, I guess her and I have something in common, then," she said just above a whisper.

Hearing her say that instantly made me feel like shit. It was true that over the past few years with Myesha, never once had I expressed that I actually loved her. After losing my mother, I had sworn to myself that I would never be that vulnerable with another person again. Because even after seventeen years of my mother being buried in the ground, that shit still hurt like hell. And although I proclaimed that I loved only one woman, which was Perri, I knew deep down I loved Myesha too. Even more so now that she'd had my son. I swear, in that moment I tried to say just that, but for some reason, the words just wouldn't come out.

# Chapter 18

## *Perri*

With Derrick wedged in between my legs, sleeping on top of me, I peeled my eyes open and looked over at the digital clock on his nightstand. It was already a little after seven in the morning, and since I knew we had a flight to catch in just a few hours, I swirled my finger in his ear. As he stirred in his sleep, he slapped my hand away before trying to reposition his head on my breasts.

"Derrick, wake up," I said.

"Give me five more minutes, Ma," he pleaded with a deep, groggy voice.

I gently pushed him off me and sat up straight in the bed. "No. We gotta get ready to catch our flight," I said. When he didn't respond, I shook his shoulder and nudged his head. "Come on. Yo, get ya ass up!"

"Damn, Ma! Just let a nigga sleep," he fussed.

"Derrick, today is your big day. It's draft day!"

And just like that, I could see a lone dimple pierce the side of his freckled face. Although he quickly covered his head with the pillow, trying to hide his smile, it was too late, because I'd already seen it. Today was the first round of the NBA draft, and Derrick and I were due to be in New York by five o'clock to meet up with his mother. I was so nervous and anxious, you would have thought that I was being drafted into the NBA. Under the covers, I bounced my legs up and down against the mattress before letting out a girlish squeal.

"Oh my Gawd, yo! Can you believe you about to go into the NBA?" I asked.

Derrick sat up in the bed, revealing his beautiful smile once again. He shook his head and said, "Shit is like a dream come true, ya know."

Just when he leaned over and tenderly kissed my lips, his cell phone vibrated on the nightstand. "Your breath stinks, Ma. You need to go handle that," he joked, reaching over me to grab his phone.

I looked down at his flashing screen, only to see a picture of Mia appear. She was a beautiful Latin girl with long silky black hair, creamy vanilla skin, and dark almond-shaped eyes. She had been calling him a lot more lately, and because I didn't want to come off like some nagging, jealous-ass girlfriend, I hadn't bothered asking him about it. Besides, I still talked to Plus all day every day, and most times not even about Camille. So I knew if I were to question him about Mia, he wouldn't hesitate to throw Plus up in my face.

"Whassup?" he said, casually answering the phone. As he leaned back against the headboard, he brushed his hand forward over the top of his freshly cut hair. I watched as light from the morning sun skimmed across the muscles of his bare chest and arms, which seemed to flex with each movement.

"Nah, I'll be touching down about three. Why?" he said, still running his hand down the top of his fade.

Noticing the sporadic faint nodding of his head, I sat back against the headboard next to him. I pretended to play with my freshly polished nails while eavesdropping.

"That's what's up. Well, thanks again, Mami," he said, ending the call.

I could feel my left eyebrow arch. "Mami?" I repeated.

Derrick let out a little snort of laughter before saying, "Don't start bugging, Ma."

Rolling my eyes, I jumped out of the bed and stormed into the bathroom. I wasn't even in the shower a good five minutes before Derrick came in to join me. He wrapped his arms around my waist and pulled me into him so that my head rested against his chest.

"You mad at me?" he asked, his mouth against my temple. His voice was so deep that it caused goose bumps to rise all over me as he slid his hand across my stomach.

I shook my head, because honestly, I didn't know how I felt. I knew I didn't like the sound of him calling another woman Mami, but the sense of jealousy I felt was no comparison to what I had previously endured when Plus was with Tasha.

"I just better be your only mami, I know that much," I said.

Derrick spun me around to face him before planting a deep kiss on my lips. His hands gripped the sides of my face as his tongue invaded my mouth in the most sensual manner. It wasn't long after that our lip locking turned into a full blown lovemaking session right there under the water. Ever since I had told Plus he couldn't stay at the house with me anymore, things between me and Derrick had definitely improved. And it was times like this when everything between us just felt right.

It was exactly 2:05 p.m. when our plane touched down at JFK Airport. Derrick had refused to drive from DC to New York because he didn't want to take a chance at getting stuck in major traffic. I enjoyed the quick flight, so it didn't matter to me that we hadn't driven. After we walked through the busy airport and made our way down to the baggage claim, I called Plus on my cell to check in on Camille.

"Hey, what's up?" I said when Plus answered. With the phone tucked between my ear and shoulder, I reached down to grab my suitcase off the conveyor belt.

"Sup, P? You made it there safe?" Plus asked.

"Yeah, we're here. Just landed. How's my baby?" I said.

"I'm doing good—"

I started laughing. "Boy, quit playing. How's Camille?" I said, rephrasing the question.

"Oh, how's *our* baby?" he asked knowingly. I imagined the slick little grin that was most likely spread across his handsome face.

"Yes, dummy," I said, laughing. By this time Derrick was rolling his suitcase in front of me, with his own phone attached to his ear, so he wasn't paying me any mind.

"She straight. Taking a nap right now, though."

"At two thirty, Ahmad?" I fussed, because he knew she took her naps from 11:30 a.m. to 1:30 p.m. every day.

"How you gon' try to regulate shit here while you way up there in New York with *that* nigga? If you wanted shit done yo' way, you should've stayed yo' ass here."

I rolled my eyes, because he was right. With a heavy sigh, I changed the subject. "Anyway . . . I'll be back in two days." I cast my eyes forward and saw that Derrick was still talking on the phone. Then I whispered, "We still on for the movies next Wednesday, right?"

His laughter erupted on the other end of the phone before he said, "Fuck you whispering for, yo?"

"Shut up! Ain't nobody whispering," I lied.

"Yeah, whateva. But yeah, *Spider-Man 3* . . . it's on like popcorn."

"Well, I'll call back a little later on to talk to Camille. Love you," I told him.

"A'ight. Be safe. Love you too."

After getting our rental car from the airport, Derrick and I headed straight to the DoubleTree downtown. As expected, the traffic was moving slowly due to the many cars that had flooded the popular city all at once. Thanks to Nika taking me to get my hair and nails done yesterday, I didn't have much to do to get ready for the main event, so we were still good on time. The biggest decision I had to make concerning my look for that night was which dress to choose. Nika had had me buy two dresses, just in case I put one on and didn't like it for whatever reason.

*Her and all her girly strategies*, I thought.

We walked into the hotel suite, and I took in the king-size bed, which was covered in thick white linens. The room wasn't lavish or anything to write home about, but I was just appreciative that we didn't have to stay with his mother. I hadn't seen her in over a year, and whenever she'd call Derrick on the phone and I'd try to say hello, she would just casually reply, "Hey." It was no secret that she preferred Derrick's ex, Mia, over me. Slowly but surely, I was beginning to be okay with that.

After tossing his suitcase down on the bed, Derrick looked over at me and asked, "You jumping in the shower first?"

I glanced at the clock and saw that we had a little over an hour before we were expected to meet his mother downstairs in the lobby. Courtesy of the National Basketball Association, there was actually a limo coming to pick us all up promptly at 5:15 p.m. as well.

"Uh, yeah, sure. I'll go first."

After unpacking and laying out my clothes, I headed into the bathroom. As I was wrapping my hair up, I could hear the muffled sound of Derrick's deep voice as he spoke in the bedroom. With the towel wrapped around me, I stepped out of the bathroom.

"Were you saying something to me—" I began, but then I realized he was on the phone. He was sitting on the far side of the bed, with his back toward me.

"Yeah, I just touched down about an hour ago," he said.

Leaving him to finish his call, I stepped back inside the bathroom and got in the shower. It felt so good to wash that flight off myself that I decided to stay under the water a little bit longer than normal. By the time I was finished my shower, the entire bathroom was filled with fog and the mirror was coated in mist. After brushing my teeth and quickly moisturizing my face, I went back inside the bedroom.

"You still on that phone," I mumbled after noticing that his phone was still attached to his ear. He was sitting in the exact same spot on the edge of the bed as before, with the exact same slumped posture.

Derrick looked over his right shoulder at me before saying into the phone, "Aye, lemme hit you back, a'ight?"

"No, don't hang up on my account. Who was that? Your mami again?" I said, my voice laced with sarcasm and even a hint of attitude as I folded my arms across my chest.

Shaking his head, he got up from the bed and walked around it to stand in front of me. Gently, he grabbed the sides of my arms before licking his dark pink lips. "Why you bugging, Ma? When did you become *that* girl?"

I rolled my eyes. "Whatever, Derrick. Just get dressed so we can be on time. And did you call your mother?"

"Yeah, I called her," he said.

When Derrick went into the bathroom to take his shower, I noticed that he took his cell phone with him. Up until this point Derrick had never given me any reason not to trust him, so I suppressed all the doubts floating around in my head and started to get dressed. I decided on the simple navy blue cocktail dress with gold sandals. My long brown hair was bone straight, and in my ears was a pair of shiny gold studs that Tez had bought me for my twenty-first birthday.

"Damn. You dressed already, Ma?" Derrick said as he came out of the bathroom with just a white towel wrapped around his waist and a few water droplets resting on his shoulders. My eyes began to scan his tall, muscular build. The wide flanks of his chest and his sculpted arms were covered in faded black ink. However, when my eyes got down to his hand and I noticed that he was still holding that damn phone, I rolled my eyes.

"Yeah, I'm ready. You gotta hurry up," I simply said, grabbing my clutch purse off the bed.

"A'ight," he said, then licked his lips. He looked over at me lustfully, like I was his next meal of the day. "Well, can I just take one more minute to tell you how beautiful you look?" he asked with a wink.

I playfully rolled my eyes before a small smile formed on my face. He always had this effect on me. There was just something about the sensual sound of his voice that would make me blush and feel all girly. I slid past him with ease, purposely grazing his chest with my arm, in an attempt to make my way back to the bathroom.

"Stop teasing me, Ma," he said, slapping me on the ass.

"I'm not," I told him.

"Yeah, a'ight. Whateva," he muttered with a smirk, then walked to the other side of the suite.

After Derrick got dressed in his navy blue tux with the black lapels, we headed out of the suite and hopped on the elevator. I noticed on our ride down that he kept looking up at the ceiling, almost as if he was saying a silent prayer. His hands were nervously clasped together, and although he looked more handsome than I'd ever seen him, standing there with his big boxy shoulders drawn back, there was no mistaking that he was getting anxious.

"Everything's gonna work out, ya know," I said softly, trying to comfort him. I took one of his clammy hands in my own and peered up at him. He nodded his head in response but didn't utter a word.

When we reached the first floor and the elevator dinged, we exited and walked out into the lobby hand in hand. Seated on an ivory sofa near the front door was his mother, Ms. Scott. Her bright face was covered in what appeared to be a thousand freckles, and uncombed curls were gathered neatly at the top of her head. Even I had to admit that she was dressed to impress in her black sheath dress and pearls. Surprisingly, her dark brown eyes lit up at the sight of us, and she even gave a little smile as she waved us over.

Just as the corners of my lips began to turn upward, in hopes that she'd had a change of heart after all this time, Mia walked up next to her. Batting her eyes innocently, she gave Derrick a closed-lip smile. I looked Mia over and noticed that her bright red cocktail dress was heavily beaded around the bust and fit her slim feminine figure to perfection. Her beauty, enhanced by her cherry-colored lips and five-inch silver heels, was certain to capture everyone's attention tonight.

I could feel my own eyebrows scrunch together and my mouth drop slightly just as Derrick gently squeezed my hand. I looked up to see his apologetic eyes right before I snatched my hand away from his. Stopping mid-stride, I turned to him and asked, "Yo, why is she here?"

Derrick's jaw flexed as he peered down at me. "Calm down, Perri. It's not that serious, Ma," he said.

"Not that serious!" I repeated, with my voice raised. My eyes were stretched to what felt like the size of quarters. "Are you fucking kidding me right now!"

Derrick held one hand up in an attempt to calm me down, but that hardly did anything. I could literally feel heat stirring inside me as my chest heaved up and down. My heart was racing at a high rate of speed.

"Look, we had an extra ticket, and Ma Dukes invited her," he tried to explain.

Shaking my head, I cut my eyes back over to Ms. Scott and Mia, who were no more than fifteen feet away now. Both appeared prim and proper, and they had these sheepish little grins across their faces. Suddenly, Ms. Scott stood up from the ivory sofa, and she and Mia began walking over to us, their arms linked, like they were the very best of friends.

The stench of cigarette smoke coming from Ms. Scott greeted me before she could. She was the first to pull Derrick in for a hug, and then Mia took her turn. I noticed how Mia just had to wrap her arms around his neck, instead of his waist, and how she closed her eyes when they embraced.

*Bitch.*

It wasn't until she stepped back that Mia actually acknowledged my presence. "Nice to see you again . . . ," she said, allowing her voice to trail off. She tilted her head to the side and pressed her finger to her chin, indicating that she had forgotten my name.

"It's Perri—" Derrick began, but I cut him off.

"That bitch know my name!" I snapped.

Ms. Scott's neck jerked back at the same time that she clutched those fake-ass pearls around her neck. "Excuse me," she scoffed.

I glared at Derrick. "You heard what I said. What is she doing here?" I pointed at Mia.

Derrick placed a firm hand on my shoulder but said nothing.

In my opinion, Ms. Scott wasn't very refined, far from it, to tell the truth, but the way she had her nose in the air, you would have thought she was an active member of the black bourgeoisie. "Mia is family, dear, and she wanted to be here for Derrick's big day," Ms. Scott said.

"*Family*?" I questioned, with an arch in my brow. "Where's Shay?" I asked, referring to Derrick's sister.

"She's not here. Anyway, Derrick," Ms. Scott said, cutting my conversation short, "you look so handsome, son. You ready for your big night?" I watched as she smoothed down the front of his tie with her hands.

"Yeah, Ma," he said, providing a small smile. "I just hope I don't have to go too far."

"Wherever you go, just know I'll be right there," Ms. Scott said.

*Ugh.*

After Ms. Scott looped her arm through Derrick's, the two of them proceeded to walk out the front door of the hotel, leaving me and Mia behind in the lobby.

"I don't know what you're up to and why you keep coming around, but if I find out you on some ho shit, I swear to Gawd, I'ma beat ya ass," I warned Mia.

With her lips pursed, Mia waved me off in a pooh-pooh manner before strolling away. After taking a couple of deep breaths and reminding myself that this was the biggest night of Derrick's entire life, I walked out behind the rest of them. We had to wait for only a few minutes curbside before the black stretch limo appeared. Thankfully, when we slid inside, Mia sat next to Ms. Scott, which allowed me to sit directly next to Derrick.

The ride over to Madison Square Garden was a quiet one, with only Ms. Scott and Derrick making small talk along the way. When we finally arrived at the arena, it was eight minutes past six, although judging by the sunny June sky, you'd never know it was evening. After the driver opened our door, bright lights from numerous cameras flashed in our faces. You could even hear several reporters yelling out Derrick's name. I instantly felt like I was with a celebrity.

We all stepped out of the limo, and I caught sight of the small red carpet laid out just before the entrance. When Ms. Scott looped her arm through Derrick's on his left side, he made sure to grab my hand on his right. He was keeping me close, and I appreciated that because my nerves were starting to get the best of me.

"You all right?" he asked me, deep voice vibrating, as he peered down at me.

When I glanced up and our eyes locked, I forgot all about the cameras in our faces and even about Mia being there. "I should be asking you that," I said.

He gave my hand a gentle squeeze before kissing me on the cheek. After Derrick posed alone for some pictures and answered a few of the reporters' questions, we all headed inside. We were seated right up front, by the stage, and at seven o'clock on the dot the draft began. This particular year the Chicago Bulls had the very first pick in the first round of the draft, and I was silently praying that they didn't call out Derrick's name. ESPN had been buzzing all month about him being a top first-round pick, and while I was happy for him, I just didn't want him to be too far away. With each second that passed, my heart galloped faster in my chest and my stomach had more knots.

The NBA commissioner, David Stern, stood before the podium and looked out at the waiting crowd. The room was so quiet and intense, you probably could have heard a mouse poop. Slowly, he grabbed the microphone and cleared his throat. "And this year's number one pick in the first round of the NBA draft belongs to the Chicago Bulls. Coach Vinny Del Negro, please come up here," he said.

As coach Del Negro walked up to the podium, the rumbling in my stomach intensified, and I felt as if I might vomit from the anticipation alone. After shaking the commissioner's hand, the head coach grabbed the microphone. "This year's number one draft pick is Derrick . . ."

I didn't even hear what he said after that, because I gasped so loud and covered my face with my hands. As the loud applause and cheers from the audience intensified throughout the arena, I felt Derrick's warm mouth against my ear.

"Derrick Rose, Ma. Not me," he whispered.

Uncovering my face, I inhaled deeply before clapping my hands for Derrick Rose. I had to admit that he looked good standing tall on the stage in front of us, in his gray suit. After he gave his thank-you speech and they put the Chicago Bulls hat on his head, the crowd went wild. It took everyone a few minutes to calm down after he exited the stage, but once they did, the NBA commissioner came back up to the microphone, and my nausea started all over again.

"And this year's number two pick in the first round of the NBA draft belongs to the Washington Wizards. Coach Eddie Jordan, please come up here," the commissioner said.

This was what I had been praying for these past few months: that Derrick would play for Washington. As I bowed my head and closed my eyes, I muttered, "Come on, come on, come on." It felt like minutes passing rather than seconds as we waited for Eddie Jordan to speak. I could even hear an imaginary drumroll going off inside my head.

"This year the Washington Wizards select Javale McGee as the NBA's number two draft pick of the first round."

I sucked in a breath so loud, I was sure that the entire front row, and probably even Eddie Jordan himself, heard me. Derrick suddenly gripped my hand, then softly rubbed the top of it with his thumb. I knew he was only trying to comfort me, but inside, I was feeling crushed. More than anything in this moment, I had wanted Derrick to play for the Wizards. Honestly, I knew that this was a little far-fetched, but that didn't stop me from wishing.

*I guess some things just aren't meant to be*, I thought.

After sitting through two more draft picks, and a lot of loud hoots and hollers, Pat Riley, head coach of the Miami Heat, took the stage. By this time, all my nerves had subsided and I was getting impatient. Reality had already set: I knew that wherever Derrick was going, I wouldn't be able to see him on a daily or even a weekly basis. With my legs cocked open wide and my dress draped down in between, I slouched back in my chair, awaiting whomever Coach Riley was going to call.

"We are proud to announce that this year's first-round draft pick for the Miami Heat is . . . Derrick Scott!"

When the crowd cheered, Derrick's fist instantly covered his mouth in surprise. He beamed with such happiness as he lifted his eyes up to the stage. Cameras flashed in his face from every angle as photographers tried to capture his excitement and apparent state of shock. All the while, Coach Riley continued to sing Derrick's praises, talking about his good grades and all his community service. I had watched the NBA draft every year for as long as I could remember, but being here in the flesh and actually seeing all the action was on another level.

Just as Derrick was about to stand up to take the stage, I reached over for a quick congratulatory hug.

"Oh, my Gawd, Ma. Shit is crazy," he said against my ear, his tone hushed. The excitement in his voice couldn't be missed.

After pulling away, he turned around to hug his mother, who was doing the most. As you might imagine, this freckled-faced, big-boned woman was jumping up and down, clapping her hands and shouting as though she was the next contestant on *The Price is Right*. Derrick practically had to grab her by the shoulders just to give her a hug. And then, of course, there was Mia. She was already standing up, waiting for her turn to congratulate him. I could feel my eyes narrowing into slits as I watched the two of them interact. Luckily for both of them, he gave her only a quick half hug before making his way up to the stage.

Derrick's speech was brief, as he gave thanks only to God, his mother, and me. When he pulled back from the podium, I instantly shot up to my feet and began clapping my hands together so hard, they actually stung. I was so happy for him that I didn't even realize I was whistling through my fingers like a nigga until Ms. Scott and Mia turned to look at me. Eventually, we ended up meeting him backstage, where the cameras were rolling and the reporters had their mics shoved in his face. I had to admit that he looked like a million bucks, though, standing all tall in his navy blue suit. With his angular face, full lips, and bright white teeth, he looked every bit like a model as he flashed his dimply smile.

After a couple more hours in the arena, we headed over to the rooftop after-party at the Chatwal Hotel to make an appearance. I immediately became starstruck upon seeing all the NBA players whom I had admired over the years alongside their wives. However, seeing the overwhelming abundance of people with breast and ass enhancements sauntering throughout the space had me feeling a bit insecure. These ballers' wives were nothing short of vixens who, in their sexy, high-priced attire, were always ready to pose for the cameras. And it didn't make it any better that over half of them hanging on the brothers' arms were either white or of Hispanic descent. But then I remembered that Derrick had chosen me for me: a nappy-headed, bright-eyed girl from the Millwood Projects who could ball better than half the men her age.

As I leaned back against a wall and sipped slowly from a flute of champagne, I watched Derrick mingle in the crowd. He was fitting right on in, making small talk and giving handshakes to everyone he came in contact with. Unfortunately, that list included the groupies that had probably snuck their way into the party. It was all good, though, because Derrick kept conversation with them to a minimum and pushed right on along. He had introduced me to several people when we first got there, but I didn't want to overcrowd him, so I'd left his side. I just wanted to sit back and watch him do his thing, because after all, this night belonged to him.

Meanwhile, on the other side of the rooftop patio were Mia and Ms. Scott. Both of them sat in chic white lounge chairs and were tossing their heads back and cackling with a group of industry folks. For Ms. Scott to be as ghetto as she was, I had to admit that she could put on a good act and hang right on in there with the best of them. I found myself laughing at the sight of her dangling a cigarette between two fingers, her pinkie pointing straight up in the air, as though that made her look more sophisticated.

"What you over here looking at?"

Engrossed in the happenings on the other side of the patio, I hadn't even noticed Derrick walk up beside me. I turned my head to see that the smile that had been plastered on his face all day had yet to fade. I didn't know if it was from the moon, the stars, or some of the fancy string lights that they had draped around this place, but the glimmer in his eyes was unmistakable.

Unexpectedly, Derrick took me by the hand and led me through the crowd of mingling partygoers. When we got to the edge of the roof, both of us peered down over the railing to take in the busy Manhattan street below. Although the night's air was still quite warm, a gentle breeze traveled past us, blowing my hair and skirt slightly. With a tender sweeping motion across my cheek, Derrick hooked his finger around a wispy piece of hair that had fallen in my mouth and put it in its proper place.

"Did I tell you how beautiful you look tonight?" he asked.

I tucked my lips in to hide my smile, but it was of no use. "Yes, you've told me a thousand times today."

He let out a snort of laughter before saying, "Why you always exaggerating, Ma?"

I laughed. "But thank you, though."

"I know that Miami is kinda far, but I really want you to come and live with me," he told me.

Letting my head fall back a bit, I released a small sigh. "I know, but I have Camille and school. And what about basketball?"

He shook his head. "Look, stop making excuses, Ma. I mean, shit. We're engaged to be married, and right now I need you by my side more than ever. Bring Camille with you, and if you still wanna go to school, just enroll somewhere down there."

"You make it sound so easy," I muttered, rolling my eyes up toward the dark blue sky.

"'Cause it is easy. You the one that makes shit so hard."

I turned to face him and intertwined my arm with his. "I'll make it work, a'ight?" I said softly, looking into his eyes. "Just give me a minute to figure it all out, okay?"

When he didn't respond, I tilted my head to the side. "Okay?" I repeated.

With a tight jaw and a quick lick of his lips, he nodded his head. "A'ight, Ma. I'ma hold you to it."

# Chapter 19

## *Myesha*

It was a little after one in the afternoon when Perri and I walked into the house from a long morning of shopping. From the foyer I could see MJ sitting in his high chair while Tez spoon-fed him his lunch. It had been almost six months since I put Tez out of the house, and although every time I'd seen him since, I had wanted to forgive him, I just couldn't. Today was no different, I thought as I watched him, admiring his sexiness and his ability to operate in complete Daddy mode. His long locks pulled up into an untamed ball on top of his head, he smiled and cooed at our son and made airplane noises as he moved the spoon through the air in a circular pattern, to MJ's sheer delight.

"I'm taking my bags upstairs," Perri said, pulling me out of my trance. "You want me to take yours?"

"Uh . . . um, yes," I stammered, passing her my shopping bags.

While Perri climbed the stairs, I made my way into the kitchen. Tez was now standing at the sink, shirtless, and rinsing out our baby's bowl. MJ, who was now almost six months old, sat in his high chair, his chubby legs and arms moving about. His mouth had gooey baby food all around it, and all you could hear was him babbling the word "Dada" over and over again.

"Hey," I said to Tez as I walked past him and made my way over to the baby.

I lifted MJ out of his seat and kissed his cheek before going back over to where Tez was standing.

"Excuse me," I said before reaching over him to grab a paper towel.

I purposely grazed his arm with my breasts to get a reaction, but all he did was step back out of the way. When I looked down in the sink, I noticed that it was filled with soapy water. Not only was he washing our baby's bowl and bottles, but he was also doing the dishes I had left in the sink this morning. As I turned on the faucet to wet the paper towel in my hand, I tried my best to hide my embarrassment.

Lately, I'd been rather lazy, especially since Tez hadn't been around as much to keep me on my toes. The dishes wouldn't always get done after every meal, a week might pass before the clothes got washed, and making my bed each morning was now a thing of the past. Shit, I was tired after six long months of broken sleep and depression. Tez was used to me keeping the house immaculate, and him seeing the dirty dishes from earlier immediately made me feel a bit self-conscious.

After he finished up the dishes, he came over and picked MJ up off my lap. He held him up in the air before bringing him back down for a little kiss. As he placed him back in my arms, my eyes couldn't help but roam his bare chest and abs. Tez had always been fine, with long brown locks, light eyes, and a body built just like a tight end's. But, for some reason, it seemed like the nigga was somehow getting finer now that we were no longer together. As I inspected every inch of him, I found myself having to squeeze my legs together, and this filled me with shame.

"A'ight. I'll check on y'all later," he said, putting his white T-shirt back on over his head.

He didn't even look at me before walking toward the front door. Over the past six months Tez would occasionally flirt with me, and every once in a while, he would even hint around about me letting him come back home, but over the past few weeks, things had gradually changed. Our exchanges had become shorter and shorter, each time with more formality than the last. To be honest, I couldn't even remember the last time Tez and I had shared a laugh, and that was bothering me.

On his way to the front door, he stopped at the bottom of the staircase and yelled up to Perri. "Aye, yo. You coming out tonight, right?"

Although she was out of view, I could hear her yell back from the top of the steps. "Yeah, I'll be there."

Tez couldn't get out the door fast enough. After he left, I hurried up the stairs, with MJ in my arms. As I walked down the long hall, I could see light shining beneath the bathroom door. I peeked in to see Perri plugging her flat-iron into the wall. It was crazy how she could transform herself from this cool tomboy of a girl into a beautiful swan in no time. I mean, either way she was pretty, but even she had to admit that she was really starting to get the hang of this femininity thing.

Leaning up against the door frame, with MJ propped up on my hip, I looked at her in the mirror. "So where you going tonight?" I asked.

"Oh, you don't know?" she asked, with a hint of surprise in her voice, as she parted her hair with a rat-tail comb.

Feeling a slight frown form on my face, I asked, "Know what?"

"Tez started his own security firm. Supposed to be for, like, 'high-profile' celebrity clients or some shit," she said, making air quotes with her hands. "I 'on't know."

My eyes instantly stretched wide from shock.

As if she hadn't told me some big news, Perri casually reached back down for the flatiron before pulling it through a long section of her hair.

I felt completely left out of the loop, and a million and one questions instantly flooded my mind. "He put all of it together himself?" I asked.

"Nah, Plus helped him put together a business plan, and my dad even helped him with the operational designs. But the investor . . . Tez got him all on his own," she explained.

"Wow," was all I could say. Tez was doing big things, *legal things*, and it was sad because I wasn't even by his side to be a part of it. Suddenly I thought that if it was true that beside every strong and successful man was an even stronger woman, then what woman had Tez been dealing with? I felt pretty certain that he hadn't been dealing with that psycho bitch Shayla anymore, but there had to be someone. Tez had been giving me the cold shoulder for almost a month now, and in my mind only another woman could be the cause of that.

"Is your brother seeing someone else?" I blurted out all at once.

Perri looked at me in the mirror before setting down the flatiron. Lowering her eyes, she released a low breath before turning around to face me. "Look, I don't know if Tez got another girl or not. You should know by now that that nigga keeps his secrets close. But the fact that you even asked about it tells me you still care. Maybe y'all should talk."

Twisting my lips to the side, I shrugged my shoulders. "I don't know. I mean, I just don't want Tez to think he can cheat on me whenever he wants or go fund another woman's lifestyle just for the hell of it. I mean, I know he's the man out here in these streets, but he can't expect me to be okay with shit like that." I shook my head. "Perri, I've been through so much in my life . . . endured so much pain and heartbreak, I honestly just can't take any more."

"Technically, Myesha, he didn't cheat on you. You left, remember?"

"Well, either way, he wasn't honest with me," I reminded her.

Perri shook her head and raised her right shoulder in an "If you say so" fashion before turning back around. There was no mistaking that she was loyal to her brother through and through. However, even if I wanted to be mad at her, I couldn't, because their close bond had always been something I silently admired.

"So what time do we need to be ready?" I asked.

As she glanced at me in the mirror again, a cute little smile crept on her lips. "You going?"

"Yep. Just gotta call Aria," I said, looking down at my son, who had already fallen fast asleep against my chest.

"Oh, no worries. She'll already be here for Camille."

Later that night Perri, Plus, and I pulled up right in front of the valet at a building on Washington Avenue in the downtown. Seeing bundles of black and silver balloons surrounding the entrance and a long line of people snaking down the block, I knew exactly where we were. When I stepped out of the car, I immediately took in the sight of the tall bricks-and-mortar buildings smack-dab in the heart of the business district. Right away I was impressed at the location Tez had found.

After pulling down the little turquoise dress I was wearing, I followed Perri and Plus up to the door. Sauntering over with my gold clutch in my hand, I could literally feel my hair slowly rising from the muggy night air. Once we had fought our way through the crowd and had reached the door, we were met by a big, tall dark-skinned fella. Quickly, I looked over his face and realized that I'd seen him a time or two before.

"What up, Levar?" Plus greeted, dapping him up.

Levar nodded to both Perri and me before letting us all pass by. When we walked inside, the lights were low and the music was playing loud. People were dancing in the center of the room, and large round tables sat around the perimeter.

Leaning my head over to Perri's ear, I said, "Is this a nightclub or a security firm?"

She cracked a little smile. "Girl, it's a party. We're celebrating the grand opening of his security firm," she said loud enough for me to hear over the music.

I began to scan the room once more, in hopes of finding Tez. Although I didn't find him, I did notice all the offices and elevator doors that bordered the room. Despite the club-like atmosphere, I could tell that the space was used for official business, and that made me feel proud of Tez.

"What y'all want to drink?" Plus asked.

"You mean there's an actual bar in here?" I said, my eyes searching around the room.

Perri pointed toward the back of the place, where, sure enough, I could see that a long bar had been set up and that three bartenders were working behind it.

"Get me a pink nipple please," I told Plus.

"Ah, look at you, trying to get grown tonight. Lemme find out," Plus teased.

"Yo, just get me a Henny and Coke, a'ight?" Perri said.

Plus let out a little snort of laughter and shook his head at just how mannish she sounded before walking off toward the bar. Meanwhile, Perri stood there, oblivious, taking in the scene. I had to laugh to myself at how sometimes she would sound totally the opposite of the way she looked. This night she wore a mustard-colored romper that exposed her thick toned thighs. Flat gold gladiator sandals snaked up her legs, a counterpoint to her gold hoop earrings and the bangle bracelets that jingled around her wrists. Perri was a rare breed, and beautiful, to say the least.

When Perri and I both started to snake our hips to the music, still on the edge of the dance floor, my eyes landed on Tez, who was sitting across the room. Although he was seated with a group of people, my eyes instantly zoomed in on the woman beside him. She was a pretty, fair-skinned woman with spiral golden curls all over her head. But more than her beauty, I noticed how she kept laughing and touching Tez's arm. If I had to bet money on it, I'd definitely say that she was the woman who had been occupying his time.

My chest tightened as I tapped Perri on the shoulder and said, "I see your brother. Come on."

Without even waiting for her to respond, I stormed across the crowded dance floor and made my way to the other side of the room. Seething, I approached the table and saw Tez sitting there, with his freshly twisted locks. His bright eyes twinkled from the disco lights as he joined the table in laughter. Neither a single gold tooth nor a tray or fronts could be seen in his mouth. And although I could see only his torso, since he was sitting down, I quickly took note of the fancy blue tie around his neck and the tailored jacket he wore.

*How dare this nigga step his game up without me?*

When Tez finally looked up and noticed me, his smile faded a little, and then he chucked up his chin. He stood up from the table and smoothed his hand down the front of his jacket like a distinguished gentleman. As he made his way toward us, I took in his complete attire. If it hadn't been for the cocky swagger in his stride, I would have barely recognized him in that sleek black fitted suit, which clung to his muscular frame. When we briefly hugged, I could smell the sexy scent of his cologne, which only intensified my anger. How could he be out parading around with the next chick, while looking and smelling good like this?

"Let me introduce y'all to some people," he said casually, nudging me in the small of my back.

We walked over to his table. There were two white men and two black men, all of whom were dressed in fancy business suits, and a lady was seated between them. However, Miss Goldie Locks was now sitting all by her lonesome. The restraint it took for me not to roll my eyes and start acting all ghetto—like in front of these people was nothing but the grace of God.

Tez cleared his throat before leaning forward and addressing the table. "Everybody, I would like for you to meet my family," he said. He got everyone's attention, and all eyes were suddenly pinned on me and Perri. "This here is my baby sister, Perri," he announced. After everyone said a quick hello to her, he turned to me. "And this here is my son's mother, Myesha," he announced, sounding all proper like.

I didn't know why, but hearing him reduce me to his baby's mother caused pangs in my chest. However, I swallowed back my emotions, because I knew I had to push through and not embarrass him on his special night. Waving at the group of prominent onlookers, I did my very best to disguise the heartbreak and humiliation I felt in that moment.

After that, Tez went around the table and introduced his new group of associates one by one. Finally, the only person left to introduce us to was the pretty woman who appeared to be his date. Instead of staying seated like the rest of the group, she actually had the audacity to stand up and walked around the table to greet us formally.

Hand already extended and a fake smile plastered on her face, she sashayed over, swishing her hips. Naturally, my eyes looked her over from head to toe. She was dressed in a crisp white pencil skirt, a fitted blazer to match, and nude-colored heels. As much as I hated to admit it, her style was on another level. I was becoming more insecure, more intimidated, by the second.

"Harley Anderson, please meet Myesha Young," Tez said.

Over the years I had always prided myself on being a class act—sophisticated and always respectable. But I swear, in that moment something just came over me. Instead of shaking her hand, I folded my arms across my chest and shifted my weight to one side. "And who exactly are you supposed to be?" I asked boldly, snaking my neck.

Little Miss Harley cut her eyes over to Tez before letting out a little chuckle.

When I glanced up at him and saw the angry scowl etched on his face, I could no longer hold my tongue. "Fine, Montez! Fine!' I yelled dramatically, swinging my arms up in the air. "Go on and be happy with the next bitch!"

Fuming, I turned around, and as I stormed off, I heard both Tez and Perri calling my name. Nonetheless, I charged across the crowded room, bumping into strangers along the way, my hands trembling. *If I can just keep it together*, I thought. Just when my eyes landed on the front door, Plus walked in front of me. He was struggling to hold three cups of liquor in his hands as he greedily sipped through one of the straws.

"Here," he said, passing me my drink. "Where's Perri at?"

When I turned and glanced back in the direction I'd just come, I saw Tez and Perri heading toward us. "I just gotta get outta here," I muttered. But before I could make a U-turn and head for the door, Tez grabbed me by the arm.

"Myesha, fuck is wrong wit' you, yo?" he spat. In just a matter of seconds, all that proper English he was speaking disappeared like a burst bubble. And before I even realized what was happening, the tears that I had been trying so hard to hold back started pouring from my eyes. When I felt his arms wrap around me, a loud cry came from the back of my throat, embarrassing me. Before I knew it, I was sobbing into his chest like a baby, not even caring that a crowd of more than two hundred people surrounded us.

Feeling Tez's lips connect with the top of my head caused me to peer up at him. Rather than speaking, he wiped my wet face with his hands, then kissed me softly on the lips. If that wasn't enough to confuse me, the little smile that formed on his lips when he pulled back surely did.

"Tez, I don't understand—"

Leaning his mouth against my ear, he whispered, "Shh," cutting off my words. He held his right hand up in the air, abruptly silencing the music. He then led me back through the mob of people that was out on the dance floor. And as always, people showed the utmost respect for this man, making a clear path for both of us. The DJ then stepped down from his platform and handed Tez the microphone.

Still holding one of my hands, Tez addressed the crowd. "I just want to thank everyone who came out tonight to support me. For those of you who don't know, my father . . ." As his voice trailed off, my eyes followed Tez's to the right, where both Mr. Phillip and Ms. Tonya were standing among the crowd. Tez then pointed directly at Mr. Phillip. "My father has been working in security for almost sixteen years. Whether he knows it or not, he's the one that actually planted this idea in my head. It was his continuous encouragement for me to get my shi—." Tez tucked in his lips after almost cursing.

He continued. "He's always encouraged me to do better with my life, and that, among other things, is what pushed me to open up this firm." Tez then turned so that he and his father were standing face-to-face. "Pops, I just wanna say thank you." Tez pounded his chest two times, just above his heart, before chucking up his chin. Mr. Phillips's chest swelled with pride as he nodded his head softly, and a round of applause filled the entire room.

Tez then pointed across the room, and my eyes followed and landed on Perri and Plus. "And this guy . . ." Tez let out a light snort of laughter. "Mr. Ahmad Taylor. My brother from another mother. My A-one since day one," he said with a wide grin on his face. "This guy is one of the smartest young men I know, if not *the* smartest. Helped me put my entire business plan together. Over the past few months we've stayed up late many nights, going over the facts and figures." He shook his head. "I owe a lot to you, little brother. Thank you."

Plus pounded his chest in the same manner as Tez had done just moments before. Then he mouthed the words *I got you*, which couldn't be heard over the loud clapping in the room.

Tez then turned around, and with his back now facing me, he said, "Ms. Harley Anderson."

I sucked in a deep breath when he said her name, and then watched as she appeared from the back of the crowd. Her pointy nose in the air and a perfect smile on her pretty, pale face, she pulled down her white blazer to straighten it.

"Ms. Harley Anderson took a chance on me. A young nig—" He cleared his throat in an attempt to cover up his last word. "A young *man* from the Millwood Projects with only a GED. She invested heavily in this business based on my solid business plan and my presentation alone. And for that, I'm forever indebted to you."

His words caught me by surprise, and my eyes stretched wide before a wave of embarrassment washed over me. This Harley woman wasn't his girlfriend; she was merely his business partner. If it wouldn't have humiliated Tez, I probably would have smacked my own self for acting like such a jealous fool.

After the noise from the crowd faded, Tez turned back around and stared at me. I was so ashamed of how I had acted earlier that I couldn't even look him in the eye. After softly taking hold of my chin with his hand, he forced our eyes to connect. Then he licked his lips before taking a nervous deep breath. The room was so quiet that the onlookers could probably hear my fast-beating heart pick up speed. When Tez dropped down on one knee and took me by the hand, I and what sounded like every person in the room let out a series of loud gasps.

"Myesha Young," he said, gazing into my eyes, "I know that I haven't always been the best to you. I know I haven't always done the right things and said the right words . . ." He paused mid-sentence and took another deep breath and swallowed hard. "But I do love you," he confessed, his voice cracking, as he looked up at me with those beautiful bright eyes. In that moment I couldn't have stopped the tears from falling down my face even if I'd tried.

He went on. "After losing my mother, I promised myself that I would never feel that vulnerable again. Promised myself that the only woman I would ever love like that was my sister. But when I met you . . ." He shook his head. "When I met you, My, all that shit changed, yo. It didn't matter that I never said that I loved you back, because I felt it. Every day that we were together, and even more on the days we were apart, I loved you. Now that we have a son, I'm trying to right my wrongs. I'm trying to secure a future for all of us. I know it won't be easy, but . . . I need you to forgive me." He pulled a small white leather box from his jacket pocket.

"Yes," I breathed, nodding my head while crying uncontrollably. Truth be told, I had forgiven him the moment that he told me he loved me, but just seeing that little white box sent my emotions over the edge.

"With that being said, Myesha Young, will you do me the honor of being my wife?" he asked.

Before he could even open up the box to expose the diamond ring, I shouted, "Yes!" I dropped down to the floor and kneeled in front of him. After placing my hands gently on both sides of his face, I pulled him in for a deep kiss. And there, in the center of the dance floor, amid the applauding crowd, our mouths greedily engaged in a passion-filled exchange. Our hearts thumped loudly in our chests and our eyes filled with tears as Keith Sweat's "Make It Last Forever" could suddenly be heard playing softly from the speakers. It was the happiest moment in my life.

After sipping champagne and celebrating for another hour with our family and his business associates, Tez and I left the party. We climbed in his car and held hands as he drove. A comfortable silence filled the car on our ride home. When I glanced over at my fiancé and took in all his handsome features, from his full dark pink lips and strong jaw to his amber-colored eyes, I couldn't help but think that all was right with the world.

"What you staring at a nigga for?" he asked, his eyes still locked on the road.

I laughed, hearing the old Tez, *my* Tez, come back to life. "Just admiring you, baby," I admitted softly. Then something dawned on me. "Say, how did you even know I would be there tonight when you didn't even invite me?"

Tez let out a light laugh. "'Cause I know you, baby. There wasn't no way yo' nosy ass was going to miss a chance at seeing what I had going on. Perri knew that shit too."

"So basically, you guys set me up," I said, shaking my head.

"Whatever you wanna call it, shorty." He lifted my hand and softly kissed my wrist before turning up the radio.

Leaning back and melting into the leather seat, I replayed the events of the past year in my head. Suddenly I realized that everything Tez and I had been through had just been a minor roadblock on our way to our final destination. No matter how hard I had tried to get over Tez these past few months, I just couldn't. I was just thankful that he didn't give up on me and move on to someone else. Closing my eyes, I vowed always to love Tez unconditionally.

*No more running*, I silently promised.

From that day forward, we would forever be a family.

# Chapter 20

## *Perri*

"The fuck you mean, you going to Miami?" Plus barked. Furiously squinting those dark brown eyes, he stood back and watched me pack my suitcase.

Without even looking at him, I rolled up another pair of basketball shorts before tossing them into the suitcase. "I told Derrick I would come down and check it out. I'm only gonna be gone for a couple of weeks . . . until school starts," I explained.

Although Plus's nose was still flared, his body relaxed a little as he took a seat on the edge of my bed. "What the fuck are you going down there to check it out for?" he asked knowingly.

Feeling irritated, I flung another T-shirt down in the suitcase before snapping my neck in his direction. "I'm engaged, Ahmad, or did you forget?"

Heaving a deep sigh, Plus shook his head, which was full of overgrown curls. He rubbed his hand down the front of his face. "You really are something, you know that?" he said.

"And what's that supposed to mean?"

"You finally get into Georgetown and make the girls' basketball team. And now that I'm finally able to be here on a daily basis to help out with Camille, the shit still ain't good enough! Perri, that nigga's not thinking about what you got going on here. He's thinking only about himself."

"Well, you would know about being selfish," I mumbled under my breath. Once the overstuffed suitcase was packed, I jumped on top of it and tried my best to zip it closed.

With a hard glare in my direction, Plus stood up from the bed. "Move," he said.

I hopped off the suitcase, and he took over and zipped it up with ease. "And please stop bringing up that shit with Tasha from two whole years ago. A nigga's done suffered enough."

I wanted to scream at him, "It's not just about Tasha!" It was about the fact that I had put off my hopes and dreams of playing college ball to raise our child, while he got to play at Georgetown. It was about the fact that I had to stay home and get a job while his mom helped me raise Camille. And yes, it was also about Tasha. He had chosen someone like her over me after all the sacrifices I'd made. That hurt me.

I simply ignored his comment and said, "Thanks," before easing past him. I grabbed the smaller matching suitcase from my closet and casually stepped out of the room. However, Plus was hot on my heels as I made my way into Camille's bedroom. From the doorway he watched intently as I grabbed items from her closet and from inside her dresser drawers.

"And what are you packing Camille's stuff up for?" he inquired.

"Plus," I sighed, with a roll of my eyes.

"Plus, what? You not taking my baby nowhere, Perri, and I mean that shit."

"She's not just your baby, Plus! She's *our* baby, and I want to take her out there with me. It'll just be for two weeks," I said, poking out my bottom lip and attempting to bat my eyes.

"And just stop wit' all that pouting shit. Shit don't even look right when you do it," he teased, with a cute little smirk.

I waved my hand dismissively in his direction. "Whatever!"

From my peripheral, I could see Plus dragging his hand down over his jaw, like he was mulling things over in his head. "Look, why don't you go and just figure things out with ole boy first before dragging my baby all the way down there?"

Plus's voice had softened a bit, and I could tell that at this point he was only trying to reason with me. Truth be told, there was no real justification for not leaving Camille here for a couple of weeks. Although I could probably count on one hand the number of full days Camille and I had actually spent apart, I fully trusted her father. There wasn't a doubt in my mind that she would be in the best of hands while I was away.

"Fine. I'll just leave her here with you," I said.

"Perfect!" he said arrogantly before walking away.

After about another twenty minutes of me getting the rest of my things together, I headed downstairs. The sounds of guns blazing, helicopters flying, and grenades dropping from the air quickly got my attention. But before I even reached the bottom step, I knew that it was only Plus playing a game of *Call of Duty* on the PlayStation without me. He was seated on the hardwood floor in front of the living-room sofa, with a half-eaten sandwich on a paper plate beside him. His free hand reached up for the open can of grape soda that stood dangerously on the edge of the coffee table. He pulled the can up to his lips for a swig before noticing me walk into the room.

"Tez would kill you if he saw you eating in here," I said, flopping down on the sofa behind him.

Plus sucked his teeth before wiping his mouth with the back of his hand. Then he grabbed ahold of the controller before allowing his eyes to focus back on the screen.

"Yo, why didn't you wait for me?" I asked. "You knew I wanted to play."

"Gotta get used to playing by myself anyway," he said, shrugging his shoulders. Judging by the saltiness in his tone, I knew he had to be in his feelings.

"Don't say that," I whispered. I plunged my fingers in his hair and gently grabbed a handful of his soft curls. "You need a haircut. *Bad!*" I said emphatically.

"I thought you liked my hair." He looked back at me over his shoulder with a set of sad dark brown eyes. I had known Plus almost my entire life, which was long enough to know that he didn't give a shit what I thought about his hair. He simply didn't want me to leave.

Tugging on his silky curls once more, I said, "You know I'll be back in a few weeks, right?"

Licking his full brown lips, he nodded his head before saying, "Yeah, but I'ma miss you, though." We stared into one another's eyes for what felt like aeons. When he turned back around to play the game, I stretched back on the sofa and stared up at the ceiling, wondering how things would all pan out.

Having the house all to ourselves, Plus and I played that game for almost three hours straight, until darkness had just begun to overtake the summer sky. Early this morning, Tez and Myesha had taken Camille and MJ for a visit to see Pops and Ms. Tonya, and had yet to return. With exhausted eyes and cramping muscles in my hands, I got up from the sofa and stretched. I gave a little yawn as I lifted myself upward on the balls of my feet.

"You going to bed already?" Plus asked.

"Nah, I'm getting ready to get us something to eat."

With a sharp turn, he cocked his head in my direction. "You not cooking, right?"

My eyes narrowed into evil slits as I looked down at him. He was still seated on the floor.

"I mean, don't worry about cooking nothing. I can just place an order," he added, correcting himself.

I knew Plus still didn't believe I could cook, but I had been practicing on a regular basis. With the help of Ms. Tonya and Myesha, I had learned how to make spaghetti, tacos, and macaroni and cheese from a box.

"Shut up. I know you're trying to be funny," I told him.

"Nah," he said, standing up to stretch. He walked up to me, then grabbed me by the shoulders before pressing his forehead right up against mine. Tired, hooded eyes peered into mine as we both breathed slowly. Warmth emanated from our bodies as he pulled me in real close. Gradually, his hands slid down my arms and circled my waist until we were pelvis to pelvis and chest to chest. "You know I love you, right?" he whispered.

*God. Why*? I thought as soon as I closed my eyes. "I know you love me, Ahmad," I breathed. Standing this close to Plus, feeling the warmth of his flesh against my very own was creating a warm tingle between my thighs. When he tilted his head to the side and began to make his move, I swallowed hard. Prepared for his mouth to crash against mine, I licked my lips with anticipation. And just as we were about to share this spontaneous and very intimate moment, the doorbell rang.

"Fuck," he muttered under his breath. As he turned around to go answer the door, I raked my fingers through my hair before blowing out a deep breath.

Seeing that the only source of light in the house now was the glow from the TV screen, I walked over to cut on the living-room lamp. Just as I was picking up the mess Plus had made, he and Jorell appeared in the light.

"What it do, baby mama?" Jorell asked, walking farther into the room. Gold teeth flashed when he gave me a wide smile, and I noticed that his locks had just been cut up to his shoulders.

I rolled my eyes before shaking my head. "Hey, Jorell. What are you doing over here?"

"Just got back in town from summer break and came to holla at y'all for a minute. What's good wit' ya?"

With a shrug of my shoulders, I stretched my lips in a downward motion. "Nigga, same shit, just a different day," I said.

"Gangsta," he muttered with a light chuckle before plopping down into a seat. "So y'all still been keeping in touch with my li'l baby or what?"

"Uh, nigga, the real question is, Have *you* been keeping in touch wit' yo' li'l baby?" I said mockingly, trying to mimic his Southern drawl.

"Breh, shawty been dodging my calls for the longest." He shook his head. "It's like ever since she seen me with Meechie at y'all baby's birthday party, she don't want shit to do with me."

I chucked up my chin and pursed lips to the side. "Nigga, stop lying. She stopped dealing with you well before that," I said, correcting him.

Plus turned to me. "Hell, yeah, shorty was mad as fuck on the way back home from Alabama. 'Member that shit?" he said.

I nodded my head, recalling all the tears and curse words that had flown from Nika's mouth on our ride back home. "And then she called me that day you tried to pull up on her at school."

"Damn! Shawty out here putting all my business in the streets," he said, causing all of us to fall out laughing.

"You know what? I should hook you up with someone," Plus said out of the blue.

I could feel my eyebrows instantly knitting together before I asked, "And who do you know?"

"Shorty that I be tutoring from time to time. Why?" he answered.

Although I gave a nonchalant shrug, inwardly I felt jealous. Obviously, he didn't have any interest in the girl, or else he wouldn't be trying to hook her up with Jorell, but the fact that he was giving another woman his undivided attention made me feel . . . possessive. Here I was, twenty-one years old, with a tall, fine NBA first-round draft pick of a boyfriend, yet I was still worried about who Plus spent his time with. I quickly shook off the thought and headed toward the kitchen.

"I'm about to order something. What y'all want to eat?" I said.

While Jorell shrugged his shoulders, Plus called out, "Chinese."

"What you want, Jorell?" Plus and I always shared two boxes of orange chicken and pepper steak from Hunan Delight, so I didn't even bother asking what he wanted.

"Just get me a bag of fried wings and a shrimp egg roll," Jorell simply said.

With a nod of my head, I walked away, leaving the two of them in the living room. After placing our orders over the phone, I went upstairs to get my luggage. My flight to Miami was leaving bright and early the next morning, so I wanted to make sure I didn't forget anything. As I was dragging my bags down the steps, I could feel Plus's and Jorell's eyes on me from across the room.

"Damn. Where you going?" Jorell asked.

Before I could even answer, Plus let out a throaty groan and said, "All the way down to Miami to be with that nigga."

"Damn, breh. I didn't even think about that shit. You 'bout to be a whole basketball wife," Jorell said, then let out a little laugh. "Mane, I can so see you on TV, fighting with Shawnie and the rest of them manly chicks."

After flipping him my middle finger, I continued stacking my luggage against a wall in the foyer.

"But nah, fa' real, though, when you coming back?" he asked.

"Two days before school starts," I replied.

He glanced over at Plus and gave a cheesy little grin. "And what's this knucklehead gon' do without you for the next two weeks?"

With a soft suck of his teeth, Plus stood up from the sofa and then said, "I'm sure I'll figure some shit out."

As he walked off to head down to the basement, I felt the exact same way as I had for the past two years. *Torn.* If I was sure about anything in this world, I knew I loved Plus with all my heart, but then there was Derrick. While Plus was a risky gamble for me, Derrick was a safe, foolproof bet. And not only that, I truly loved Derrick and would never want to hurt him intentionally. It was like every time Plus and I were getting ready to take things to another level physically, something would stop us in mid-act.

*That has to be some sort of sign*, I thought.

With that thought in my mind, I carried on with the rest of my night. Eating dinner alone up in my bedroom, I tried my best not to feel guilty for leaving Plus and Camille for two whole weeks. Thankfully, Derrick and I texted back and forth for most of the evening, saying things to get each other, excited about the time we'd be spending together under the hot Miami sun. Every so often he would hint about us getting married or me at least moving in, but I didn't want to go there just yet. I just kept reassuring him that everything would happen like it was supposed to in due time.

# Chapter 21

## *Nika*

Hesitantly, I walked into Crab Cake Café, feeling like a ball of nerves. Eyes quickly darting around the restaurant, I held my cell phone up to my ear. "You said he'd be wearing a red cap and a white shirt?"

"Yes," Plus groaned emphatically through the receiver, like I was getting on his nerves.

"And you sure he ain't no corny nigga, right?"

Plus sucked his teeth. "Man, Nika, if you don't get off this damn phone."

"Okay, okay," I whispered before disconnecting the call.

After failing biology this past semester, I had found myself in summer school, repeating the course all over again. Luckily, Plus had agreed to tutor me during most of the summer, which had resulted in me making a B. That was one thing about Plus: he was smart as hell and didn't mind bringing others up to speed. Occasionally, during our study sessions at Ms. Tonya's house, he had asked me about my dating life and had even mentioned Jorell. I was so over that nigga that I had told Plus not to even say his name around me anymore, because I couldn't even stand the sound of it.

During our final study session, Plus had convinced me to go out on this little blind date. I was reluctant at first, but after the lonely year I'd had, I said, "Why not?" Hell, I had turned down every good-looking guy on campus that had asked for my number, instantly assuming that they were most likely players. I swear, Jorell had injured my mind so bad that I was avoiding anyone who even resembled him. I'm talking tall niggas, dread-head niggas, gold front–wearing niggas, dark-skinned niggas, even country niggas . . . I was avoiding them all like the plague.

With a lot of convincing, I had even allowed Grandma Pearl to set me up a few more times over the summer. Yes, even after that sensationalized performance with Clarence back at the church, I had decided to give Grandma another try. However, that had been an epic fail, because all Grandma Pearl knew were the societal rejects at the church. I'm talking about the closeted gays, who she would try to convince me were straight, the nerdy nose pickers, who went out just to feel a sense of popularity and acceptance. And then there were the old men who were trapped in twenty-year-old bodies. These were the young guys you saw wearing the polyester pants and the short-sleeve button-up shirts every day of the week. The ones with the heavy keys latched onto their belt loops and big old bulky wallets sticking out of the back pocket of their pants. All the while, these young old men would say and do shit that only old niggas did. I just couldn't relate.

"Um, I'm supposed to meet someone here," I said to one of the hostesses. "I believe he's wearing a red baseball cap."

Her eyes suddenly widened. "Ah, yes. He's been waiting on you," she said.

As I followed her through the restaurant, smelling nothing but garlic and seafood, I began to get nervous. *Am I really this desperate that I have to go on a blind date?* I thought. My palms were growing sweaty, and my heart was gradually picking up speed, as we trekked between the crowded tables. I was almost at the point of turning around when we finally reached the very back and I saw the red hat. Since his back was toward us, this guy was still a mystery to me, but I did notice the dreads that hung right to his broad shoulders. Almost instantly, I could feel my bad attitude beginning to form as I discreetly rolled my eyes. Plus was definitely going to get cussed out after this, because I had specifically told him no dread heads.

When the hostess extended her hand toward our table, which was next to a window, I timidly slid past her and sat down in the booth. At first, his face was hidden beneath the brim of his hat as he looked down at the menu. But as soon as he noticed that I was seated directly across from him, he lifted his head. Jorell's face appeared.

"Oh, hell nah!" I spat and immediately slid back out of the seat.

"Shawty, hold up! Wait a minute!" With his long, lanky arm, he reached out in the aisle and grabbed ahold of my waist. I hadn't felt his touch in over nine months, and although I'd never admit it, his hand on my body felt good.

Snaking my neck in his direction, I rolled my eyes. "You and Plus must really think you're funny, don't you?"

"Shawty, I got set up, just like you," he said, standing up from the table to tower over me.

I didn't know what got my attention more in that moment: the mere fact that he was out on a blind date or that he was finer than the last time I'd seen him. Slowly, my eyes traveled up from his chest to the dark, tight skin covering his chiseled face. I noticed that his locks were freshly cut underneath the Jacksonville State fitted cap before I connected with those piercing brown eyes. My breath hitched as he pulled me in close.

"Damn, shawty. A nigga can't get no hug? I see you checking ya boy out," he mumbled, his mouth now buried in my hair.

Refusing to hug him back, I merely closed my eyes and inhaled his fresh scent. Standing there in his embrace, I felt a sense of familiarity course through my being, thanks in part to the smell of his Creed cologne and the soft cotton T-shirt he wore, which was pressing against my cheek. When he pulled back, he looked down at my small frame. Lustfully licking his lips, he cracked a tiny smile.

"You ain't gon' at least have dinner with me?" he asked, attempting to sound hurt. His eyes pleaded with me as he slowly ran his tongue over the gold in his mouth.

Letting out a deep sigh, I shrugged. "I guess," I said.

When I spun around to take my seat, I could practically feel his eyes glued to my ass. He even had the nerve to let a low grunting sound escape from his lips. I mean, I didn't think I was wearing anything too sexy for a first date. Just a casual pair of flat gold sandals and a peach maxi dress that clung to my frame. My curly hair hung up in a loose ponytail, while simple gold hoops swung from my ears. Jorell had never been shy about expressing his physical attraction to me. So even with my back still facing him, I could imagine him rubbing those big old hands of his together while biting down on his bottom lip.

"Damn, li'l baby. I see you been taking care of yo'self," he said.

I could feel my face ball up before I rolled my eyes again. Him calling me his "li'l baby" made me want to run for the high hills. I mean, this man could practically charm the panties off a nun, and at this point I just refused to be caught under his spell.

"Boy, just sit down, so we can eat," I snapped.

Another little smile crept upon his face before he sat down across from me. We shared a few moments of silence between us as we both scanned the menu. But while my nerves began to subside, hunger took over, and a series of soft rumbles came from my stomach. I tried tightening my muscles to make the sounds stop, but that seemed only to make the growling louder.

"I'm gon' feed ya, li'l baby. Just hold on a minute," Jorell said playfully.

"You don't need to feed me. I can pay for my own," I said, still looking down at the menu.

When I felt Jorell's hand connect with mine from across the table, I quickly jerked it back. "Look, let's just get this over with, okay?" I snapped.

"Damn," he muttered, squinting his eyes. "You hate me that much?"

I let out a low snort before staring out the window. "*Hate* is a strong word."

He let out a low snort. "Is there any way we can start over?"

The sincerity in his voice caused me to look back at him.

He removed the cap from his head before licking his lips. His face had the most serious expression that I thought I'd ever seen. Slowly, he reached his hand back across the table, and with his palm facing up toward the ceiling, he waited. "Let's just start over and see if we can at least be friends," he offered again.

After a few seconds, I reluctantly placed my hand in his. "Deal, but just as friends."

He nodded his head before wetting his lips with his tongue. Then he peered at me with lust-filled eyes as he crack a devious smile. "So what do you know about being friends with benefits?"

My jaw dropped as I pulled my hand back from his. "See, this is why I can't—"

Laughing loud enough for most of the patrons in the restaurant to hear, he held one of his hands up in the air. "Shawty, I'm just playing. Relax," he said.

"I swear, you always did play too much," I said before going back to my menu.

After we both decided on our meals and placed our order with the waitress, he cleared his throat and then began making small talk. "So what did ya pretty ass need to come out on a blind date fa?"

Releasing a small laugh, I hunched my shoulders. "I don't know. I've been meeting all the wrong kind of guys, I guess. The thugs, the wannabe players, even the corny dudes. I just can't seem to click with anyone."

Nodding his head, he took a sip of lemon water through his straw.

"And what about you? You and Meechie not working out?" I asked, pretending to care. I knew we were supposed to be starting fresh, but I couldn't resist taking one last jab.

He twisted his full dark lips to the side before giving me a little smirk. "Me and Meechie ain't been together for over two years now," he said, his voice low.

I was a little caught off guard when he said that. "But what about when I saw y'all at the birthday—"

"Breh, you always assuming shit," he said, cutting me off.

"But you hit, though, right?" I asked, secretly hoping that he'd deny any type of sexual relationship with her.

Releasing a low snort, he raised his right eyebrow before licking his lips. "Do it even matter?"

I'm not even going to lie: when he said that, my jaw slightly dropped, but luckily, the waitress approached the table with our food at that very moment. We both got the crab cake, shrimp, and french fry platter and a glass of their signature lemonade. During the course of dinner, we somehow ended up moving on to other topics of conversation, like school, the NBA draft coming up, and my grandmother. The natural chemistry we shared reminded me of old times, and even though I hated to admit it, I actually missed being around him.

When we were both just about done eating, I asked the waitress for my check and she told me that Jorell had already paid it. I cut my eyes over at him and cocked my head to the side.

"What!" he asked before a small chuckle escaped his lips. "Look, I paid that bill early on. Had I known you was gonna put me in the friend zone and not give up the booty, I would have let you pay your part," he joked.

Shaking my head, I laughed, then said, "Let's get out of here. You ready?"

"Yuh, let's go."

After placing the red Jacksonville State cap back on his head, he slid out of the booth. When he held out his hand for me, I peered up at him, taking in his tall stature, before cautiously grabbing ahold of his hand. Even though I tried pulling away once I stood up from my seat, Jorell wouldn't let go. He literally held on to my hand until we were out in the parking lot, in front of my car door.

"Did you enjoy yourself?" he asked, swiping a rogue curl out of my face.

"I did, actually," I said. Tucking my lips inward, I paused briefly. "I know I said we could try being friends, but can I just ask you one question?"

"Fa' sho'," he said, his thick Alabama accent coming through, before hiking his chin up in the air.

"Why did you lie to me about having a daughter?" I knew that I had been telling myself that I was over Jorell and what we once had, and after the way he had hurt me, I knew things could never be the same between us. But more than the cheating and the blocking of my calls, the fact that he hadn't trusted me with the most sacred part of his life hurt me to the core, and I needed answers.

Jorell let out a deep sigh before running his hand down his face. "Shawty, I didn't lie. I just didn't say—"

"Well, then, why didn't you just tell me about her?" I asked, cutting him off. He wanted to play the proximity game, and I wasn't up for it. I simply wanted him to be truthful for once.

"You want me to be honest?"

"No, just lie to me, like you usually do," I said, sarcasm dripping from my tone. "Of course I want you to be honest, Jorell. The fuck?" I yelled, flinging my hands up in the air.

Grabbing me gently by the sides of my arms, he compelled me to look into his eyes. "When I first met you . . . ," he began, his voice low. He took a deep swallow. "I . . . I just wanted to fuck."

Sucking my teeth and rolling my eyes, I quickly attempted to move away.

"Nah, hold up and let me finish," he said, firming up his grip to keep me in place. "That's what this college shit was for me. Just a place to party and have fun, ya feel me? I mean, I also figured I would get my degree and then get drafted. But, shawty, I wasn't expecting to . . ." His voice trailed off.

"You weren't expecting what?" I asked, demanding he finish.

"I wasn't expecting to fall for you, a'ight?" he confessed, almost sounding angry.

My eyes widened and a lump quickly formed in my throat before I collapsed back onto the car. I was stunned, not so much by Jorell's choice of words but by the way in which he said it. He'd always been a jokester, so the numerous times he'd told me that he loved me in the past had always been part of some sort of joke or somehow tied to sex. But tonight, as I listened to him tell me for the first time that he actually fell for me, his words had never sounded more true.

"But that still doesn't explain why you didn't tell me about your daughter, Jorell," I said softly, needing more.

As he shook his head and closed his eyes, I could see his jaw clench out of frustration. "Shawty, I didn't think you'd still want me if you knew I had a kid. You too fucking good for me," he admitted, his voice so low that I barely even heard him.

"That's not true—"

"Look, li'l baby, I gotta go. You take care of yourself, a'ight? And make sure to stay in touch," he said, cutting me off.

I watched as Jorell strolled across the parking lot, heading toward his red Chevy Impala. Seeing nothing but the back of his tall, slender frame growing smaller in the distance, in that moment I started to cry, though I didn't know why. But then I realized that at the start of this evening, I had envisioned a budding friendship on the horizon, but everything about his last words had felt final. Like I'd never see him again. A wave of emotions had hit me all at once, letting me know that after all these months, I had just been kidding myself. I wasn't over Jorell by far. In fact, I was still in love with him.

# Chapter 22

## *Perri*

These past couple of weeks with Derrick had felt indescribable. All the days and nights spent lying on the beach, in his arms, and hearing the Miami waves crash against the shore had felt like more than just a vacation. They had actually felt like a dream. And although I missed Plus and Camille like crazy, I knew that Derrick and I had really needed this alone time together. He'd been spoiling me left and right with spa days, fancy dinners, and even shopping sprees. He'd truly been giving me the basketball wife experience and treating me like a queen. Surprisingly, on the days he had training camp, Derrick would find time to Skype so that we could talk face-to-face. He had thought of everything, leaving no room for error in his attempt to have me in Miami on a permanent basis.

It was late on a Saturday night when I found myself lying back and soaking in Derrick's whirlpool tub. After drawing me a hot bubble bath and pouring me a glass of champagne, he had stepped out for a quick workout session in his home gym. His beachfront condo was very lavish and extravagant. It had lots of amenities, from floor-to-ceiling windows that showcased the best Miami views to a gourmet kitchen that was wrapped in fancy Italian marble. Almost the entire three thousand square feet of space featured Brazilian tigerwood floors. And if that wasn't enough to brag about, the hottest bars and nightclubs in town were all within walking distance. Derrick had undeniably acquired the perfect celebrity home.

As soon as I closed my eyes and allowed my head to rest back against the wall, my cell phone started to vibrate. When I glanced down at the ledge on which it sat, I saw a picture of Plus and Camille flash across the screen. I hurriedly dried off my right hand with a nearby towel picked up the phone, and answered.

"Hello."

"Say hey to Mommy," I heard Plus say in the background. Then the sound of Camille's heavy breathing could be heard through the receiver, causing me to smile instantly.

"Hey, baby," I cooed, trying to grab her attention.

"Mommy, Mommy," she said excitedly.

"Yes? Hey, baby. Mommy's here."

"Mommy, Mommy," she said again just before I heard the phone crash to the floor.

Seconds later Plus came on the line. "Hey, P."

"Hey. What's Camille doing?" I asked.

"I don't know, running around here without her clothes on. I was trying to have her call you before I put her in the bathtub."

"Aw, I miss her," I said more to myself than to him.

"Is she the only one you miss?" he asked.

"Plus," I whined.

Hearing his hearty laugh instantly brought another smile to my face. "It's all good, shorty. I know you can't tell me how much you love me while you all laid up with that nigga."

"Nigga, ain't nobody laid up. I'm actually in the bathtub," I replied.

"Hmmm," he mumbled in a suggestive manner.

"Boy, let me get off this phone."

"I'll let you off the phone, but just tell me you love me first," he said. All of a sudden I could hear Camille again. She was saying something in the background.

"Plus, let me talk to Camille."

He put her on the phone again, and I could hear him instructing her as to what to say. "Tell Mommy you love her," he said.

"I love you, Mommy."

"I love you, too, sweet girl. You getting ready for your bath?"

"Yes."

"Guess what? Mommy's taking a bath too," I said.

Then I heard Plus say, "Tell her you miss her and that you'll see her tomorrow."

Well, she completely failed to tell me that she missed me, but she did say, "See you morrow, Mommy."

"See you tomorrow, baby."

"P?" Plus said, making sure that I hadn't hung up.

"Yes? I'm still here."

"Well, I'm getting ready to put her in the tub and in the bed, but you have a safe flight home tomorrow, a'ight?"

"Thank you. I will," I assured him. After a brief pause, I said, "Oh, and . . . Plus?"

"Huh?"

"I love you."

"I love you too, P. You be safe," he said, then ended the call.

As I turned to lay the phone back down on the ledge, I saw Derrick lurking in the doorway. His face was expressionless, with the exception of a small frown, as he glared at me. It didn't take a genius to figure out that he'd overheard me talking to Plus on the phone. In an instant, a surge of guilt swept over me, and I found it hard to look him in the eye. We'd had the best time together over the past two weeks, and I really didn't want to ruin our last night by arguing. So I ignored the elephant in the room and lathered my shoulders with soap. I then rinsed off by squeezing the sponge over each of my shoulders.

"Hey, can you come wash my back?" I asked, trying to redirect his thoughts.

Derrick sat down on the edge of the tub and grabbed the sponge from my hand. After lathering it up with soap, he proceeded to clean my back, gently stroking from side to side. While if felt good to have him tending to me, the uncomfortable silence that had grown between us just wouldn't let me fully enjoy it.

After he rinsed the soap off me, he passed me back the sponge, stood up, and turned to walk out the door.

"Derrick," I called and got his attention.

He turned back, with his eyebrows raised.

"Are we okay?" I asked.

Scratching behind his right ear, he simply said, "Yeah, we straight, Perri," before trudging out the door.

An uneasiness settled in the pit of my stomach as I unplugged the drain and got out of the tub. I hated the fact that Derrick felt threatened by my relationship with Plus. It had always been one of the back-and-forth struggles in our relationship. And while I sympathized with Derrick for feeling the way he did, I couldn't deny my love for Plus. I mean, he was my first true friend, my very first love, and now he was the father of my child.

After drying off and wrapping one of Derrick's thick, ritzy towels around me, I stepped out into the bedroom. I instantly felt the cool air hit my shoulders as my eyes searched for Derrick. He was sitting on the edge of the bed, legs agape, his elbows propped on the area just above his knees, and his eyes focused on his phone. I knew he had heard me enter the room, but he was so stubborn that he wouldn't even look up and acknowledge me.

Once again, I tried to break the ice. I sat down beside him, then placed my hand around his bicep. "I'm gonna miss you, ya know?" I said just above a whisper.

After finally removing his eyes from the screen, he turned to look at me. "You don't have to miss me, Perri." He casually tossed his phone on the nightstand, then turned and angled his body square with mine. "When are you going to stop running and just let me love you?" he asked.

"I'm not running, Derrick, and I do let you love me," I replied, but he shook his head.

"You give me only half of you, Perri, and you know it," he said, firmly tapping his index finger against my chest. "I mean, shit . . . I got down on one knee in front of your entire family and asked you to be my wife. Why did you even accept my ring if you weren't gon' marry a nigga?"

My eyebrows gathered in confusion. "Yo, what are you talking about?"

"I mean, I want you and Camille to move down here so that we can be a real family. I want us to get married, Perri. How many more ways can I spell that shit out, Ma?"

I knew it wasn't the first time we'd had this conversation, but for some reason, my eyes widened, as if his desire for us to be together was news to my ears. "Uh, I . . . I," I stuttered.

"Is it because of Plus? Is he the reason you won't marry me?"

Feeling my airway constrict and my heart start to pound in my chest, I shook my head. "No," I said defensively.

"Are you sure? I mean, you tell that nigga you love him more than you say shit to me!" he shot back, standing up from the bed.

"Is that what this is about?" I asked.

Derrick began to pace the floor in his bare feet. He swiped his hand down his freckled face every so often as he tried to contain his frustration. "Just keep it real with me, Ma. Are you fucking that nigga?" he said.

My jaw dropped dramatically as I, too, shot up from the bed, clutching my towel against my chest. "No! Why would you say that?"

Grabbing the top of his head, he closed his eyes and let out a quick breath. "Just tell me the truth right now and we can end this shit with no hard feelings, a'ight? If you fucking that nigga, then just say so." He stepped into my personal space.

"I'm not! I swear, Derrick."

His eyes softened when he heard the desperation in my voice. "Then what is it, Ma?"

"What is what?"

"What's holding you back from moving down here with Camille? From marrying me?" he asked, his deep voice low and his expression one of vulnerability as he stared into my eyes.

I was so caught up in wanting him to believe that I loved him and that I wanted us to move forward that before I knew it, I said, "We'll move. Camille and I will pack up and move down here as soon as I fly back."

"Are you sure that's what you want?" he asked, lifting one of his eyebrows.

As I nodded my head vigorously, he grabbed the sides of my face and pulled me in close. Slowly, he began kissing me on the lips and unraveling the towel that was wrapped around me, until I was standing there completely naked. And without warning, Derrick dropped to his knees and threw my right leg across his shoulder. He dove headfirst between my thighs and kissed my most sacred place. Allowing his tongue to slither about my wet folds, he sent me to newly found heights of sexual pleasure.

Sitting on the floor Indian style, I heard a soft knock on my open bedroom door. I looked back over my shoulder and saw Plus standing there with Camille, who was fighting to get down from his arms. He placed her little feet on the floor before stepping farther inside the room. As his eyes quickly darted around my room, he had a look of panic and confusion on his face.

"Why is all your shit packed up?" he asked. His mouth hung slightly open as his eyes continued to scan the room.

With my long hair pulled up in a sloppy bun, I grabbed the back of my neck. "Um, I need to talk to you guys."

"Talk to you guys," he repeated.

"I'll be downstairs in just a minute. Our parents should be pulling up soon."

Plus let out a frustrated snort before shaking his head. "Come on, Mille," he muttered somberly, reaching for our daughter's hand.

After another fifteen minutes or so had passed, I could hear that my family was all gathered down in the living room. Clueless about my motives for asking them here, they laughed and talked loudly among themselves. Sucking in a deep breath, I stood up from the floor and pushed my shoulders back. I was nervous as hell, but I knew I needed to be confident when voicing my decision.

Creeping down the wooden steps, I could hear Tez talking to Ms. Tonya. "I 'on't know what she asked y'all to come over here for. You know women. Always gotta dramatize everything," he said.

"Boy, shut up! And that's not even Perri, and you know it," Ms. Tonya said, defending me.

"Yeah, you right, Godma, you right. The last time a family meeting like this was called . . ." He paused for a second before I heard him say, "Her ass ain't pregnant again, is she?"

"Nigga, don't look at me. I can't even sniff the pussy no more," I heard Plus mutter under his breath. I could only shake my head before stepping down on the landing.

As I walked into the living room, all eyes seemed to zoom in on me at once. My father, who looked up at me with a curious set of eyes, had MJ seated in his lap. Ms. Tonya, who was sitting on the couch beside him, bounced the leg she had crossed over the other. Myesha sat in the lone corner chair, and Tez rested on one of its arm. Aria sat quietly on the wooden floor at Myesha's feet, and Myesha played with her hair.

Everyone was present and accounted for, with the exception of Plus and Camille, who had just stepped out of the room. Immediately, my eyes began to survey the large open floor plan, and soon I found them in a back corner of the dining-room area. He held her high on his shoulders, and they were playing peekaboo as they stared at the large framed mirror that hung on the wall. Her contagious laughter pierced the sudden silence, causing everyone to let out a little laugh.

The laughter, however, was only temporary.

"So what's this all about, Perri?" my father asked abruptly, redirecting my attention.

Clearing my throat, I nervously clasped my hands behind my back. "I . . . uh," I stuttered.

"Just spit it out, baby. Aria's got SATs in the morning, and we need to get back," Ms. Tonya said, still bouncing her leg.

"You got us all sitting around here looking stupid, yo. Might as well gon' and tell us. What? You pregnant again?" Tez said. He showcased that gold at the bottom of his mouth as he gave a sneaky grin.

Before I could even finish rolling my eyes, I caught a glimpse of Plus's reflection in the mirror. His eyes instantly locked with mine, and his expression told me that perhaps he might have been thinking the same thing.

"Oh, uh, no! No, I'm not pregnant!" I asserted quickly, with conviction.

From my peripheral, I saw Plus make his way into the living room, with Camille still sitting on his shoulders. With her chubby hands, she was holding on to his head for dear life as she let out another series of innocent giggles. After entering the room, Plus arched forward to let her down, then stood up straight and leaned back against a wall. Arms crossed over his broad chest, as he lifted his chin, and those dark eyes peering down at me.

"Um," I said again, then swallowed.

"The fuck, yo! Just spit that shit out," Tez said, obviously impatient and annoyed. Myesha patted his leg to calm him down.

"Montez, please! I know this is your house, but please stop cussing like that in front of these children," our father said.

"Okay!" I yelled, with both hands raised in the air. "I brought you all here because I wanted to tell you that I'm leaving tomorrow—"

"Going where?" Ms. Tonya asked abruptly, cutting me off.

I hesitated at first, my mouth slightly agape. "I . . . I'm moving to Miami."

Sucking his teeth, Plus pushed himself away from the wall. Chest heaving and jaw clenched, he stepped closer to where I was standing.

With his sable eyes glaring at me, he softly shook his head. "Now *you*"—he pointed his finger at me—"you can go, but you ain't taking my daughter nowhere, yo." Although his voice was low and calm, I didn't think I'd ever witnessed him express this degree of vexation or possess such a menacing look in his eyes.

I tried to stay calm. "Ahmad—"

Tez stood up. "Nah, fuck that shit! Plus is right, Perri," he said, cutting me off.

"Now, just hold on and let the child speak, y'all," Ms. Tonya said.

I glanced over at my father, whose head was moving from side to side. Total displeasure was written all over his face. In that moment I wasn't sure if he was disappointed with me or with the way Plus and Tez were carrying on, but in either case, I knew I needed to speak up and explain.

"Derrick and I—"

Before I could even complete a sentence, Tez and Plus both sucked their teeth at the same exact time.

"Man, you letting that nigga control you already," Tez grumbled, with a simple flick of his hand.

"Let the child speak," my father said sternly.

I sucked in a deep breath, then released it. "Derrick and I have finally decided to set a wedding date." I had finally got it out. "When I visited him in Miami, we . . ." I swallowed, cast my eyes up to the ceiling. With each second that passed, I lost more confidence. But then I blurted, "We both agreed that it would be best if Camille and I move down there to get acclimated and settled in."

Without warning, Plus stepped forward, and now he was so close to me that his tall frame was towering over me. His broad chest heaved up and down as he positioned his face right next to mine. "Like I said, *yo'* ass can go," he muttered through gritted teeth, stabbing his finger in my chest.

Blinking my eyes fast, I tried my best to hold my tears at bay. I had known this wasn't going to be an easy conversation, but I swear, I hadn't expected Plus to disrespect me.

"Yo, back the fuck up off me!" I barked, pushing him hard in the chest.

However, Plus didn't budge. It was like that nigga's chest only got harder as every muscle in his upper torso seemed to flex. That only fueled my anger, so I stepped into his personal space and pressed my chest right up against his, suddenly feeling that fearless twelve-year-old tomboy resurface in me.

Then, out of nowhere, my father and Ms. Tonya appeared at my side. Their hands quickly slid in between us, and they attempted to separate us.

"That's enough, y'all. That's enough!" Ms. Tonya yelled.

"Let's all sit down and talk like adults . . . like a family, for Christ's sake," my father said.

Staring Plus down, I waited for him to take the first step back. Everybody knew that the first person to back down was considered the weakest, and even with shaky hands and tears pooling in my eyes, I refused to let him see me as weak.

"Myesha, you and Aria take the kids down in the basement for me, baby," Ms. Tonya said.

As the four of them left the room, my father and Ms. Tonya sat back down on the couch, and Plus stepped back and went to sit down in the lone corner chair. I'd admit that initially I was stubborn, as I kept my feet planted in the same spot on the floor. Arms folded across my chest, I twisted my lips to the side. That was until my father pointed to the empty seat next to him, indicating that I needed to sit my ass down.

My father turned to me and asked, "Now, Perri, how can you make a decision to take Camille all the way down to Miami without talking to Plus first?"

"Hell, or without even talking to *me*," Ms. Tonya muttered, shifting in her seat.

"Tonya, please," my father begged.

"Well, you all knew I got engaged last year, and everyone's fully aware that Derrick got drafted by the Heat. What did you expect?" I retorted, looking over at Plus, who had his head in the palms of his hands.

"To be honest, I didn't really think you'd go through with it. You know, as far as marrying him," Ms. Tonya said.

Tez ran his hand down his face before letting out a little laugh. "Shit. Me either," he said.

"Perri, what about school? I mean, you have only one year left. And what about basketball?" my father said.

I shrugged. "I looked at colleges while I was down there. I'll probably apply to the University of Miami."

"And basketball?" Tez asked.

As everyone waited for my answer, I could hear a sarcastic snort come from Plus, and for a second, this made me feel foolish about my decision. "I don't know," I said, my voice low, and gave another shrug.

"Perri, you're grown, and as much as I don't want you and Camille to leave, I'll support your decision. But you have got to figure this out with Plus. I mean, both of you know how it feels to be raised by only one parent. Is that what you want for Camille?" my father said, looking back and forth between the two of us.

"Ahmad," I called softly.

When he lifted his face, which was still buried in his hands, I could see the wetness smeared around his red-rimmed eyes. "So you just gon' up and take my baby from me, Perri? That's fucked up," he said weakly.

Seeing him cry like that caused involuntary tears to suddenly fall down my face. "I can't stay here while my fiancé is down in Miami, Plus. I mean, what did you expect?"

Plus sprang up from his seat and just stared at me for what felt like an eternity. I swear, I'd never seen him look so hurt in all my life. And finally, he broke the awkward silence and said, just above a whisper, "I expected you to love me better than that, P." And with that, Plus walked out the front door.

It was a little after six o'clock that next evening when my father pulled up to the airport terminal. While I unstrapped Camille from her car seat in the back, my father and Ms. Tonya hopped out to get our luggage from the trunk. With Camille being so heavy in my arms, I had to check my bags with the skycap outside. There was no way I could tote her and all my luggage through BWI.

As soon as I got out of the car with Camille, my father came up and wrapped his arms tightly around both of us. "Call me as soon as you land," he said against my ear.

Nodding my head in response, I glanced over his shoulder to see Ms. Tonya standing behind him. Her tired eyes were puffy, most likely from crying all night. In reality I wasn't just taking Camille away from Plus; I was taking her away from Ms. Tonya too. After my father released us, he stepped back, allowing Ms. Tonya to give us a good-bye hug and kiss on the cheek.

"I know we're family because of Camille, but the truth is you've always been like a daughter to me. When your mother died, she left you in my care. To teach you all the things she knew your father would struggle with. And I swear, over the years I tried my best. Like when you first got your period, 'member that?" she said, offering a small smile. "And then there was graduation day, when you found out you were pregnant," she added, then let out a little laugh. "I've always tried to say and do the things I knew Camille would've, had she been here. But now that you're all grown up and you're leaving . . ." Her voice trailed off into a soft cry. Shoulders shaking, she covered her mouth to barricade the sound with her hands.

"Ms. Tonya, please don't cry. We'll be back before you know it. Plus, you know I can't have Camille away from Daddy months at a time," I said, trying my best to reassure her.

Wiping the tears from her eyes, she nodded her head. "I know, baby, I know. And Ahmad . . ." She paused and pulled in her lips before releasing a deep sigh. "Ahmad will be okay. He's just hurt because him and Camille have grown so close. And not only that, Perri. You know that boy's in love with you."

In the past twenty-four hours, I hadn't seen or spoken to Plus. I'd called his dorm room and even reached out to some of his teammates, but no one had seen him at all. Now here I was, ready to catch a flight to Miami, with his only child in my arms. I felt like shit for leaving without him at least seeing Camille off, but at this point what could I do? While it was my decision to move to Miami, it was his decision to not spend our last hours here with Camille.

"Everything will be okay, Ms. Tonya. You'll see," I promised, then gave her one final kiss on the cheek.

With Camille still in my arms, her head resting on my shoulder, I walked through the automatic double doors of the airport. I saw travelers from all walks of life with their luggage rolling behind them. Overhead speakers announced cancellations and departures every other minute, and if you listened closely, even the sporadic sound of tickets being scanned could be heard. I glanced down at my ticket, saw GATE D16 stamped boldly in black letters, and then I looked up and noticed the arrow signs.

As I rode the escalator up to the second floor, I saw that the airport wasn't that crowded. Well, that was up until I reached the TSA security screening line, which looked to be at least a quarter mile long.

"Great," I muttered.

After about fifteen minutes of being in that line, which seemed to move at a snail's pace, Camille started getting heavy in my arms. We were almost to the security guy working the line, so I decided to put her down. However, Camille was so spoiled that she kept reaching up for me to hold her.

"No, Camille," I told her, shaking my head.

"Pit me up, Mommy. Pit me up," she urged, stretching both of her arms up in the air.

Just as I started to shake my head again, in an attempt to hold firm, I heard his voice behind me. "Daddy will hold you, baby."

I turned around to see Plus reaching down for Camille. My eyes instantly widened at the sight of him. "You came," I said in disbelief.

As he stood upright with our smiling daughter in his arms, we locked eyes. "Yeah, I wanted to say good-bye to her," he said before clearing his throat.

"Plus, you know I'm not gonna keep your daughter from you, right? I mean, we'll rotate holidays, and the summers . . . well, the summers will be all yours, of course," I said, taking a step forward in the line.

"Yeah," he muttered. He gave a weak nod before he added, "We'll figure it out, I guess."

As we continued to stand in line, I could hear Plus whispering to Camille behind me, telling her how much he loved her and that he'd miss her like crazy. He even told her that he'd call her every single morning and each night to read her a bedtime story. Up until this point, my emotions had been fully under control. But at that moment, as the next person in line to head through security, it was like I couldn't breathe. My chest tightened as I fought back the tears in my eyes.

"Next in line!" I heard the TSA guy say. With trembling hands, I passed him my ID card and my ticket. Feeling hot tears slide down my face, I turned around to grab Camille. I saw that he, too, was on the verge of tears. As I took her from his arms, he leaned in and surprised me by hugging us both.

"You take care of yourself, P. And take care of my baby," he said.

"Plus," I breathed.

He shook his head to stop me. "Perri, I know you used to hate the fact that I would call you my best friend, but I swear it's always been the truth. To this day, no matter how far apart we are, that's what you'll always be to me . . . my best friend. Can't shit ever change that, shorty." Just as the tears started to fall down his face, he moved in and crashed his lips against mine. Then he parted my lips with his tongue right before snatching my breath away. Our hungry mouths both battled in the most passionate kiss. When he pulled back, we stared intensely into each other's eyes for as long as we could.

"Call me when you get there, P. I love you," he said. His brown face wet and noticeably red, he slowly backed away.

"I love you too, Ahmad." I clutched the heart-shaped locket that was around my neck. It contained the picture of our little family. Holding it firmly against my heaving chest, I watched him walk away. "I love you too," I whispered again.

# Chapter 23

## *Perri*

For the past three months, I had been living in Miami Beach, Florida. Although I hated to admit it, things weren't exactly like I had thought they would be. Derrick was constantly on the road, playing one basketball game after the other, so I rarely saw him. The days of lying out on the beach beside him and stepping out on dinner dates were few and far between. My days usually consisted of being at home with Camille. It was too late to enroll in school for the semester, so I didn't even bother putting her in day care. And because I had Camille with me 24/7, with no family support, the little social life I used to have was now nonexistent. In Miami I had no friends and, sadly, no one even to shoot hoops with.

Just as he'd promised, Plus called Camille every morning and every single night. I was so lonely that most nights, after he'd finished with Camille, I'd get him to talk to me on the phone until we both fell asleep. Often I'd pull random trivia questions up on my laptop and quiz him to see if he was still the smartest boy I'd ever met. And he was. Nigga never got one answer wrong. I kept telling him that he should go on *Jeopardy*, but he'd just laugh it off like it was some sort of joke.

Now here it was Christmas Day, and I was all alone, because Derrick was traveling for a game in Chicago. Since I had had Camille for Thanksgiving, I felt it was only right that Plus get her for Christmas. As soon as his winter break began, he caught the first flight down and took her back to Maryland with him. Honestly, I wanted to go, too, since I hadn't been back home in a while, but Derrick had promised that we'd officially spend our first Christmas together this year. That plan, however, was a total bust. His new head coach, Spoelstra, demanded that the entire team fly to Chicago together on Christmas Day. In spite of that, I already had plans to fly back home for New Year's, and Camille could just return to Miami with me.

As I lay curled up on the couch, watching *Miracle on 34th Street* with a throw blanket on top of me, my cell phone started to ring. I instantly smiled when I saw my favorite picture of Plus and Camille appear on the screen. After turning the volume down on the TV, I put the phone up to my ear and answered the call. "Hey."

"Is this my baby muva?" Plus asked jokingly.

"Yo, why you playing on the phone?" I said.

He let out a small chuckle. "So what you doing?" he asked.

"Shit. Sitting here watching this boring-ass Christmas movie."

"Did you get the pictures I sent earlier?" he asked, referring to the pictures of Camille opening up her presents that he'd sent to my phone this morning. I secretly hated myself for not being there.

After releasing a heavy sigh into the phone, I said, "Yeah, I got them."

"What's wrong? Why you sound all sad?"

Sucking in a deep breath, I rolled my eyes. I really didn't want Plus to know that I had started to regret my decision to move down here. And I definitely didn't want him to know how lonely I was. But none of that even mattered, because he could sense it from a thousand miles away.

"Tell me what's wrong," he said again.

"I'm just alone, yo. And on Christmas."

Suddenly there was a knock at the door.

"Aye, hold on, a'ight? Somebody's at my door," I said. After lifting myself up on the balls of my feet, I looked through the peephole but saw no one on the other side of the door. "Man, people play too much," I mumbled as I headed back to the couch. Then I noticed the line had gone silent. "Plus, you there?"

"Yeah, P. I'm here."

As soon as he said that, another round of tapping began at my door. I hurried back to the door, annoyed, and this time I unlocked it before yanking it open. Just as I peeked my head out into the hall, Plus jumped up out of nowhere and shouted, "Surprise!"

In complete and total awe, I covered my mouth with my hands. Getting more teary eyed by the second, I watched as Nika appeared, holding Camille in her arms, and then Jorell.

"Oh my God, y'all," I said, shaking my head.

"Come 'ere, you old crybaby," Plus said, pulling me in for a hug. As I pressed my face against his chest, I couldn't help but squeeze him so tight. He had made me the happiest I'd been in a really long time.

"Oh my God, you guys. She's actually crying," Nika said when I pulled back from Plus's embrace.

I reached over and gave her a hug, as well, before taking Camille off her hip. I smothered Camille's little face with kisses and tickled her sides until I had her laughing uncontrollably.

"You gon' invite us in or nah?" Jorell asked jokingly, interrupting the moment.

With my face balled up, I gave him a half hug, then sarcastically said, "And Merry Christmas to you too, Jorell."

As the five of us stepped inside, I quickly took notice of Nika's and Jorell's awestruck expressions. While Plus had already seen the place a couple times before, this was their first time being here. In the center of the open floor plan stood a massive Christmas tree. It had bright white lights, which were all lit up, and was decorated in silver and gold. Although I had wanted to go the traditional route and decorate it myself, Derrick had decided to have it professionally done. I had felt a bit slighted at first, but the finished product was so gorgeous that I was glad Derrick had insisted. In fact, the whole house was beautiful, from the white leather furniture to the unique hardwood floors and the white alpaca rug in the living-room area.

"Damn, y'all living like George and Weezie up in the mug, fa' real," Jorell muttered, still surveying the space.

"Take your coats off," I said. They were wearing thick winter jackets. I chuckled inside, because even in December, it was seventy-five degrees outside.

As Nika and Jorell went to take a look around the place, Plus raided the fridge.

"You're just making yourself right at home, huh?" I said with a smirk.

"Yeah. I'm hungry."

"I cooked—"

"Nah, I'm good. Who delivers?" he said, cutting me off.

While I laughed, he kept a straight face. "You need to stop. I can actually cook a little something now," I insisted.

He let out a little snort of laughter as he shook his head. "Like I said, nah, I'm good. I'll just let you poison that nigga."

I sucked my teeth, grabbed my cell phone off the counter, and ordered us a pizza. Ten minutes later, we all ended up in the living room, where they gave me

Christmas presents to open up. While I had a few gifts for Camille under the tree, I hadn't bought any for anyone else. I instantly felt bad.

"I'm so sorry, y'all. I'll have to get y'all something later," I said, sitting in front of the tree, with Camille in my lap.

"Girl, please, you don't have to get me anything," Nika said.

"Me either," Plus quickly agreed.

When Jorell didn't part his lips to say anything, everyone cut their eyes over in his direction. He was laid back, unconcerned, with his arm stretched across the back of the sofa. "What?" he asked innocently, shrugging his shoulders. "Where I'm from, if you give a gift, you get a gift."

When Nika took one of the throw pillows and hit him in the face, we all fell out laughing. Once Camille was finally through opening up all her presents, I decided to open up the gift Nika had got me. It was a silver bracelet that had NIKA AND PERRI Bff engraved on it.

Plus looked at her. "What I tell you about that best friend stuff?" he asked.

At first she was laughing, but when he didn't join in, she rolled her eyes and said, "Whatever, Plus."

The next gift I decided to open up was from Jorell. After lifting the heavy bag up in the air, I jokingly shook it from left to right. "Jorell, what did you get me, yo? This bag is heavy," I said.

He casually shrugged his shoulders before he said, "Open it and see, shawty." Then he gave a little wink.

I tore into the bag, and after pulling out several pieces of crumpled tissue paper, I retrieved an extra-large bag of Twizzlers "Really, nigga? And you expecting a Christmas gift in return for this?" I said. I twisted my lips to the side as I glared at him over my shoulder.

"Hell yuh. It's the thought that counts, right?" He was so serious.

"Yo, you stupid," Plus said with a chuckle.

After the pizza arrived, everyone ate and played with Camille until it was time for her to go to bed. Even in the home I shared with Derrick, Plus took over when it came to our daughter. He gave her a bath, then put her to sleep. By the time he returned from the back bedroom, Jorell, Nika, and I were all out on the balcony, taking in the view of the bright lights of Miami, which sparkled magnificently.

Just as I was leaning over the railing and peered out at the city, I heard Jorell say, "Y'all trying to smoke some?"

I turned around to see an unlit blunt already dangling from the corner of his mouth.

"Go on and spark that shit, yo," Plus said with a lick of his lips.

While Jorell was preparing for our smoke session, Plus came up next to me. "I got you a little something," he said, passing me an envelope.

"Plus, you didn't need to get me anything for Christmas. You being here and bringing my baby are more than enough."

"Nah, it's nothing big. I mean, shit . . ." He turned around and extended his arm toward the apartment. "What can I get a woman that's got everything?"

Plus was right. Derrick made sure that in my new life with him, I wanted for nothing. The only thing missing was him actually being here. "I don't have *everything*," I said, tearing the sealed white envelope.

Inside was a folded piece of paper, which I quickly opened and began to read. The first words at the top, in bold black letters, were *National Basketball Association*. Although I knew exactly what I was getting ready to read, my eyes eagerly scanned down the page, and I quickly confirmed that Plus had entered the 2009 NBA draft.

"Oh my God, Plus," I breathed. Abruptly, I threw my body against his and circled my arms around his neck.

He hugged me tight, then lifted me up so high that my feet were inches off the floor. When he set me down, I took a step back and looked into his eyes.

"Congratulations," I said, shaking my head, still in a slight state of shock.

"Damn, P. You act like you surprised. You always knew that was the plan," he said, narrowing his smiling eyes.

"I know, I know. It's just . . . You actually did it!" I shrieked.

"Well, I mean, I gotta get drafted first." The corners of his mouth turned up into a boyish smile.

"Boy, please!" I jumped in his arms again before placing a single kiss on his cheek. "I'm so proud of you, Ahmad," I whispered. His face was now less than an inch from mine, and our lips were even closer as we locked eyes. Being this close to him, with his arms wrapped tightly around me, felt scary and safe all at the same time.

"Ahem," Nika said, clearing her throat, and breaking our intense, yet awkward moment, before passing me the lit blunt.

I put it to my lips and took a long drag. I felt the potency of the drug as it slowly filled my lungs. After one more puff, Plus took the blunt from my hand and pulled on it too.

"Don't choke this time, nigga," I said jokingly.

"Shid. A nigga ain't sixteen no more," he muttered, allowing a swirl of smoke to rise from his lips. His eyes were already low and, unexpectedly, all *sexy like*.

After thirty minutes or so of smoking and laughing out on the balcony, Jorell and Nika decided to call it a night. They were planning on staying in a hotel, but I convinced them otherwise. It was extremely late, going on one in the morning, and besides that, I had more than enough room to spare. The luxury apartment had four large bedrooms and three full baths. I quickly decided that Plus and Nika would get the guest bedrooms, while Jorell would take the couch in the media room. Of course, he wanted to stay in the bedroom with Nika, but she wasn't having it. She was holding firm on being only friends with him, and for the time being, it was actually working. They were getting along flawlessly, leaving all prior incidents in the past.

Plus looked over to me and asked, "So I guess you're ready to turn in too?" I was still leaning over the railing and feeling the cool breeze on my face as I looked out into the midnight sky.

"I guess," I said, with a shrug.

"I'm gon' need some chips or something first. I got the munchies," he said before sliding back the glass door to step inside.

Seconds later I went in behind him and saw that he was already standing in front of the fridge, with the door wide open. "Just eat that last slice of pizza," I told him.

After grabbing us each a can of grape soda, I sat up on the cold marble counter and watched him devour the single slice of meat lover's. When he was done, he took a long swig of his soda and let out a loud belch. Now I realized that I was a grown woman and my tomboyish ways were slowly but surely fading, but in that moment, I couldn't help but to release an even louder belch. That was some dumb shit we used to do as kids: challenge one another to see who could burp the loudest and the longest.

Plus chuckled and shook his head before he said, "Ew. Yo, say, 'Excuse me.'"

I whipped my neck back and raised my brow. "Why? You didn't say, 'Excuse me.'"

"'Cause I'm a nigga and you supposed to be a lady, remember?"

Playfully, I pushed him in the chest, and we both shared a laugh.

"Damn, P. You look just like your moms, yo," he muttered, coming a bit closer.

I softly sucked my teeth. "You don't remember what my mama looks like," I stated matter-of-factly.

"Shid, yeah I do. Your mama saved my ass from Ronnie so many times, it's not even funny," he said.

"Oh," I said softly, not really wanting to bring up the childhood abuse that Plus had endured, as I looked across the room.

Plus came even closer, so that he was now in between my legs. He gently cupped my chin and turned my face toward his. Stared deep into my eyes before licking his lips. "I could never forget your mother's eyes, P. They were kind, just like yours. Just like Camille's." With his fingers still holding the sides of my chin, he let out a small snort. "You know, I think out of everything we've been through, the best thing we ever did was have Camille," he said.

A smile crept upon my face at the mere mention of her. "I agree. She's . . . she's a special kid."

"If I've never thanked you for the sacrifice you made, I want to take the time to do that now," he said, his voice low, his face only inches apart from mine, as he continued looking into my eyes.

"What sacrifice, Plus?"

"Shorty, you gave up your basketball scholarship and let me keep mine. That's some real shit—"

Holding up my hand, I shook my head to cut him off. "Plus, we were kids. Besides, it all worked out, Mr. NBA."

"We'll see." He gave a modest shrug before changing the subject. "So why did that nigga just up and leave you all by yourself on Christmas? And why you didn't just come home?" he asked, with his eyebrows knit together, catching me completely off guard.

"He found out at the last minute that he would be traveling on Christmas Day, and there weren't many last-minute flights available for me to just fly back home."

He chucked up his chin and allowed his sleepy eyes to glance down at me. "Well, as long as I'm alive, you won't ever have to spend another Christmas alone, a'ight?" he said, tugging gently on my chin.

I rolled my eyes, attempting to restrain the corners of my mouth, which insisted on turning upward. "Well, what if you're traveling or playing in a game on Christmas? Then what, huh?"

"Then I'll make sure you're with me or that you're back at home with family at least," he said, slowly sliding his hand down to the front of my chest. He grasped the locket around my neck before licking his lips.

An awkward silence fell between us as we gazed into each other's eyes. The only sound that could be heard was that of my fast-beating heart. It grew louder and louder in my chest as Plus drew nearer. We were so close that I could literally feel the warmth of his body merging with my own. Our eyes stayed locked together as his hands slid down to my waist and then gently roamed underneath my shirt. He teased my skin with the tips of his fingers, sending chills throughout my entire body. And then, without notice, his lips crashed against mine.

No longer able to fight the magnetic chemistry between us, I found myself kissing him back, exploring his mouth with my tongue. Although I knew it was wrong, it was like I was having an out-of-body experience and just couldn't control myself. My hands suddenly grabbed ahold of his broad shoulders and then slid down the front of his shirt. I felt the mounds of his brawny chest beneath my palms as uncontrollable moans went from my mouth into his.

In the midst of all that fervent lip locking, he pulled my shirt up over my head. Not wasting any time, he then removed my bra with ease. And as if by reflex, my back arched when he began to flick his wet tongue over each of my stoned nipples. As he took each breast into his hungry mouth, my body shuddered and that constant thudding between my thighs returned full force. I felt as if I could just explode at any minute.

Plus peeled off my shorts and panties and allowed them to fall carelessly to the floor. When he picked my naked body up off the countertop, I wrapped my legs tightly around his waist. We attacked each other's mouths as he carried me all the way down the hall and through the door to one of the empty guest bedrooms. We were so drunk from passion and high off of loud that we didn't even care about anyone catching us. In that moment, all I could recall was how good it felt to have Plus inside me. The memory of our last time alone had me sopping wet from anticipation.

After closing the door shut with a kick of his foot, he carried me over to the bed. With lust-filled eyes, he scanned my entire body as he laid me on the bed.

"Fuck, P," he uttered, shaking his head. "I just wanna taste you. I swear that's it. Just one last time," he practically begged, murmuring.

There was something about the desperation in his voice and the way he bit down on his bottom lip that made my body instantly turn hot. Before he could even think about burying his face between my thighs, I sat up and tugged at the gray sweatpants he wore. I pulled them all the way down, until they were sitting right around his ankles. Feeling more bold and sexually alive than ever, I put my mouth directly in front of his red boxer briefs and looked up at him with wide eyes.

"You sure?" he asked, voice deep yet faint as he peered down at me with that lazy set of eyes.

"Show me," I whispered.

Slowly, he peeled down his briefs, releasing his hardened dick. I was now sitting face-to-face with what I would call a work of art. Taking in its long, perfect shape, which was covered in the smoothest of chocolate skin, I began to salivate. My sexual curiosity was starting to get the best of me, and before I knew it, my pussy was pounding as if it had a heartbeat of its own.

With one hand, Plus began stroking his length, and with the other, he massaged my scalp with his fingertips. Then, with a firm grip on my hair, he gently pulled my head back and said, "Just pretend it's a lollipop, and don't use your teeth."

I opened my mouth, and he guided it inside, feeding me inch after inch, until my lips were securely wrapped around his girth. Not being able to take any more in, I began to suck just as he had instructed, and instantly tasted a mix of salty and sweet.

"Fuck, P," he whispered. He began moving his hips against me, and before long we settled into a steady pace.

I didn't know if it was due to the blunt from earlier or my mere desire for Plus, but in that moment I was in a zone. As his hard muscle slid in and out of my dripping mouth, I unconsciously began to pick up speed. Hearing the low grunts and groans that he released, I continued to lick and suck him to no end. I looked up once and saw that his eyes were sealed tight and that he was now biting down on that bottom lip. One of his hands was now gripping the back of my head, while the other was still planted firmly on my crown as his hips collided against me.

"You 'bout to make me cum," he groaned, slowing his pace.

I was so into it that I didn't let up. I couldn't. Instead, I contracted my mouth around him and kept right on until he pulled me back with force.

"Gahdamn it, Perri," he sputtered, completely spent and out of breath.

Straightaway, he pushed me back on the bed and removed his shirt before climbing on top of me. I was so ready to feel him that I could literally hear myself panting like a dog in heat. After wedging himself between my thighs, he positioned his dick right at my entrance, which was throbbing relentlessly.

"You want it?" he asked in a teasing manner, his voice low.

"Please," I damn near whined.

When he entered me with such ease and force, I couldn't help but let out a loud moan.

"Ah, Plus!" I cried.

He began working his hips in such a steady grind that I released in a matter of seconds. Hot tears trickled down into my hair as I trembled from orgasmic pleasure. While steadily moving in and out of me, Plus kissed away my tears and held my face in his hands.

"I love you so much, Perri," he said, confessing his current state of mind, as he looked directly into my eyes.

When he kissed my lips, I clutched my legs around him tighter, allowing him even deeper access. He began thrusting in and out of me with such precision that I buried my face in the crook of his neck and held on for dear life. I experienced the most pleasurable pain as our flesh became one. That night I had thoughts only of Plus. Love only for *him*. So much so, that we ended up making love right there in the guest bedroom until the first light of day, both of us climaxing over and over again, with no regrets or self-condemnation.

# Chapter 24

## *Plus*

Waking up this morning with Perri in my arms was the best feeling in the world. While she slept, I stared at her beautiful sun-kissed face, waiting for the exact moment she would reveal her amber-colored eyes. If I hadn't known it before now, I was certain that a nigga was gone over her and that after last night there would be no turning back for me. I wanted all of Perri. No more parts, halves, or the leftovers in between. I needed her to be mine, like, yesterday and to make things official.

Just as I pulled the covers up over us after seeing the goose bumps on her arms, Camille crept through the door.

"Daddy, I want eat," she said.

I put my finger up to my lips to keep her quiet as I scooted gingerly out of the bed. After sliding my sweatpants back on over my boxer briefs, I walked down to the kitchen with Camille. I looked in the fridge first and then through the cabinets, but I found little for me to cook. Right when I was opening the pantry door, I heard someone walk in.

"She doesn't have much in here, does she?"

I looked back over my shoulder and saw Nika standing there in a silk two-piece pajama set. Cinnamon-colored curls sprouted in every direction as she let out a little yawn.

"Nah. I'm trying to see if she got some oatmeal at least," I said, turning back toward the pantry.

"I think she said they been interviewing chefs."

I let out a low snort, which I thought only I could hear.

"So how did you guys sleep last night?" Nika asked, with a hint of a smile in her voice.

After pulling out a box of cinnamon-apple oatmeal, I closed the pantry door. "We slept straight," I said, trying to ignore her. I knew it was her crafty way of asking if we'd fucked.

"Sounded more than just *straight* to me," she muttered with emphasis.

I couldn't help but grin, recalling the way Perri's body felt. And the way her mouth felt. *Fuck.*

"Plus!" Nika shouted, snapping me out of my trance.

"Huh?"

"Didn't you hear Camille? I think she wants a cup of milk."

"Oh, my bad," I said, rubbing my hand over my unkempt curls.

After I made Camille her oatmeal and served it with a cup of milk on the side, I raided the fridge again. Upon finding only a half carton of eggs, shredded cheddar cheese, and a few slices of turkey sausage on the shelves, I decided to make omelets. By the time the food was completely done, everyone was in the kitchen with the exception of Perri. I trekked back down the long hall to peek my head in the guest room, but I didn't see her. I kept walking, but before I even reached the master bedroom door, which was cracked open only a few inches, I heard her voice.

"Good luck on your game tonight," she said.

Hearing that she was already on the phone with that nigga, only hours after fucking me, I instantly grew pissed. Looking through the small opening, I saw her sitting on the edge of the bed with a white towel wrapped around her. The phone was nuzzled against her neck, and she had one smooth leg crossed over the other. No matter how angry I was, I couldn't deny how beautiful she was, sitting there with her wet hair cascading down the opposite shoulder.

Then, all of a sudden, I heard her say, "Love you too." Voice clear, even, and to the point.

Right away a nigga's heart was crushed, and my ego was beyond bruised. My chest began tightening to the point where it actually hurt, and my stomach dropped, as if I were falling from the highest peak in the sky. I quickly contemplated going in and cussing her ass out for trying to play me, but how could I? I was in this man's home without his knowledge and had fucked his fiancée without any remorse. Not only that, Perri had given me no verbal commitment or reassurance after the night we'd shared. So I didn't even have a leg to stand on.

I charged back to the guest bedroom, quickly changed our flights, and promptly packed up my shit. Then I jumped in the shower, hoping to calm myself. The entire time I was in there, I kept trying to accept the fact that Perri and I would never be. I had fucked her over too many times when we were young, and now this was my karma to bear.

No matter how many times in the past I had told Perri that I was letting her go, freeing her to go be happy with another nigga, in the back of my mind, I had always known that the story would end with her and me together.

But hearing her say those three little words to another man after the night we'd shared exposed a vulnerability within me that was seldom revealed. And although I refused to cry, even within the confinement of the glass shower walls, a nigga's heart was literally shattered.

After I got out of the shower and got dressed, I went across the hall to Camille's room to pack up her things. I was laying her clothes out on the bed when Perri came walking through the door. She stopped in her tracks when she saw the small carry-on bag sitting on the floor, and a look of bewilderment took hold of her face.

"You're leaving? I thought your flight wasn't until tomorrow," she said sadly.

"Yeah, we're heading back," was all I said, without making eye contact. I carried on as though she weren't even there.

"Plus!"

I didn't want to, but as if by reflex, I looked up at her from where I was bending down to the bed. She didn't even have to utter a word, because her bright eyes begged for understanding. But I wasn't ready to talk, and honestly, I didn't know if I'd ever be. I didn't want to appear weak by acknowledging the fact that not only had she broken my heart, but she had also made a nigga feel cheap all at the same time. Like I was some sort of side nigga, when the truth was, I was the one who had had her heart from the jump, or so I'd thought.

Swallowing hard, I said, "I just got some things I need to do back at home, P."

I picked Camille's carry-on bag up off the floor before stepping past her. When I went into the kitchen, I saw Jorell and Nika still sitting in their night clothes, while Camille sat at the table in her booster seat. I hurriedly unstrapped her and picked her up in my arms.

"Y'all need to get ready. Our flight's leaving in three hours," I said over my shoulder before taking Camille back down the hall. I could only imagine the looks on their faces, since we had planned on staying another night.

I got Camille bathed and dressed before getting all our bags to the front door. And I did all of that without saying a word to Perri. When it was time for us to leave, she held Camille in her arms and told her that she would see her in another week. Jorell and Nika both gave Perri a good-bye hug. And when it was down to just me and her, my first instinct was to just hit her with a head nod and keep it moving. But I couldn't. No matter what, she was my daughter's mother and, even more, my oldest friend.

"Are we all right?" she asked softly, still confused by my sudden behavior.

"We straight," I said curtly. Then I gave her only a half hug before taking my daughter out of her arms and heading out the front door.

In the days after we left Miami, I felt like I was in a daze. Of course, I avoided Perri's calls like the plague, only allowing communication with Camille through Tez and Myesha. Sure I knew it was petty as fuck of me, considering the fact that we had a child together, but a nigga was still in his feelings. I poured myself into basketball, Camille, and these tutoring sessions, which put some extra cash in my pockets.

As I climbed the stairs of Georgetown's Blommer Science Library with Jorell, I zipped up my letterman jacket. It was thirty degrees outside, and the late December wind was whipping something fierce.

"Mane, it's cold as a sheep's ass out here, breh," Jorell said, hiking up his shoulders.

After jogging inside the building, we headed over to where the tutoring sessions were usually held. This small corner of the library housed several round tables, only large enough to seat about six. Sitting at a table all by herself was Brianna, the girl I had been tutoring for the past three weeks. She was a pretty, petite little thing who couldn't weigh more than 110 pounds soaking wet. She stood around five feet tall, and her skin was a simple shade of brown. Brianna's jet-black hair hung right above her shoulders, and it added to her underrated beauty by framing her wide-set eyes and button nose.

"Breh, this bitch must be slow. How long you been tutoring her now?" Jorell whispered when we were about twenty feet away from the tutoring corner.

I elbowed him and shook my head at his crazy ass. "Ain't that your girl?" I pointed toward a nearby table. White Girl Amy, as we called her, sat there looking down at her book. Her long red hair fell down the sides of her face like sheets, and the glasses she wore sat on the bridge of her nose. She had been tutoring Jorell in geology for the past two weeks, so he didn't have much room to talk.

Seeing his tutor sitting there, patiently waiting for him to join her, Jorell let out a deep sigh. "Let me get this shit done and over with," he muttered. After removing the skullcap from his head, he shook out his shoulder-length dreads and dapped me up.

"And pay attention, nigga," I hollered at his back as he walked over to begin his studies. I let out a chuckle when I saw him throw his middle finger up in the air.

When I approached the table where Brianna was sitting, I quickly noticed that she was all smiles. "What up, Bri?" I said, greeting her with my fist.

She giggled, then gave me a pound. After all the niceties were over, I proceeded to get down to business. Brianna was struggling in physics, and not to sound arrogant, I could pretty much master just about any subject. I had been working with her four days a week for an hour at a time, so I was surprised that she hadn't grasped the concepts by now. However, it didn't matter to me, since I got paid twelve dollars an hour for tutoring. And between her and my other tutees, the extra cash was a nice sum and came in handy.

In the middle of our study session, Brianna looked over and placed her hand on my forearm. "Can I ask you something?" she asked.

"'Sup?"

"Do you have plans for New Year's Eve?"

Scratching behind my ear, I noticed that she hadn't removed her hand from my arm. Up until this point Brianna had never hit on me, so I quickly pushed that thought to the back of my mind. Besides, even though Brianna was a pretty girl, she wasn't exactly my type. These days I had only one woman on the brain, and that was Perri.

"I'm not really sure what I'm doing yet. What about you? You got big plans?"

"No. Actually, I was wondering if you wanted to hang out."

I cut my eyes at her, feeling my brows instantly rise.

"I mean as friends, of course," she said innocently enough, sheepishly raising her shoulders.

"Let me just see what my mans got going on, and I'll let you know, a'ight?"

She smiled and nodded her head.

After another twenty minutes or so, our study session was over. While Jorell took off to the dorms, I drove back to Bowie. Now that Perri wasn't there, I found myself staying with Tez more often than not, especially since Camille was there part of the time. This was her home away from her mother, and of course, I couldn't keep her in the dorms.

As soon as I pulled in the driveway, my cell phone started to vibrate. I looked down and saw Perri's name on the screen. I hadn't talked to her in over five days, and because I had gotten used to talking with her on the phone on a daily basis, the shit was killing me. Initially, I was just going to let the call go to voice mail, but for some reason, I decided to answer her call.

"Yo," I said, my voice low.

"Ahmad, why have you been avoiding me? What did I do?" She took off on a rant without so much as a hello.

"You ain't do shit," I told her nonchalantly.

She released a guttural groan, indicating just how pissed I was making her. "All I know is your ass better answer the fucking phone when I call. I'm not gonna be going through Tez and Myesha every time I want to talk to Camille!" she fussed.

"Yo, you done?" I purposely kept my tone calm and even to piss her off some more.

"No, Ahmad! I'm not done. I fucking. . ." She paused, then whispered, "I fucking had sex with you. I cheated on my fiancé, Ahmad! And now—"

Growing more annoyed, I cut her off. "So you just had *sex* with me, huh?" I asked, still using that even, petty tone of voice.

"I cheated on Derrick for you, and now—"

"Like I said before, I don't give a fuck about that nigga. Now, if that's all you called me for, you can get the fuck off my line."

Perri let out a loud grumble before hanging the phone up in my ear. It didn't take a rocket scientist to figure out that she was furious. *But fuck it.* I was pissed at her too. *Shit!* As far as I was concerned, she and I weren't even close to being even. While a nigga was sitting here hurt, because I had actually thought we would finally be together, she was worried about the fact that she had cheated on her fiancé. *Fuck him!*

At this point I didn't know what the future held for me and Perri, but one thing I knew for sure was that I needed to get her out of my head and, by some means, out of my heart.

# Chapter 25

## *Perri*

The passion-filled night Plus and I had shared was one I had been dreaming about ever since I was fifteen years old. He had taken me to new heights of sexual pleasure and had made me feel things that only he could. That next morning, when I had heard them all talking in the kitchen, I had decided to jump in the tub first. My body had felt achy from all the provocative positions he put me in, and I'd hoped that a hot bath might take away some of the soreness.

Right after I'd bathed and gone back into my bedroom, I had heard my cell phone buzzing on the bed. I'd glanced down and seen a kissy picture of Derrick and me flash vividly across the screen. My heart had begun galloping inside my chest, and I swear, in that instant, I could barely even breathe. It was sad to say that my fiancé had been the furthest thing from my mind up until this point. And seeing that he was trying to reach me had caused an instant rush of guilt to consume me.

After everything that had happened the night before, I was certain that morning that I needed to call it off with Derrick. No matter how much we loved each other, that love would never surpass the love I felt for Plus, and stringing Derrick along would never be an option. He just didn't deserve that. Right after I let his call go straight to voice mail, I quickly got my nerve. Immediately decided that I would break it off with him face-to-face when he returned home rather than over the phone. So after taking a few deep breaths, I mustered up the courage to call him back.

The exhaustion in his voice was readily apparent, so I tried my best to sound upbeat and pleasant. I wished him luck during that night's game and even told him that I loved him. Because I did. After I ended the call and got dressed, I went to join Plus and the rest of the crew. But to my surprise, when I found them, they were all packing up to leave. I was pretty disappointed because I was expecting them to stay at least one more day, but even that I could've lived with. It was the way that Plus was behaving, as if the night before had never even happened, that left me feeling totally hurt and confused.

I was supposed to leave for Maryland the day before New Year's Eve, but I just couldn't. At least not without talking to Derrick first. I needed to come clean and break things off before things ended badly between us. The day before my scheduled flight, which was also the day Derrick was coming home, I busied myself with taking down Christmas decorations in a failed attempt to calm myself. When I finished with the decorations, I realized that Derrick would be home at any minute, so I sat down in the living room and waited patiently for him to arrive.

While I was waiting, my father called. I picked up on the first ring.

"Hey, Daddy."

"Hey, Perri. I wanted to wish you a safe trip. You're leaving tomorrow, right?"

"Yeah, my flight leaves tomorrow morning at eight." Just then, I heard the jingling of keys at the door.

"I gotta go, Pops. Derrick's coming in now," I said.

After ending the call, I blew out two quick puffs of air, preparing myself for the heart-to-heart we were about to have. Imagine my surprise when little Miss Mia strolled through the door, then tossed her keys down on the foyer table, as though she'd been here before.

"Derrick!" she hollered. She kicked off her high-heeled shoes by the door.

I shot up from the chair and marched over to her. "Mia, what are you doing here? And why do you have a key to our house?"

Mia's eyes damn near popped out of her head as she clutched her nonexistent pearls with her hand. The horrified look on her face told me that, for some reason, she wasn't expecting to see me here.

"Derrick said you'd be gone this week," she said under her breath.

At this point I was so furious, I literally felt my hands trembling. I moved in so close to her that she took a step back out of fear. "Now, I'm gon' ask you one more time. What the fuck are you doing here, and why do you have a key to my house?" I repeated through gritted teeth.

Although her mouth opened, she appeared to be at a loss for words. She said nothing and just kept shaking her head and holding her hands up in surrender. But just as I was about to reach out and touch her ass, forcing her to give me honest answers, she shouted, "Derrick gave me a key!"

I could feel my left eyebrow rise as I cocked my head to the side. "And why would Derrick do that? Why are you here?" I asked again.

She swallowed hard as she tucked a strand of her silky hair behind her ear. "Derrick and I have been seeing each other for over a year now, Perri," she confessed.

My neck whipped back, as though I had been slapped in the face. "What!"

"Derrick told me that you two had been on the outs since last Christmas. And sometime after that, we seemed to find our way back to each other." She let out a deep sigh, like she was tired of explaining herself. "Look, Mami, I'm sorry to tell you this, but Derrick has and always will be mine."

Feeling gut punched, I suddenly became short of breath. With my mouth hanging ajar from shock and my eyes blinking fast, I began to recall the events of Christmas past. Then it hit me that last Christmas was when Derrick drove down from New York to see me and gave me that cheap-ass bottle of perfume. Feeling that my knees were about to give out on me, I walked over to the couch, sat down, and softly grasped the pendant around my neck. I sat there in silence for a few seconds, with one hand covering my mouth, trying to figure out just how all of this could have happened.

"I'm sorry, Perri," Mia offered, breaking the dead silence in the room.

My neck snapped around so fast. "Bitch, are you serious right now? You knew good and goddamn well that Derrick and I were still together." I jumped up to my feet, feeling a newfound surge of energy. "So then why would Derrick tell you I would be gone this week? Why was I on his arm during draft night and not you? Just admit it! You knew, and all along you've been playing your role."

My words must have struck her the wrong way, because all of a sudden I could see her nose starting to flare and her eyes narrow. "Tuh!" she spat, throwing her head back for dramatic effect. "Perri. Sweet dear. It was never going to be you. Do you think that Derrick would actually end up marrying some manly-looking bitch from the projects?"

Wounded by her words, I stood there in my oversize white tee and signature ball shorts and clenched my jaw.

Feeling my fists gradually tighten at my sides, I mentally prepared for war.

"I mean, out of all the women that come on to Derrick, especially now that he's in the NBA, you think he'd actually settle for you?" She let out a sarcastic snort as she raised a perfectly arched brow. "Take care of another man's child when he doesn't have to? Let's be for real," she added.

Just that little reference to Camille and Plus was all it took for me to pounce on her. I leapt off the couch with such fury that she ran for the front door. I chased after her and pushed her back against the apartment door so hard that a picture on the adjacent wall fell to the floor. She immediately put her hands up to shield her face, but after fighting niggas for many years, I knew how to remedy that. I punched her hard in the gut, and when she brought her hands down to her belly to protect it, I smacked fire from her pretty face.

"You wanna talk about my daughter, bitch!" I hollered, this time getting a clean punch.

She screamed and cried out loud, like I was actually killing her. "Please, Perri, stop! Help!" she wailed dramatically. When her hands went back up to cover her face, I dragged her down to the floor by that long silky black hair. Once her thin body hit the floor, I hopped on top of her and proceeded to drill my fists into her face. It didn't matter that her hands were in the way, because I was still doing damage. Just as the blood from her face began to leak through her fingers, the house phone started to ring.

Completely spent and out of breath, I stood up and towered over her. "Saved by the bell, bitch!" I muttered before going to grab the phone.

"Hello," I answered.

"Perri, you need to get home now." I could barely hear my brother speak with all of Mia's loud crying and moaning in the background.

"I need to come home? Why? What's wrong?" I asked.

"There's been a fire."

That night I took a cab from the airport straight to UM Prince George's Hospital. As I stared out the backseat window, I watched snow flurries fall from the sky the entire ride there and just prayed that Aria would be okay. Tez hadn't elaborated over the phone, but from what I'd been able to gather, Ms. Tonya's house had somehow caught fire. Aria had been trapped inside, and as a result, she was now in a drug-induced coma, with third-degree burns covering more than half her body.

Since Tez had already told me what floor Aria was on, I didn't bother checking in with the receptionist. I immediately hopped on the elevator and pressed the number four. When I got out on the fourth floor and made my way to the waiting room, I saw Tez sitting down, with his elbows resting on his thighs. His face was buried in the palms of his hands, and his shoulders were slumped, as if he was carrying the weight of the world. Doing her best to comfort him was Myesha, who was sitting at his side, with a sleeping MJ strapped to her chest. She was rubbing his back, her head against his arm.

"You made it," Myesha said somberly when she looked up and saw me enter the room.

When she stood up to greet me, I gave her a quick hug before Tez pulled me from her arms. With his sandy-brown locks pulled back, his red-rimmed eyes were completely exposed, giving away the fact that he had been crying. Immediately, my stomach dropped, and I began to think the worst. I wrapped my arms tightly around him and buried my face in his chest as we rocked from side to side. And before I knew it, I was crying too.

"Is she gone?" I murmured.

"No, but she's in the ICU," Tez explained with a sniff.

As I stepped out of his embrace, I saw my father enter the waiting room. He was carrying a cup of coffee in one hand and was holding on to Camille with the other. She was walking by his side, and as soon as she saw me, her amber eyes lit up like two flickering candles. She didn't hesitate to break free from her grandpa's grip and rush full tilt toward me.

"Mommy! Mommy!" she shrieked.

I scooped her up in my arms and kissed her cheek.

"Perri, you made it. Thank God," my father said before giving me a hug. He, too, had worry lines etched on his entire face, which told me that it had been a rough night.

"Where's Ms. Tonya and Plus?" I asked.

"They're back in the room with Aria," he said. He shook his head and dragged his free hand down his face. "She's pretty bad off, but it could've been much worse."

"So what happened?" Up until this point, all I had was some vague information. I had so many unanswered questions, such as how this fire had occurred, and I simply needed to know more.

My father released a deep sigh and shook his head once more. "It was Ronnie. He was in the house, smoking—"

"Smoking? Since when did he start smoking cigarettes?"

My father's hand went up to stop me. "Ronnie was smoking crack in a pipe at the house, and somehow it caught fire."

I could feel my mouth drop slightly. "Where was Ms. Tonya?"

As soon as I said that, Plus and Ms. Tonya came through the waiting-room door. The cold look on Plus's face when he saw me was one of disgust. So much so that it instantly sent chills down my spine. He didn't even greet me; instead, he just walked past me toward the other side of the room. I followed him with my eyes, and for the first time, I noticed a petite brown-skinned girl sitting alone in the corner.

When Plus sat down next to her, I instantly realized that they were here together. Although I didn't know the nature of their relationship, I felt a sudden sense of betrayal. After all, no matter how tragic the events in our lives were, Plus and I had always gotten through them together. We had never held grudges toward one another in the midst of a crisis, yet here he was breaking the code.

"Thank you for coming, baby," Ms. Tonya said, snapping me out of my thoughts.

I turned and gave her a hug, then asked, "So how is Ronnie?"

Ms. Tonya's breath hitched before she swallowed hard. "Ronnie didn't make it, baby," she explained, allowing a single tear to drop down her face.

From across the room, Plus hollered, "Fuck is you crying for? For that nigga?" He shot to his feet, with a scowl on his face, and stormed over to us. His angry eyes were filled with tears, and his wide chest was inflated with rage.

"Don't you start with me, Ahmad. Not today," Ms. Tonya cried.

"Nah, fuck that! You let that nigga beat my ass growing up, and you didn't do shit. Now that the nigga done burned down your house and damn near kilt your daughter, you still don't got shit to say?"

Clearly, Plus was furious, and with good reason, but I couldn't stand there and not say anything. I put Camille down and placed my hands on his chest. "Calm down, Ahmad, please," I urged.

"You ain't seen her, P. She's in there, all fucked up, yo," he croaked, pointing back in the direction of Aria's room.

"I know, I know," I whispered. I placed my hands on his face and forced him to look me in the eye. "Everything is going to be okay. Aria's going to be just fine. You hear me?"

"That's my sister, yo," he said weakly as he shook his head. He sounded as if he was on the verge of crying uncontrollably.

When I felt like I was getting through to him and he was actually letting me be there for him, I took him in my arms. "She's gonna be fine," I told him again.

All of a sudden, I heard someone call, "Perri!" from behind me.

I released Plus and turned around to see Derrick's cheating ass standing next to my father. "Derrick? What are you doing here?" I asked, confused.

I knew that Mia had to have told him what had happened between us, so why he was here was beyond me. But before he could even answer me, Plus stormed out of the waiting room, bumping into my shoulder in the process. The little brown-skinned girl was on his heels.

"Fuck," I muttered under my breath and briefly closed my eyes.

"Perri, can we talk?" Derrick asked, sounding so pitiful, as he walked into my personal space.

"What is there to talk about, Derrick? You've been cheating on me for a whole year!"

A look of shame covered his entire face as he glanced over his shoulder and saw my family gathered around. "Can I please just talk to you in private?"

Tez walked up to us. "Nah, homeboy. Whatever you got to say to my sister, you can do that shit right here," he said. His fists were balled tightly at his sides, and his jaw was clenched, so I knew that he was prepared to fight.

Lifting his chin in the air, Derrick took a corner of his bottom lip between his teeth. "I just wanted to say I'm sorry, Ma."

Without even realizing what I was doing, I slapped him hard across the face. "That's for having that bitch even come around me, knowing you had been fucking her the whole time!"

Derrick's hand instantly went up, and he grabbed his jaw as he let out a low snort and narrowed his eyes. "How you gon' be mad at me for some shit you been doing since day one? You think shit was sweet for me, playing second to another nigga?"

"I never cheated on you—"

"Bullshit!" he said, raising his voice.

Tez stepped in even closer, attempting to make his presence known.

"You may not have laid down with that nigga, but you cheated, Ma. Admit that shit," Derrick said.

Twisting my lips to the side, I quickly gave his words some thought. "You're right. Clearly, we're both in love with someone else," I stated matter-of-factly.

"I never said I was in love with Mia. You've always had my heart, Ma. But it's obvious you don't feel the same way about me."

Guilt immediately consumed me when I recalled all the not so innocent kissing, touching, and late-night calls Plus and I had shared over the past year. Over the years I had cheated on Derrick not only physically but emotionally as well. I was just as guilty as he was, if not more so, for stringing him along. "I'm sorry, Derrick," I finally admitted as I slid his engagement ring off my finger. With tears welling up in my eyes, I gently placed the ring in his hand before collapsing into Tez's arms.

From Aria, Plus, and now this thing with Derrick, I was an emotional wreck. Tez rubbed my back and held on to me while just letting me cry. He made me feel like that same little girl from the Millwood Projects who had always been under her big brother's protection.

"Look, I need you to pull it together so we can go back and see Aria, a'ight?" he said.

After pulling back from Tez's embrace, I quickly wiped my face and saw that Camille was now up in my father's arms. I gave one final sniff and said, "I'm good. Let's go."

# Chapter 26

## *Plus*

It had been over a month since that tragic night of the fire, and although today was my birthday, I could barely stand to form a smile. Aria was still in the hospital, where she was preparing for major skin-graft surgery. The procedure would cover the right side of her body, including a small area on the right side of her face. Since her burns were so severe, she had been in constant pain and was currently trying to wean herself off the morphine the doctors had prescribed. Even though I was thankful she had survived, her condition was still depressing.

Not only was I messed up in the head over that, but my mother and I were still beefing. I just couldn't get over the fact that she would actually shed tears over a sorry-ass nigga like Ronnie. And then there was my friendship with Perri, which at this point was practically nonexistent. Despite the fact that she had moved back home and had broken it off with Derrick, my pride just wouldn't let me look at her the same way. I had even moved back into an apartment-style dorm with Jorell on a permanent basis just so I wouldn't have to see her as much.

Although I wasn't rocking with Perri like that anymore, I had to admit that she continued to impress me. Somehow she was able to reenroll at Georgetown for the spring semester, and she also got a part-time job. But even with us attending the same school, we moved like two ships passing in the night. While my classes were during the day, hers were mostly scheduled in the evenings. And I also had my basketball games and the practices I had to attend. Perri, on the other hand, was unable to regain her spot on the girls' basketball team.

I didn't feel up to doing anything for my birthday other than maybe having a few people come through, but Tez insisted on throwing a small party for me at the house. He was like my big brother, so I always found it hard to turn down his generosity. He went all out, ordering food and liquor. He even sent my mother and the kids over to Mr. Phillip's for the night, so I knew the least I could do was appear to be enjoying myself.

It was around ten o'clock that night when I found myself down in the basement, taking shots of Henny with Jorell at the bar. Lil Wayne's "Lollipop" blared through the surround-sound speakers, and the faint scent of Kush drifted through the air. Several of my teammates were already there, playing pool, and even a few girls that I was cool with were in attendance. Everything was all good until Perri and Nika came downstairs.

Perri was dressed in a simple pair of black skinny jeans and a red long-sleeved crop top that revealed a sliver of her flat belly. On her feet were a pair of red and black Jays, and her long hair was slicked back into a high ponytail. Although her attire was casual, she looked good enough to eat. I hated the fact that I was still attracted to her.

"Hey, Plus. Happy birthday," Nika said, giving me a hug. "I see you got that bush cut off yo' head," she said jokingly, rubbing her hand over my fresh new haircut.

"Had to," I simply said. I hugged her again and saw that Perri was standing not far behind her. When our eyes met, she gave me a small smile and a coy little wave before saying, "Happy birthday, Plus."

I raised my chin to her and kept my conversation short. "Thanks."

Nika then went over to Jorell and gave him a hug as well. "Hey, big head. What y'all over here drinking on? We wanna take a shot too," she said.

"Nah, lightweight, you don't know how to hold ya liquor. I done already seen you in action, remember?"

"Oh my God, it was one time, Jorell. Will you just let that go?" she whined.

While those two fell out laughing at their own inside joke, Perri and I just stood there awkwardly, looking at one another. She twiddled her thumbs and rocked back on her heels, while I did my best to get through the uneasy moment by scratching a spot behind my ear that didn't even itch. I looked her over once more. I was just about to tell her that she looked nice tonight when Brianna walked up and put her arms around my waist.

"What's up, birthday boy?" she said, giving me a tight squeeze.

"What up, Bri?" I offered, leaning down to hug her back.

When I looked up, I saw a glower appear on Perri's face that was undeniably intended for Brianna. She was jealous. I chuckled inside, because Brianna was just a friend. Even though she sometimes flirted with me, I never took it there with her, because I didn't see her that way. However, now that the opportunity had presented itself, I couldn't help but be a little petty.

I threw my arm around Brianna's shoulder and looked at Perri. "I guess I'll catch you later, then," I said before walking off.

Perri's eyes followed Brianna and me as we trekked across to the other side of the basement. When we plopped down on one of the leather couches and started playing drinking games with a few people from school, I could feel Perri's eyes burning a hole through me. Just to be spiteful—because I knew she was watching—I leaned over and whispered in Brianna's ear.

"So did you have trouble finding the house?" I asked over the music.

Brianna shook her head and was all smiles, probably because I was finally paying her some attention. Either that or she was beginning to feel the effects of that green monster concoction in her cup. Before I knew it, Perri got down from the barstool that she was sitting on and rushed past me, with Nika in tow. Judging by her expression and the way she cut her eyes over at me before she climbed the stairs, I knew she was pissed at me.

I released a deep sigh of frustration and ran my hand over my low-cut waves. "I'll be back, yo," I told Brianna before getting up from my seat.

Seeing Perri hurt didn't bring me as much pleasure as I had thought it would, and I knew I needed to go make things right. I had been avoiding her by seeing Camille only in the evenings, when she was away at class, or on the weekends, during those hours when she was at work. The shit had to stop. I was twenty years old and needed to start acting like a grown man rather than a childish little boy. Whether I liked it or not, we would be bonded forever, and I needed to remember that.

After going upstairs, I immediately looked for Perri in her bedroom, but she wasn't in there. As I came back out into the hall, I heard crying. I leaned my head up against the bathroom door and heard Perri and Nika talking on the other side of it.

"He's found someone else," Perri cried.

"Well, have y'all talked?" Nika asked. Perri must have shaken her head no, because Nika then said, "Well, just go tell him how you feel."

All of a sudden, I heard the sound of someone gagging and vomiting in the toilet.

"See, girl? This shit with him is making you sick," Nika said.

The next thing I knew, there was silence on the other side of the door.

Then Nika gasped dramatically. "No, Perri," she breathed. "Please tell me you're not pregnant."

My mouth damn near fell to the floor, and my heart instantly began to race. But before I could even get my emotions in check and wrap my head around what I had just heard, I could hear Jamal calling my name. I walked down the hall and stopped just before the first step of the staircase and peered down into the foyer. Standing there were Jamal and Shivon, with their coats still on, as though they had just arrived. I opened my mouth to speak, but something behind them caught me completely off guard. . . .

A familiar set of bright blue eyes.

*The fuck?*

Dear readers,

I hope you all enjoyed reading Part 2 of *Love and the Game*, in which Perri, Plus, and Derrick's love triangle continues and we also learn more about the other couples. I didn't plan to make this a three-book series, but there is just way too much left of the story to cover . . . so Part 3, the finale, will be coming soon. Also, if you haven't read my two-book series entitled *Loving a Borrego Brother*, please do so. I promise you will fall in love with these men and their leading ladies.

Also please stay connected with me to keep up with my future book releases and upcoming projects:

Facebook:
https://www.facebook.com/johnni.sherri.3

Facebook Author page:
https://www.facebook.com/johnnisherri1

Instagram: @johnnisherri

Twitter: @Johnni_Sherri

Thanks, everyone, for your continued support.


Love always,
Johnni Sherri